HEART OF ICE

Center Point
Large Print

Also by Lis Wiehl with April Henry and available from Center Point Large Print:

Face of Betrayal
Hand of Fate

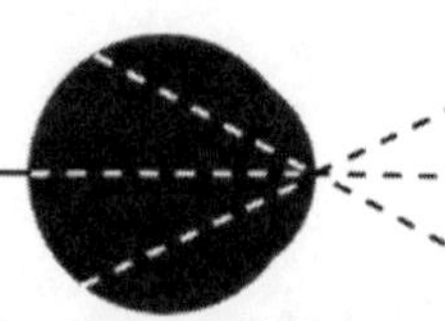

A Triple Threat Novel

LIS WIEHL
with APRIL HENRY

Center Point Large Print
Thorndike, Maine

This Center Point Large Print edition is
published in the year 2011 by arrangement with
Thomas Nelson Publishers.

Publisher's Note: This novel is a work of fiction.
The events in this novel are inspired by actual events,
but all characters are entirely fictional.

The text of this Large Print edition is unabridged.
In other aspects, this book may vary
from the original edition.
Printed in the United States of America.
Set in 16-point Times New Roman type.

ISBN: 978-1-61173-033-3

Library of Congress Cataloging-in-Publication Data

Wiehl, Lis W.
Heart of ice : a triple threat novel / Lis Wiehl with April Henry. —
Center Point large print ed.
p. cm.
ISBN 978-1-61173-033-3 (library binding : alk. paper)
1. Women journalists—Fiction. 2. Public prosecutors—Fiction.
3. Large type books. I. Henry, April. II. Title.
PS3623.I382H43 2011b
813′.6—dc22

2010052638

For the wonderful followers of Allison,
Nicole, and Cassidy,
especially Miss Margaret Ralston
of Philadelphia, Pennsylvania,
who said the Triple Threat books got her
through the "terrible pain" of a broken wrist.
And for Dani and Jacob.

"The air around him seemed to buzz, and the eye contact he made with me was so direct and intense that I wondered if I had ever really looked anybody in the eye before."

—ROBERT HARE

WITHOUT CONSCIENCE: HE DISTURBING WORLD OF THE PSYCHOPATHS AMONG US

CHAPTER 1

Southwest Portland

The fuel sloshed inside the red metal gas can, splashing in rhythm with Joey Decicco's steps. As soon as the house at the end of the long driveway came into view, he stopped and took stock. Sprawling. Lots of windows. Two-story. Wooden. On the porch, two Adirondack chairs and a blue bike with training wheels. And no lights on, no car parked in front. Nobody home.

Just like Sissy—or Elizabeth, as she called herself now—had said.

Because Joey didn't want to kill anyone. He had already caused enough death.

The sun was setting, but the fading light was enough for what he needed to do. Joey walked to one corner, carefully tilted the can, and began to trace a line around the house, drawing an invisible noose. By the time he finished, it was almost fully dark. He trailed the last of the gasoline and diesel mixture back up along the driveway.

Pulling a silver Zippo from his overalls pocket, he flipped open the cover. The thin metallic clank gave him goose bumps, as it had every time since he was eleven.

It was showtime.

Fire made Joey powerful. He could cause ordinary, boring people to wake in fright. He made the alarms sound. Made the fire trucks race down the road, sirens wailing. And right behind them stampeded the television cameras and reporters. All of them eager to look upon his handiwork.

Without fire, Joey was nothing. People made a point of not looking at him. At the patchwork skin on his face and his scarred left hand. But fire drew their eyes like iron filings to a magnet. They couldn't *not* look at fire.

He flicked the lighter and then bent down, shielding the quivering blue flame with his free hand. With a *whoosh,* a line of fire raced away from him, advancing into the dark.

This was Joey's favorite part. The beginning. He had surprised the night. What was supposed to be dark was suddenly filled with light and heat.

The flames circled the house like a lasso, then began to crawl up the sides. Joey's hands were clenched, his eyes intent as he followed the spreading fire. But like a kid determined to spot the magician's sleight of hand, sometimes even Joey was surprised by the fire's next move. The blaze leapfrogged over the open porch and to the top story. A window shattered. With another *whoosh,* the curtains caught. For a second, Joey thought he saw a flicker of movement, but he told himself it was a trick of the shifting light. There was no one home. Sissy had promised.

Heat tightened his skin. He stood at the end of the driveway, ready to slip into the woods as soon as he heard the sirens. But with no nearby neighbors, they were slow in coming.

Then came a moment when Joey knew the fire would win. The sound had shifted, like an engine shifting to a higher gear. The flames must have found a new, more concentrated source of fuel. Cans of paint in the basement, a natural gas line—something. He sniffed but couldn't smell anything except the sweet smell of burning wood. But still, the crackle and hiss became a roar, building and echoing until it was a wall of noise.

Finally he heard sirens in the distance. He moved farther back into the trees. As soon as he saw the first fire truck, he would slip away and make his way back to his El Camino. Like a man leaving his lover before a long journey, Joey feasted his eyes on the fire's beauty—the undulating colors, the flickering flames licking the sky, and the great pillar of smoke visible only because it blocked out the evening's first stars.

Tomorrow morning the house would be nothing but charred timbers and puddles, gray ash still drifting through the air. And the fire would be dead.

But for now, it was alive. And so was Joey.

"Believe me, she deserves it," Elizabeth had told him through gritted teeth as she gave him a hand-drawn map and five hundred bucks. Joey had been desperate for cash. It wasn't easy to get a job when you looked like he did. Not when a background check—even something as simple as typing his name into Google—turned up the truth of who he was. What he had done. So he needed the money.

But the thing was, Joey thought, his heart beating wildly in his chest as he watched the hungry flames, he would have done this for free.

CHAPTER 2

New Seasons Market

Elizabeth was pushing her cart down the aisles of New Seasons when she saw it. A beautiful royal-blue silk scarf tucked into the corner of another cart. The color, she thought, would complement her auburn hair and blue eyes. The cart also held a block of cheddar cheese, a half dozen cans, several boxes of pasta, and a gallon of milk. Not that much different from the contents of Elizabeth's own cart.

She looked around. An observer might have thought she was scanning the shelves for the next item on her list. But Elizabeth never shopped with a list. And what she was looking for was the cart's owner.

But she was all alone in aisle seven.

Without a second's hesitation, Elizabeth walked away from her cart. She didn't even think of it as her cart anymore. It was *the* cart. Or *a* cart. In a few more steps, in the time it took for her to begin pushing the second cart, to put her big black purse on top of the blue scarf, Elizabeth had completely forgotten the first cart. She could have just taken the scarf, but the idea of eating the other woman's food made her feel powerful.

Having Joey burn down Sara's house had awakened something in Elizabeth. Something strong. Something hungry. Something she hadn't felt in a long time. She had built up a perfect life for herself, and she wasn't going to let anyone spoil it. Sara had needed to be punished.

Feeling bubbly, almost buoyant, Elizabeth pushed her new cart toward the front of the store. The skin between her shoulder blades tingled as she imagined a woman, much like herself, looking in bewilderment for her cart. Her cart with the beautiful blue scarf.

As she pushed the cart toward the line of registers, Elizabeth added a half dozen more items, like a dog marking its territory. A golden-yellow beeswax candle, a clear plastic box of sixteen perfectly iced cookies, a log of goat cheese rolled in silver-gray ash. New Seasons had a reputation for carrying the best organically grown produce, the finest cuts of pasture-raised meat, and cheeses and pastas imported from all over the world.

It also wasn't cheap.

But Elizabeth did not believe in treating herself cheaply.

At the register, she transferred her groceries to the black rubber conveyor belt with one hand. With the other, she bunched up the scarf and in one quick motion tucked it into her purse. When she lifted her head, she caught the clerk staring at her. His name tag said *Clark S.* His brows drew together as he saw her hand emerge from her purse.

Elizabeth realized he thought she was shoplifting.

He wasn't her type—a grocery checker would never be her type—but Elizabeth gave him her very best smile, and his face smoothed out. Well, smoothed out as much as it could. Clark S. was about twenty, with horrible acne, red pustules alternating with old cratered scars. His eyes were striking—large, a deep greenish-blue—but who would ever look past those scars to see them? Or to see how he flinched every time someone looked directly at him?

Elizabeth bet she was the first woman who

had smiled at Clark in a long time. She felt him falling into her smile. His shoulders straightened, his hands moving mechanically as he slid each item past the scanner. He only had eyes for her.

She signed the check with a flourish and handed it over. Technically, it belonged to her old roommate, but Elizabeth had taken a book of checks from the bottom of the box before Korena moved out. With any luck it would be weeks before she noticed. And New Seasons prided itself on its friendly neighborhood atmosphere. An atmosphere that included accepting customers' checks and not asking to see any ID.

"Korena?" Clark asked, staring at the name on the check. "That's pretty."

Elizabeth let her eyes drop, as if in shyness. She was calculating what she could get from him. He was only a checker, but she had always had a sixth sense about people who might prove useful to her. This could be the beginning of a beautiful friendship.

"Why, that's the nicest thing anyone has said to me all day." She lifted her gaze and let her smile reach her eyes. Behind her she could hear a woman saying the words *blue scarf,* but Elizabeth didn't turn, didn't let her expression change even as a thrill raced down her spine. She didn't know if Clark heard it, or understood what it meant, but he didn't turn either.

As Clark placed her bags—half filled with items she hadn't chosen—into her cart, Elizabeth let her hand trail over all the impulse buys hanging on the wall behind her. Her fingers closed on an imported chocolate bar with hazelnuts. She slid it into her pocket just as he turned back to her. Giving Clark one last long smile, she began pushing her cart out the door.

By the time she reached her car, Elizabeth was already sucking the last of the chocolate bar from her fingers.

When she pulled out of the lot, she left the grocery cart right where she had unloaded it. Twenty feet from the cart corral.

CHAPTER 3

¿Por Qué No? Taqueria

Spring could be a tease in Portland. Today, she was in full flirt mode. Yellow daffodils edging a curb bobbed their heads in the light breeze. The sky was a pale blue, as if it had been washed clean and hung out to dry. Even here on North Mississippi Avenue, where telephone poles outnumbered trees, the birds were striving to outdo each other with trills and warbles.

Urban hipsters had turned this once-blighted area into a neighborhood filled with funky boutiques, tattoo parlors, and the city's hottest new restaurants. Most weren't special occasion places, but rather offered pizza, tapas, or breakfast all day. And even though the offerings were often modeled on Mexican or Filipino street food, they still used top-shelf ingredients like regional line-caught snapper or locally farmed organic greens.

Although the thermometer had barely broken sixty degrees, the open-air tables at ¿Por Qué No? Taqueria were crowded. Surrounded by colorful plates, sun-starved Portlanders people-watched, read newspapers and novels, pushed back sleeves to expose pale or tattooed arms, and in general sprawled like contented cats. Allison Pierce leaned back against the hot pink wall, but straightened up when she felt how it still held the chill of winter.

There were days when that was how Allison felt. Still a little cold inside.

"You okay, girl?" Nicole Hedges asked. She had an uncanny ability to read minds. "Too cold out here for you?"

"No, it feels good." Allison tilted her face up to the sun, listening to the driving beat of an old Clash song coming from inside the restaurant.

The waiter, a tall guy with a shaved head and a half dozen earrings, walked up with their drinks. "One Coke." He set the glass bottle, which the restaurant imported from Mexico, in front of Allison. "One iced tea"—this went to Nicole—"and one pomegranate martini." The last was for Cassidy Shaw, who rewarded him with a smile Allison thought her dentist could use as an advertisement.

"Hey, haven't I seen you on TV?" the waiter asked, prompting Cassidy to add a few more teeth.

"Channel Four," she said.

"That's it! The crime reporter." He pitched his voice like a TV anchor's. " 'This is Cassidy Shaw, reporting live . . .' "

"That's right." She ducked her head in a show of modesty. "Thanks so much for watching."

After giving her another starstruck smile, the waiter left. As Cassidy picked up her drink, Allison wondered if it would be comped. Probably. Cassidy had that effect on people. She also wondered if Channel Four had a policy against drinking during the middle of the day. Probably not. And even if it did, Cassidy wasn't a stickler for the rules. You didn't break the big stories without occasionally coloring outside the lines.

As a federal prosecutor, Allison would never drink during the workday. And no matter whether it was day, evening, or weekend, because she was an FBI agent, Nicole had to be fit and ready for duty at all times. She rarely drank more than a single glass of wine in the evening, and she carried her Glock to dinner, to the grocery store, and to her kid's third-grade play.

The waiter forgotten, Cassidy leaned forward and put her hand over Allison's. "So, are you feeling better?" Her nails were perfectly manicured, a contrast to Allison's, which were short and bare.

A few weeks ago Allison had miscarried, joining the imaginary club of Mothers Without Children. Only there was no color-coded ribbon to wear, no walkathon or T-shirt. Nobody talked about it. It was the kind of secret that women whispered to each other—if they said anything at all.

Allison had told only a few people, including Nicole and Cassidy. They understood, or at least they tried to, even though they came to it from different places. Nicole had a nine-year-old daughter and had never been married. Cassidy had had a string of boyfriends, but never talked about wanting kids.

The pain, the mess, the inexplicable shame—all of it was behind Allison now. Everything except the emotional aftermath. Maybe she wasn't meant to be a mother. Maybe it wasn't God's plan for her to have a kid. She was thirty-three, and every day she saw women a dozen years younger or even, occasionally, a dozen years older pushing a stroller. It seemed like any other woman—any girl—could have a baby as easy as pulling a letter from the mailbox.

Allison held out her hand, palm down, and wiggled it back and forth. "Some days I'm fine. Other days I wake up and wonder why I should bother to get out of bed."

"What happens then?" Nicole asked.

"Marshall brings me coffee, lets me talk about it, and doesn't try to tell me it happened for a reason."

Her husband believed, and most times Allison did, too, that they might not ever know why it happened. Just that it had, and that God could bring forth good out of bad, just as He had brought forth the flowers and the birds after what had seemed like an endless winter. On days like today, the deep sorrow lifted and Allison felt hope tugging on her sleeve. Now she offered up a silent prayer of thanks for her friends.

Fifteen years earlier, the three of them had graduated from Catlin Gabel, one of Portland's elite private schools. They had barely known each other then, although they had known *of* each other. Nicole had stood out by virtue of being one of the fewer than a half dozen African American students. Cassidy had been on the cheerleading squad. And Allison had captained the debate team.

At their ten-year high school reunion, they realized they all had something in common: crime. Cassidy covered it, Nicole investigated it, and Allison prosecuted it. At the time, Nicole was working for the Denver FBI field office, but not long afterward she was transferred to Portland. At Allison's suggestion the three women met for dinner, and a friendship began. They had half-jokingly christened themselves the Triple Threat Club in honor of the Triple Threat Chocolate Cake they had shared that day.

"Marshall's a keeper." Taking a sip of her drink, Nicole smiled her enigmatic, catlike smile.

Cassidy spoiled the effect by nudging her in the ribs. "You should know. How are things with Leif?"

But Nicole was not one to spill any details about her new relationship with a fellow special agent. Raising her eyebrows, she simply shrugged one shoulder and broadened her smile. Allison knew that might be all the answer they would ever get. Nic kept herself to herself.

The waiter set down their food, and the three women fell silent for a few minutes as they traded bites of crisp fish tacos, pork carnitas, and tingas made with spiced beef.

"So what's the latest on the Want Ad Killer?" Cassidy spoke around a mouthful of mango-and-cabbage salad. "Do you guys really think it's Colton Foley?"

A man had been attacking women who advertised "erotic massages" in the alternative paper. He would lure them to a hotel, where he tied them up and robbed them. And sometimes more. Three women had ended up dead—two in Portland and one in Vancouver, Washington. But the alleged culprit had been a shock. Even the judge was a little surprised when Allison brought him an arrest warrant to sign. Colton Foley was a medical student at Oregon Health Sciences University.

"You've seen the hotel surveillance tapes," Nicole said. "It's clearly him." Nicole was also on the Want Ad Killer task force; the FBI had been brought in since the murders had taken place in two states.

"Yeah, but he's a medical student," Cassidy protested. "Someone who is supposed to save lives, not take them."

"We've been told he has gambling debts," Allison said, although to her it didn't seem like much of an answer.

Cassidy wrinkled her nose. "His friends are all coming forward and saying he's the most wonderful human being."

"Well, he might be—to them," Nicole said. "Most people make a decision about someone within five seconds of meeting them. And then filter out any new information that contradicts it, only letting in stuff that supports it. Foley seems likely to be a sociopath or a psychopath. Basically, they mean the same thing. Lots of people love sociopaths, because they never get to see behind the mask."

Cassidy's perfectly arched eyebrows shot up. "What, are you saying Colton's like Ted Bundy? But look at him! Why does somebody like that need to kill? Everyone says he's smart, friendly, funny." She slurped her martini. "And it's more than just that first-five-seconds stuff. He's got a beautiful fiancée and a career as a doctor ahead of him. He's too successful to be nuts. Wouldn't other people in his life realize he was crazy?"

"Sociopaths aren't the kind of people you see hanging out on Burnside, talking to themselves," Nicole said. "They aren't out of touch with reality. Foley wasn't suffering some compulsion he couldn't fight against. If he were, he wouldn't have worn gloves or used disposable cell phones. He wanted money, so he targeted people he thought wouldn't go running to the police. It was his choice."

"And just because someone kills somebody else doesn't mean they're crazy, at least by a legal definition," Allison said, thinking about some of the cases she had prosecuted over the years. "Some people kill because they're overcome by passion and have a weapon available. And some kill very deliberately." Those were the ones she had trouble understanding.

Cassidy wrinkled her nose. "But really, wouldn't anyone have to be crazy to kill or torture another person? Isn't doing that by itself a kind of definition of insanity?"

Nicole snorted. "That's the kind of thinking that overloads our mental health system with people who can't be cured and don't want to be. Some people are just plain evil. Period. Doctors can label them, society can make excuses for them, but in the end, they are just a waste of good oxygen. Don't forget that Ted Bundy was a Boy Scout, president of his church youth group, and a good-looking law student."

"But still, why *kill* someone?" Cassidy asked. "If this guy needed money, why not just rob them and leave it at that?"

"But sociopaths don't see other people as people. Something's wrong with their wiring," Nicole said. "They don't have any empathy, and they don't feel fear. So they don't feel guilty when they kill. If anything, they feel powerful. This guy shot his victims and then robbed them. It's quite possible that the last thing Kimberly Stratton felt was Foley yanking the engagement ring from her finger."

"How could he be that cold?" Cassidy shivered. "It's not human."

Nicole shrugged a shoulder. "We all choose when—or if—to harden our hearts. Doctors can't break down when they see some little kid come into the ER with his leg torn off from a car accident. They can't freak out over some sweet old lady with a heart attack. So they laugh and make jokes and work as hard as they can. Soldiers, gang members, and terrorists—they all view certain groups as less than human, as objects. How do you think Hitler got the Germans to go along with what happened to the Jews? By telling people they were more like rats than people."

"So are you saying," Allison asked, "that there's a little bit of sociopath in all of us?" Nicole's view of humanity could be amazingly downbeat.

"Maybe there is. When we choose." Nicole spread her hands. "The real question is, why *not* kill someone? Most of us have something inside us that will tell us to stop, that is, if we don't override it with drugs or alcohol or prejudice. But a sociopath can do anything he wants because there's nothing inside him telling him to stop. To a sociopath, a human life has as much value as a wadded-up Kleenex."

"Maybe something happens to make them like that." Cassidy took the last sip of her drink. "Didn't Ted Bundy come from a messed up family, like his sister was really his mother, and his father was supposed to be his grandfather or something? Maybe Foley's family's not as apple-pie as they seem."

Nicole pointed at Cassidy with her fork. "You're acting like sociopaths don't have any choice about how they act. But they know enough about right and wrong to know they should hide their behavior. They're not like a schizophrenic who really believes he's hearing voices."

"Well, the only voice I want Colton to hear is mine," Cassidy said. "I'm trying to get a jailhouse interview with him. Something like that could get our ratings up—which we really need. People don't watch television for the news anymore. They go online if they need to know what's up. They only turn on their TV if they want visuals or some color. But an interview might bring them back to the set."

"At least until it shows up on YouTube," Allison said, causing Cassidy to make a face.

Nicole looked thoughtful. "Foley just might agree to it. That kind of person craves attention. Try to get him to brag—it might help Allison build her case. It's clear that Foley thinks he's smarter than any three people put together. People like him like to run their mouths."

Cassidy tucked a strand of her blonde bob behind her ear. "Just as long as it still makes for great TV."

They were all looking at the same guy, Allison realized, but seeing him through different lenses.

"No matter what, be careful. And don't believe everything he tells you." Nicole took her last bite. "A guy like that will only let you see the surface. Maybe the only people who really know what he's like are the women he's killed. Remember the parable about the scorpion that asks a frog to carry it across the river, then stings it halfway across?"

Allison hadn't thought of that story in years. Along the way it had gotten mixed up in her mind with the riddle about a man with a row-boat who needed to transport a fox, a chicken, and a bag of corn. Now she suddenly remembered how the first story had ended.

"And the frog says, 'Why did you do that?' And the scorpion answers, 'You knew what I was when I climbed on your back.' "

Nicole nodded. "Exactly. A scorpion is a scorpion. It can't help it. But that doesn't mean you shouldn't kill it if you get a chance."

CHAPTER 4

Portland Fitness Center

"Looking good, ladies," Elizabeth chanted, her unfocused eyes not seeing the women in the boot camp class at all. In a few hours Ian would be in for his workout, and she would make sure to run into him.

"Eighteen, nineteen, twenty! Great job!" She clapped her hands. "Time for fire hydrants. And they look like this." She got down on her hands and knees and lifted one leg like a dog, then jumped back to her feet in a single motion.

The women in the class regarded her enviously. So many of them were fat or old or clumsy. At least compared to her. It was one of the reasons Elizabeth enjoyed this class so much.

Calling out the count, she walked around the class. She bent down and lifted one woman's leg until the angle seemed impossible for the human body. "This is where you need to keep your leg." Inside, she smiled at the tears that now sparkled in the woman's eyes.

She looked at the clock, as so many of the women in the class did. Just a little over five hours until she would see Ian.

Ian McCloud was Elizabeth's boyfriend. Even if he didn't use the word yet. But for the past two months they had been seeing each other nearly every weekend. And Elizabeth didn't plan for things to end there. Boyfriend was good, but husband would be better.

Ian, Elizabeth believed, was her destiny. She deserved nothing but the best, and that's what Ian was. Not only was Ian drop-dead gorgeous—he had even been the prom king in high school, twenty years earlier—but he was also one of the city's top defense lawyers. The only fly in the ointment was his moneygrubbing ex-wife, Sara.

Thousands of dollars of alimony he paid her every month, just because she had waitressed to put Ian through law school. Now he billed nearly $900,000 a year, but his ex-wife and kid were like a drain, constantly sucking it away.

Which was why Elizabeth had hired Joey. To teach Sara a lesson.

She finished putting the class through its paces, leaving them red-faced and gasping.

As she left the room, she ran into frumpy Georgia, who worked at the front desk. Georgia was twenty years older than Elizabeth. She wore big blue plastic earrings, and even though she worked at a health club, she was forty pounds overweight. Elizabeth thought she was pathetic.

She flashed Georgia a smile. Georgia was the one who put together the schedules.

Georgia immediately brightened. "Oh, my goodness, don't you look cute today."

Elizabeth was wearing a turquoise-and-black tank top and black low-rise pants from Nike—an outfit that showed off her taut belly.

"Why, thank you, Georgia," she said with another big smile. "I can always count on you to brighten my day."

Georgia pressed a bulging manila envelope into her hand. "I'm glad I ran into you. You're one of the last people who needs to see this. It's to buy a baby gift for Bethany." A staff list for the gym was stapled to the outside of the envelope. Most of the names had already been crossed off. "We're all chipping in for a stroller."

"Oh, how sweet," cooed Elizabeth. Which one was Bethany again? The one with the ankles like a Russian peasant's? Why would any woman allow herself to be used like an incubator, to lose her shape, to have some parasite growing inside her?

Elizabeth took the envelope with her into the women's locker room, opened her locker, and sat down on one of the benches. She took her wallet from her purse. Then she pulled the white envelope and card from inside the manila envelope. The card was covered with signatures, but she wrote, *Congrats! XO! Elizabeth* across the photo of the baby on the inside.

She riffled her thumb over the stack of bills. A lot of singles, but some bigger bills too. She plucked out a twenty, a ten, and two fives and transferred them to her wallet.

A noise behind her made Elizabeth start. It was the housekeeper with her plastic cart of cleaning products. Her brow was furrowed and her gaze was fastened on Elizabeth's wallet.

"Just making change," Elizabeth said brightly.

She was already deciding how to get the cleaning lady in trouble. Maybe she could start dirtying up areas the woman had already cleaned, and then point them out to the manager. With a show of reluctance, of course. It shouldn't be too hard to get her fired. She was pretty sure the woman didn't even speak English.

CHAPTER 5

Mark O. Hatfield Federal Courthouse

The group of forty-nine fifth-graders stood open-mouthed in the huge open atrium, staring at the three-story waterfall that fell silently between two long panes of glass.

"Welcome to the Mark O. Hatfield United States Courthouse," Allison said as the kids gawked at the marble, limestone, and granite walls carved with quotations ranging from Mark Twain to Maya Angelou.

She gave these tours a few times a year. Fifth grade was a good age—old enough to understand, but not so old they tried to impress each other by acting out. She let herself think for a minute of the baby that had been growing inside her—the baby she had lost. Would it have looked like the girl with the long brown hair, or the boy with the wide blue eyes? Then she caught sight of a girl wearing a shiny metal brace on one leg. The left side of her face was markedly smaller, and white elastic bands held a small clear plastic plug in the hollow of her throat.

Allison brought herself back to her talk. "During your visit you'll see judges, jurors, lawyers, and other people involved in court cases. I'm a federal prosecutor, which means it's my job to prove to a jury that a person committed a crime and needs to be punished. To help you understand what I do, let me tell you about a case that really happened in Chicago a few years ago.

"Two middle school boys were on their way home from the doctor. But they got off their city bus at the wrong stop. They didn't recognize the area they were in, but they thought, 'No big deal, we'll just ask someone for directions and head on home.' " As she spoke, Allison made eye contact with each of the students.

"But before they could ask directions, some neighborhood boys started to tease them and told the lost boys that they weren't wanted in that part of town. Then they left, and the lost boys thought things were okay. But the neighborhood boys came back—with a baseball bat." Allison saw a few mouths drop. "Before the lost boys could run away, the neighborhood boys beat them up. Just because they didn't want the lost boys in their neighborhood."

Kids winced, and a couple of them felt the backs of their heads, as if in sympathy.

"Finally, the neighborhood boys took off. Luckily, the lost boys survived the beating and the other boys were arrested." She paused. "Are you with me so far?"

"But why did they beat them up?" asked a girl with huge dark eyes. "Why did the boys do that to them?"

She reminded Allison of Estella, a little Mexican American girl whose family she tried to help.

"Maybe they were afraid of the other boys. Maybe they came from families where the parents beat them, so they felt it was okay to beat others." Allison raised one shoulder. "Maybe they just did it because they could."

The girl pressed her fingers to her lips before asking her next question. "Was it because they were a different color?"

It hurt Allison's heart to think that the child might have experienced something similar herself.

"That was the theory of the case," she admitted. "The lost boys *were* black, and the neighborhood boys were white. But in this country, you can't treat people differently because of the color of their skin, or where they're from or what church they go to." She took a deep breath. "So, in Chicago, there was a federal prosecutor who does the same job that I do. And he got a call about what happened. He started working with an FBI agent. And the FBI agent and the prosecutor talked to the parents of the neighborhood boys, went to their school to talk to their teachers, and talked to witnesses."

Allison held up two fingers. "They were looking for two kinds of evidence." She switched to her index finger. "*Direct* evidence is information from a witness—or even a security camera—that sees or hears the crime. In this case, the direct evidence was the lost boys saying the neighborhood boys beat them up for no reason. There was also a four-year-old girl who saw the whole thing from her grandmother's window."

She added a second finger to the first. "The second kind of evidence is *circumstantial.* It's not based on firsthand experience. For example, say your mom comes home and finds cookies missing from the cookie jar. And there's a trail of crumbs leading to your bedroom." She tilted her head to one side. "But that does not *definitely* mean that you took them. Even if you are the only person in the house. In fact, it could mean that you have . . . *mice.*"

Several of the kids giggled.

"In this case, the neighborhood boys were charged with a hate crime. They were the defendants. They were told they could either hire a lawyer or get a free one—a public defender—provided by the government."

A girl wearing worn boots and a sundress that didn't seem warm enough for a cool spring day observed, "That's not fair. Why should they get a lawyer for free? They're the ones who did something wrong."

"Yes, but the government needed to prove it. In this country you can't just accuse someone of doing something bad. You have to provide evidence. That's why we say 'innocent until proven guilty.' " As she spoke, Allison wondered how many people had judged this girl solely on her worn clothes and tangled hair. The law was far more black-and-white than the real world.

"After someone is charged, there's a trial." She was simplifying things. In reality, eight out of ten of criminal defendants pled guilty and never stood trial. "At the trial, it's like there are two teams." She held out her left hand. "As the prosecutor, I'm on one team, and my goal is to have the defendant found guilty." She lifted her right hand. "And the defense's goal is to have the defendant found *not* guilty." She brought both hands together in the middle. "And the judge is like the referee. But before the trial can begin, the prosecutor has to do homework. He or she has to study the evidence, understand all the facts, and talk to three kinds of witnesses. A *lay witness* is a person who just watched what happened. An *expert witness* is a specialist. Like the prosecutor in this case called a fingerprint expert to testify that the prints on the bat matched the prints from the neighborhood boys."

"Like on *CSI*!" a boy wearing a red baseball cap said.

Allison winced. In her opinion, *CSI* was far too graphic for an eleven-year-old to watch. And the show sometimes led to unrealistic expectations. Leif Larson, who headed up the Portland

FBI's Evidence Recovery Team, had recently complained to Allison that jurors now expected him to be able to pull a fingerprint off running water.

Allison settled for a simple nod. "Like *CSI*, yes. And then a *character witness* is someone who knows someone involved in the case. They can say good or bad things. In this case, the prosecutor talked to people who said the neighborhood boys were known to be bullies. The federal prosecutor had to prove that the defendants, the neighborhood boys, committed the crime. And in this case, the neighborhood boys were found guilty."

"So what happened to them?" asked the boy in the red cap. "The neighborhood boys?"

"They were sent to a juvenile detention facility for several years."

"You mean like a jail?" He looked startled. "For kids?"

Allison nodded. "Just for kids, not adults."

The girl with the leg brace asked, "Why didn't they go real jail? They did something really bad."

It was the age-old debate about what the justice system was really about: punishing the perpetrators, deterring would-be criminals, rehabilitating lawbreakers, or protecting future victims.

"Well, our justice system believes that juveniles —children—can be rehabilitated."

Blank faces looked up at her.

"You know, that by sending them to these places, which are like special schools, they can learn how to be better people. That they can be fixed."

At the word *fixed,* the girl in the leg brace let out a soft snort.

Allison finished the tour by taking the kids to the sculpture garden off the ninth floor. The metal sculptures were whimsical or nonsensical, depending on your point of view. One showed an owl sitting atop a tree. Allison knew the owl was supposed to be wisdom, but she wasn't sure what the rest of it meant. A snake crept up the tree, while a beaver gnawed through the trunk. The snake probably represented sin or the devil. But the beaver? Maybe that was the sculptor's nod to Oregon, which was officially "The Beaver State." But then what was the meaning of the piece of paper and the computer—both portrayed with faces—fleeing the scene?

The kids didn't seem to care, though. They crowded around the sculptures or pointed out landmarks as they took in the panoramic view of the city, with the snowcapped peak of Mt. Hood in the distance. Below them the steel gray artery of the Willamette River cut through the city's heart. And they especially liked the ice-cream sandwiches Allison and their teacher handed out.

If Allison hadn't turned her head at just the right moment, she might not have seen it. The boy in the red cap snatched the ice-cream sandwich from the girl in the leg brace. Allison opened her mouth to call him on it, but before she could say a word, the girl met her eyes and gave her head one swift shake.

CHAPTER 6

Portland Fitness Center

Elizabeth stood in front of the mirror in the women's locker room and wished for the thousandth time that she were not merely pretty, but beautiful. Life would be so much easier.

She was only thirty-two, but she looked much younger. Her skin still looked good. No lines yet. Her arms were a little pale. Summer was just round the corner. She made a mental note to start hitting the tanning bed.

Leaning closer to the mirror, she brushed on another coat of mascara. It paid to look her best for Ian. Even seen from an inch away, her eyes were unshadowed. Since Joey had torched Sara's house, Elizabeth had been sleeping like a baby.

When she walked into the weight room, Ian was already there. His eyes were closed as he did a lat pulldown, the weight set at 140 pounds. Elizabeth's gaze roamed over the V of his shoulders, his strong arms, his black hair silvering at the temples. *Yum*.

He started when Elizabeth put her hands on his shoulders. "Open up your chest a little bit," she said, pretending to correct his form.

He turned his head to grin back at her. "You're a pleasant distraction for a Thursday." As he stood up, he let the weights stack back into place.

Elizabeth bit the tip of her index finger and gave him a naughty smile. Even though no one was close enough to hear, she lowered her voice. "Want to go someplace where you can be even more distracted?"

Last Monday they had ended up in the pool supply closet. Ian was clearly charmed by her impulsiveness and turned on by her firm body.

His expression turned serious. "I wish I could, but I need to cut my workout short. Our new house burned down Monday night."

Elizabeth put a hand to her chest and let her lips part. She had a whole repertoire of gestures, gleaned from careful observation and practiced in front of the mirror. "Are your ex-wife and Noah okay?"

Noah was Ian and Sara's five-year-old son.

"Yes. Thank God Sara was visiting her parents, or it could have been a whole different story." Ian shook his head, his eyes unfocused. "But the house is a total loss. It was our dream house, and now it's nothing but ashes."

Ian's marriage had broken up while the new house was under construction. Of course Sara had ended up with the dream house, leaving Ian with their old one. That woman did nothing but take and take from him.

Elizabeth touched his arm and broke the spell. His eyes refocused on her.

"So it was like an electrical fire or something?" she asked.

"No. Arson. They didn't make any attempt to hide it, either."

"Why would someone do that?" It gave Elizabeth a secret thrill to discuss something she already knew everything about.

"Sara just broke up with her boyfriend a few weeks ago, although he really doesn't seem like the type." Ian's mouth twisted. "If he did, I would never have let him near Noah. And she had kind of an ongoing argument with the neighbor, someone whose land is next to where we built the house. The police are looking at both of them."

Elizabeth had no idea the universe would supply such ready suspects. Things were looking up. Sara had been punished, and no one would ever be able to connect it to Elizabeth. And now Ian was letting his eyes run up and down her body, clearly thinking only of her again.

He added, "They already know we were at the Ringside when the fire broke out. I don't think anyone will talk to you, but you never know."

"I hope they catch whoever did it soon." Elizabeth leaned closer and walked her fingers up his chest. "Are you sure you can't spare a few minutes? I've missed you. It's been nearly three days."

"Sorry. I promised Sara I would help with the insurance paperwork."

Fury stiffened Elizabeth's spine and turned her fingers rigid as claws as she let her hand drop to her side. *Would that woman ever stop thinking of excuses to try to get Ian back in her life?* Taking a deep breath, she made herself relax and give him a playful smile. "Okay. But you owe me one."

CHAPTER 7

Northeast Portland

Nic was in the shower, humming an old Al Green song at the end of a long day, when her fingers found something in her left breast.

A lump.

Time seemed to stop. The inside of Nic's head emptied out. Or maybe there was a lid, a lid on her thoughts. If she lifted it even a fraction of an inch, her sickening fear would come boiling out.

The jets of water drummed against her back. She couldn't think. Didn't want to think.

She felt like she was out of herself, above herself. Part of her was standing in the brown-tiled shower. Part of her denied that she was even in the shower. Maybe she was already in her warm bed, dreaming this moment, and she would soon open her eyes, sit up, and forget this terrible nightmare.

She stood suspended, her fingers hovering just above the spot.

Then she pressed in again, rolling her index and middle fingers back and forth. Still there.

Some part of her brain must still be working, because Nic found herself cataloging what she found as if it were a piece of evidence, like a fingerprint or a blood spatter. Not perfectly round. Hard. Painless. She imagined laying one of the photo evidence rulers next to it. About a third of an inch across. The size of a large pea.

It was a lump. There was no other word for it. A lump. In her breast.

Could something so small kill her?

Nic couldn't move, couldn't draw a breath. The shower beat down on her.

Maybe it was a cyst.

But maybe it wasn't.

It could be cancer. Breast cancer. Loretta, their

old receptionist, had fought breast cancer for three years.

Fought and lost. When Loretta finally died, she had been reduced to bones and slack skin. With her naked, drooping head and her unfocused eyes, she had looked like a broken baby bird.

No. It was just a cyst. Nothing else. Certainly not cancer.

Nic couldn't die. Not now.

She couldn't leave Makayla alone.

CHAPTER 8

Portland Fitness Center

Cassidy was changing into her workout clothes for spinning class. She had perfected a method of getting dressed and undressed that involved showing as little skin as possible. She wasn't like some of the women at the gym who paraded to the shower wearing nothing but a pair of flip-flops and a towel thrown casually over a shoulder.

A woman with short dark hair sat down at the end of the bench. With a moan, she reached forward to turn the dial for her locker. "I can barely move my fingers, I'm so worn out."

Cassidy managed to pull on her sports bra at the same time as she took off her regular bra. "What class were you in?"

"Boot camp. They've only had it about six or seven months. And the instructor is brutal." The woman mopped her red face with one of the gym's thin white towels.

Cassidy remembered a quote, if not who said it: "What doesn't kill me makes me stronger."

"With boot camp, it's kind of a toss-up which is going to happen first. But look." The other woman hiked up her top to expose her midriff. "I'm starting to get a six-pack. I've never had one of those before."

Even though the woman was clearly sucking in her stomach—and Cassidy didn't begrudge her that; Cassidy always sucked in her stomach in the changing room—she did have the beginnings of a sculpted abdomen.

Cassidy poked her own stomach. "I've pretty much got a one-pack."

Thanks to the arch in her back, she had always had a shape like a jelly bean—perky butt, but a little bit of a belly—perched on slender legs. She had always wanted a six-pack. And fiercely muscled arms, the way all the celebrities had now. You wouldn't want to meet Madonna in a dark alley. Cassidy wanted to look fantastic in a sleeveless shell.

But she also knew she wasn't capable of doing it on her own. She needed someone standing over her, yelling.

The other woman ran her hand through her

sweat-soaked hair, making it stand up in short spikes. "If you want to get in the best shape of your life, then you've got to take this class. But you won't thank me for it. Not at first. A lot of people can't hack it and drop out. But if you keep with it, Elizabeth will whip you into shape."

Cassidy thought of Jenna. Jenna Banks was her chief rival at Channel Four, as ridiculous as the thought would have been a few months earlier. And Jenna had an amazing body.

"When is the class?"

"Six a.m. on weekdays. But by seven fifteen you are done for the day."

When the alarm went off Monday morning, Cassidy hit the snooze button three times before she managed to pull herself out of bed. She yanked her hair back into a ponytail and pulled on some sweats, all the while cursing Jenna under her breath. Jenna, with her tiny skirts and her waterfall of blonde hair, so shiny it looked like it had been polished. Jenna, who sat on a blue exercise ball during story meetings to "exercise her core." Like her core needed it. Jenna, who was supposed to be Channel Four's intern, but who had somehow managed to talk her way into a couple of actual assignments. Jenna, who pretty much sucked up all the male attention whenever she walked into the room.

Jenna, who was only twenty-two years old.

Eleven years ago, Cassidy had been a Jenna. Fresh out of college, eager to learn, eager to do whatever it took to get ahead. She had reported from state fairs and gruesome accident sites. Done her share of standing on icy overpasses while hyperventilating about a "winter storm watch."

She had paid her dues, and Jenna hadn't. Yet Jenna was occasionally picked for stories that Cassidy wanted. Cassidy was determined to fight fire with fire. She knew how to turn a head or two. But she needed to kick it up a notch.

It was 6:02 when she opened the door to the exercise studio. The room was completely full, intimidatingly full with women on their hands and knees kicking their bent right legs into the air like donkeys. The slender red-haired woman standing at the front of the class turned and looked at her. Really looked. It made Cassidy feel like she had never been looked at before.

"There's a spot right up in front," the redhead said, pointing at a mat in front of her.

Cassidy picked her way to it.

"I'm Elizabeth. Elizabeth Avery," the instructor said. Then she called out to the room, "Left leg now," and the women switched obediently, like some kind of synchronized dance team dreamed up by a sadist.

"I'm Cassidy." She got down on her hands

and knees, already counting the minutes until the class was over. Why had she ever thought this was a good idea?

"Okay, Cassidy, do you have any back or shoulder problems I need to know about?"

Cassidy briefly considered claiming a host of them. It would probably get her out of the worst of it. Then she thought of Jenna and her long, lean legs. Jenna was as single-minded as a shark. And what she was focused on was going right over Cassidy on her climb to the top. This was no time for shirking. "No."

"Okay, on your backs, everyone, fingertips on either side of your head. Abs in." Elizabeth lifted her hands, fingers spread, to demonstrate, revealing a slice of her flat belly. Then she shot her arms out, punching the air with fingers straight, miming legs. "The legs go in and out. Don't forget to breathe. And we're on our way to 100. One, two, three . . ."

Cassidy complied, although curled up from the floor as she was, her chin kept getting stuck in her cleavage. Which was all hers, no matter what the viewers who left stupid comments on Channel Four's website said.

By the time the hour was finished, Cassidy wanted to die. Or possibly she already had, although she had thought that when you were dead you were beyond the reach of pain. She lay on her back, spent, and felt the sweat run into her ears. Around her, women picked up their mats and gathered their things.

She couldn't move. She couldn't even twitch.

Then a hand entered her line of vision. Cassidy managed to look up without moving any other muscle in her body. With a groan she raised her own hand and Elizabeth, smiling, pulled her to her feet.

Even though Elizabeth had done most of the exercises right along with the class, not a drop of sweat darkened her color-coordinated outfit. "Did you survive?" she asked as she wiped off Cassidy's mat and hung it on the wall.

Cassidy managed a smile, although she guessed it looked as fake as it felt. "Barely."

"So, Cassidy, what do you do when you're not donkey kicking?"

Cassidy was taken aback. Her face was on billboards along I-5 and I-84. Granted, it was just one of four faces, but still. She hoped that it was just that dressed down, she was somewhat incognito. "I'm a TV crime reporter."

Elizabeth tilted her head. "For which channel?"

"Channel Four."

Elizabeth seemed to be doing a rapid calculation. "Oh, that's where I've seen you. And you're even prettier in person. I guess it's true what they say about the camera adding ten pounds."

Cassidy forced a smile.

"Want to grab a cup of coffee or something to eat?" Elizabeth asked. "My treat."

Cassidy looked at her watch. The morning story meeting wasn't for another hour and a half. She guessed that was the bright side of getting up before the sun. "Sure, I'd love that. Just let me take a quick shower, and I'll meet you in the café."

Ten minutes later Cassidy let her teeth sink into a buttered bagel. After all that exercise, she could afford it.

Elizabeth was only drinking a cup of Earl Grey tea. Pulling her tea bag from the water, she said, "Too bad they don't have loose tea here."

"Why?"

"When I was a kid, I learned how to read tea leaves."

"Cool!" Cassidy had been to a psychic, had her palms and her aura read, and checked her horoscope every day. She thought of it as getting a leg up on the future. "About the only thing I learned when I was a kid was how to hide the school cafeteria spinach in my milk carton. Did you grow up here?"

Elizabeth waved one hand. "Oh, here, there, and everywhere. My mom was kind of a free spirit."

"And your dad?"

"Have you heard of—" And Elizabeth named a famous rocker who had made a name for himself in the early seventies. When Cassidy nodded

—who *hadn't* heard of him, even if he looked more like a lizard every year—Elizabeth said, "I don't tell many people, but that's my dad."

"Your dad?" The guy, as far as Cassidy knew, had never been married.

Elizabeth shrugged. "One-night stand with my mom after a concert. But he was always good about paying child support."

"Do you ever spend any time with him?"

"Now and then." Elizabeth smiled, a little mysteriously, which whetted Cassidy's appetite even further. Elizabeth could probably tell a million stories about the rich and famous people her father hung out with.

Normally, Cassidy would have been jealous of someone like Elizabeth, with her perfect body, flawless complexion, and fascinating past. But it didn't feel like they were competing.

Instead, it felt like Cassidy had met some missing piece of herself.

CHAPTER 9

Portland Fitness Center

Elizabeth sipped her tea, noting the slight shine on Cassidy's upper lip where she had bitten into her buttered bagel too enthusiastically. She had been terrible in boot camp, not pushing herself at all, but Elizabeth was willing to overlook that.

For now.

"How long have you been teaching here?" Cassidy asked.

"About nine months." Elizabeth had started out as just a patron. A patron who wanted to look good. Having a great-looking body made everything so much easier. As a bonus, the gym attracted a lot of rich, divorced men from Portland's West Hills.

Then one day the guy who taught the sculpting class was sick. Elizabeth volunteered to fill in—and did such an outstanding job that she was asked to replace the teacher. Of course, it didn't hurt that she dropped a few hints to the manager about the original teacher's occasionally slurred words and erratic behavior.

And Elizabeth had even taught at health clubs before. At least that's what it said on her resume.

The resume was a work of art. It listed jobs she had never held at health clubs that never existed, promotions that had never happened, professional memberships in nonexistent organizations, awards she had never received, and a fake degree. Accompanying it were letters of recommendation she had written herself.

Personal trainer was just Elizabeth's latest incarnation. For a few years she had been a graduate student who managed to qualify for generous scholarships by lying on her application, cheating on tests, and finding others who were willing, even anxious, to write her papers. After an unfortunate occurrence with a provost, she had been forced to leave school.

For a few years she had been a rich man's mistress. Donald Dunbar, who was heir to a family fortune, liked to surround himself with fine things. He leased a condo and a new Lexus for her, and furnished the condo in the quietly moneyed style he expected to be surrounded by. He even bought Elizabeth a fur coat, which was anathema in the relatively warm and more than relatively progressive Portland. Don taught her how to dress, how to appreciate quality in everything from liquor to tailoring, and how to shoot his extensive arsenal of guns. He'd died while they were on safari in Africa, leaving his wife a multimillion dollar estate and Elizabeth nothing but the things he had kept at the condo and the gifts he had bought her. But after a frank talk in which Elizabeth was forced to spell out just how much damage she could do to the dead man's reputation, Don's widow had offered to reimburse her for her time and energy.

During the boom years, when houses were on the market for less than a day, Elizabeth had reinvented herself as a real estate agent. She steered clients to bigger and bigger houses—which meant bigger and bigger commissions—and to mortgage lenders who didn't ask too many questions and who were willing to kick back a little something to her for her business.

But when the bottom fell out of the market, Elizabeth had to remake herself yet again. It wasn't too hard. All it took was a little imagination. She couldn't fathom why people would wait their turn or work hard for things they wanted, not when it was easy enough to find a shortcut.

The owners of the Portland Fitness Center—part of a small local chain—were thrilled to have her on staff. As were most of the students. Most, but not all. Certain people tended to drop out over time—the chubby, the clumsy, the ones who couldn't take a joke. The ones she had no use for.

Telling people what to do was a good fit for Elizabeth. And rotating among the chain's three clubs gave her the chance to meet a wide variety of people and gain power over the ones she chose to single out.

In her head, Elizabeth called what she did "The Game."

The rules were simple: to pretend to be whatever someone else needed until they gave you whatever *you* needed. After that, there were no rules. The Game was fair, at least to Elizabeth's way of thinking. Anyone could play it. In fact, she was sure most people *were* playing it; they just didn't like to admit it. Sure, there were a few losers and idiots, suckers who, for whatever reason, didn't mind getting played. And some people were so weak that they played poorly, basically inviting anyone to take advantage of them.

Living with Grandma had taught Elizabeth the basic rules. At Grandma's she had learned that you were either a giver or a taker, predator or prey.

And Cassidy Shaw had all the hallmarks of prey. The corners of her mouth turned up any time Elizabeth praised her job, her highlights, her French manicure. And turned down any time Elizabeth mentioned calories, age, looks, or career advancement.

Elizabeth had a gift. Within a few minutes of meeting people, she could identify what they liked least about themselves. Did they think they were too shy, too fat, too ugly? She knew. If it was worth her while she then pretended to accept them exactly as they were: shy, fat, poor, bulimic, whatever. Even if they disgusted her. To deepen the bond, she would reveal that she secretly shared the same flaw as her newfound friend.

She could be whatever anyone needed. Patriotic or prissy. Worldly or naïve. Strong, if someone longed to be dominated. Submissive, if they wanted to dominate. She might pose as a celebrity, a suffering artist, a misunderstood spouse. Sometimes her lies came so easily that she almost believed them herself as she heard them come out of her mouth.

Elizabeth adjusted her message to match whatever she saw in the recipient's face, read in the body. The feedback allowed her to build and maintain control—at least until she was done. Or bored. Her most recent best friend had lasted just long enough to cosign the loan for Elizabeth's new car.

All Elizabeth had to do was to give people what they longed for. Or pretend to give it to them, which was basically the same thing. After that it was like the Latin saying Elizabeth had learned at the Spurling Institute—*quid pro quo*. A trade. For as long as she needed them, she offered people acceptance, love, understanding. And in turn, people gave her what she needed. Money. Power. Sex. Secrets. Admiration. Thrills.

Now Elizabeth tried out another topic, like a fisherman casting a new lure into the water. Leaning closer to Cassidy, she whispered, "How come if this is a health club, the men all look so schlumpy?" She cut her eyes to two guys drinking coffee a few tables away. One man's shorts and sweat-stained T-shirt were accented with black socks and brown shoes. His friend had a comb-over that consisted of about five extremely long strands of hair curled in a spiral.

"Men," Cassidy said with a shrug.

But Elizabeth caught the shadow that crossed her face. She gave her imaginary line a tug.

"I've had terrible luck with men. Sometimes I think that all men are just, just . . ."

"Users?" Cassidy supplied.

"Exactly." Hook, line, and sinker. Elizabeth took a sip of her tea. "What about you? You can't be single, can you?"

"My last boyfriend—well, he had some issues. And he took them out on me."

Elizabeth bit her lip. "I dated someone like that." She hadn't, of course, but she trusted her mouth to come up with the right words even before her mind knew what they were. "He seemed to think he wasn't abusive if he didn't leave actual bruises. Instead he just did a number on my self-esteem."

Cassidy's next words came in a rush. "Once Rick pulled a gun on me." She put her hand over her mouth, looking surprised.

Around Elizabeth, people readily offered up their secrets.

"Yeah, like that made him some big man." Elizabeth snorted.

"I sprayed bathroom cleaner in his eyes."

"Good for you!" Elizabeth made a mental note. Maybe this one wasn't as weak as she looked.

Cassidy looked around, leaned closer. "I don't tell too many people the details."

The first part of The Game was to win the other person's trust. But you didn't really win until he or she was willing to give you whatever you needed.

Elizabeth continued to exchange stories with Cassidy, only hers were just that: stories. She didn't tell her new friend about Ian. Let her think they had loneliness in common.

As she wove her web, Elizabeth thought that Cassidy offered so many possibilities. Her clothes were expensive, so she probably had money. And she seemed to know everyone, name-dropping like crazy. *My old boyfriend, the radio host. My pal, the mayor. My good friend, the federal prosecutor. My other good friend, the FBI agent.*

Elizabeth didn't like the sound of those last two. She'd seen prosecutors and even FBI agents up close. They were the enemy. They only existed to entrap people. They didn't understand that sometimes you were forced to do something distasteful. That it was a matter of self-defense. She filed their names away. Allison Pierce and Nicole Hedges.

She couldn't—wouldn't—allow them to get in the way of her playing The Game.

CHAPTER 10

Mark O. Hatfield Federal Courthouse

Colton Foley had been arrested six days ago. Two days later he had gone before a judge. Declaring Foley both a flight risk and a possible risk to the community, the judge had denied bail. Now Allison had only a little more than three weeks to give a grand jury cause to indict him for the crimes attributed to the man the media had dubbed "The Want Ad Killer."

The judge had signed Foley's arrest warrant after Allison showed him several pieces of evidence. The first were surveillance videos taken in hotels where the three women had been found murdered. Each showed a dark-haired man wearing a baseball cap and a navy-blue Columbia jacket walking down a hotel corridor or through a hotel lobby. The second came from an Internet service provider that had tracked an e-mail sent to one victim back to Foley's seven-story condo building. And the third was a videotape the FBI had secretly made, beginning at dawn the day before, of every man who entered or exited that building. The videotape showed a man with the same color hair, the same physique, the same gait, and even what appeared to be the same Columbia jacket, walking out of the building and then getting into a car registered to Foley. Of course, Colton Foley wasn't the only five-foot-eleven guy with brown hair who lived in the condominiums. The clincher was an e-mail the victim had sent to a friend shortly before she died. In it, she had said her next client was a med student.

But Colton Foley was no dummy, and neither was his lawyer, Michael Stone. So Allison had to move carefully and make sure the case was airtight.

Mike Stone was Portland's premier lawyer—if you were in deep, deep trouble. He took on clients other lawyers avoided—swim team coaches accused of child molestation, surgeons who had operated while three sheets to the wind, bank presidents caught embezzling millions.

When you were in the fight of your life or your career, Stone was the guy you wanted sitting at the defense table. If you could pay his steep fees, you got the slickest lawyer in town, one who always had an ace—or two or three—up his hand-tailored sleeve.

Foley's parents certainly didn't have the money. His mother was a cashier, his father a TriMet bus driver. But the med student did have a great-aunt who had plenty of money and who was sure that "dear Colton could never have done these terrible things."

Just being defended by Stone was a sure sign

that you were involved in something embarrassing or off-putting. But if you were one of the people who came to him, then you couldn't afford to be choosy. Couldn't afford not to pay his high fees. Because otherwise Stone would be more than happy to leave you to the services of a public defender.

Allison checked her watch. 11:58. Getting up, she turned on the small TV in her office to Channel Four. Cassidy had told her that Stone had announced plans to hold a press conference at eleven. The media-savvy Stone had picked a time that would ensure it would get the most play. Most stations wouldn't risk a live news conference in case it turned out to be filled with nothing but hot air, but the eleven o'clock time frame allowed them just enough time to film and edit a two-minute segment.

Allison would never have gone—it would show weakness—but she would watch all the coverage and order transcripts. The catnip Stone had offered the media was Foley's fiancée. Until now, she had been in hiding. Stone had promised that she had something important to reveal to the press.

After briefly running through the day's top national and local stories—flooding in Ohio, a child left stranded on a MAX rail platform, a tease about the week's weather—the news anchor cut away to Mike Stone standing in front of a bank of microphones in what looked like a hotel conference room.

In ringing tones, Stone said, "My client, Colton Foley, is not guilty of these ridiculous trumped-up charges. I am confident that at the end of the day, given the facts of this case, the lack of evidence, and the faulty investigation, my client will be freed. Colton has the full support of his family, his friends, and his fiancée, Zoe Barrett, who is with me here today. I have not received any document or report or piece of evidence other than what I heard in the courtroom. All I have at the moment are words—no proof of anything."

Seeing as how Stone's clients literally lived and died by words, Allison found it grimly amusing that he dismissed them so blithely. But it was true that they needed more evidence to convict Foley. The search of the condo that he shared with his fiancée had turned up a roll of duct tape and a single pair of plastic flex-cuff restraints—no gun or weapon, and nothing from any of the victims.

Stone continued, "The police completely searched my client's condominium but found absolutely nothing of any significance. A roll of duct tape? Heck, if that's all it takes to be guilty of these crimes, 75 percent of Portlanders could be indicted."

A few of the reporters laughed.

"And as for the plastic handcuffs, Zoe has a few words she would like to say."

The young woman, her eyes downcast so that her shoulder-length blonde hair obscured her face, stepped to the microphone. "This is very embarrassing for me to say, but Colton and I sometimes used those plastic restraints to play games." She exhaled, and the microphone caught how her breath wobbled. "They were my idea. Of course, I had no idea that my personal and private life would have to go on display to right this travesty of justice. I love Colton and will continue to stand by him until he is freed and we can resume our wonderful life together."

Oh, honey, Allison thought as she looked at the trembling girl. *Did someone put you up to that? Or was your boyfriend clever enough to have covered his own tracks in advance?*

Then it was back to the news anchor. "Our own Cassidy Shaw was at the press conference this morning, but neither Foley's attorney nor his fiancée took questions."

The camera pulled back to show Cassidy sitting next to the anchor.

Cassidy looked into the camera, and it was like she was looking right into Allison's eyes. "I understand the crime lab is trying to link the single plastic restraint found at Foley's condo to the ones that bound the victims' hands. But Foley's attorney is right—the federal prosecutor needs more than circumstantial evidence to win this case."

• • •

It was dark by the time Allison got home. As she walked up the path, the rhododendron in front of her rustled. She stopped, the back of her neck prickling. You couldn't be a federal prosecutor for five years without making enemies. Was one of the many threats she had received about to become a reality? Should she scream for Marshall, try to get back in her car, dial 911?

But before she could move, a voice broke the stillness.

"Ally?"

"Lindsay?" Her sister. The perennial bad seed. Or the bad penny, always turning up.

Allison had been sixteen and Lindsay thirteen when their dad died. As their mother lost herself in loneliness and a bottle of brandy, Allison became the adult and Lindsay became the trouble-maker. Each finding her own way to cope. Only Lindsay's had led to a rap sheet by the time she was eighteen. She had even spent six months in the Spurling Institute. As an adult, her life wasn't much different. In and out of jail, in and out of rehab, off-again, on-again boyfriends with problems of their own.

Accompanied by the sound of snapping twigs, Lindsay pushed her way out of the bushes. Allison hoped it was just her hiding place that had left her black hair so tangled, the overhead porch light that made her eyes and cheeks dark hollows. The prettiness, the enthusiasm, the energy that had been there at thirteen had long ago dissipated. Now, at thirty, Lindsay looked far older than her older sister.

Allison was torn between crossing her arms and reaching out to hug Lindsay. She compromised by leaving her hands dangling loose by her side. "Why are you here?" How many tears, how much money, how many sleepless nights had Lindsay cost her?

"I need a place to stay. I broke up with Chris. For good this time." Lindsay swiped the hair from her eyes. "And I'm clean, Allison. I really am."

Which of those things were true? Any of them? Lindsay couldn't seem to keep away from Chris. And she couldn't seem to keep away from drugs. Pot, coke, and for the past few years, meth. At least, as far as Allison knew, her sister had never done any needle drugs. Thank heaven for small favors. Of course, she still might have Hep C or HIV, but if she did, it hadn't come from sharing a needle.

"Why aren't you at Mom's?" Allison worked to keep her voice neutral.

"She won't let me in. Mom stood in the door to our house—our house!—with the chain on and said she couldn't. Said her counselor told her she had to let go of me." Lindsay's voice broke. "But where am I supposed to go, Ally? What am I supposed to do?"

Allison was on the verge of echoing her mother's words. Then she thought of Peter. Peter asking Jesus, "How many times must I forgive my brother? Up to seven times?" And Jesus' answer, "Not seven, but seventy times seven."

She reached for her sister's hand while she found her house key with the other. "Come on in."

And Allison prayed she was making the right choice.

CHAPTER 11

Bridgetown Medical Associates

The white paper on top of the examining table crackled under Nic's thighs as she shifted restlessly. Her fingers reached up and found the lump. Still there. At odd moments during the day—and even while she slept—she kept touching it. Trying to prove to herself that she had been wrong.

Now she ordered herself to stop. She was wearing a blue exam gown patterned with snowflakes. It concealed her body about as well as a cape. Around her wrist was a bright-green plastic spiral bracelet holding the key to the locker where she had stashed her clothes and purse. Her Glock was locked in a gun safe in her car. And on the exam table next to her left thigh was a pen and a small notebook. She didn't want to chance forgetting something important.

Nic couldn't remember the last time she had been to the doctor for anything besides a physical. Even today, with everything going on, her blood pressure and pulse had been low when the assistant took them. It had taken her nearly a week to get this appointment, which was both too soon and not soon enough. What if the cells were dividing at an exponential rate? What if those few days turned out to be the difference between life and death? Whenever she thought about it, her breath seemed to only go as far as the hollow of her throat.

Nic wanted to be anywhere but here. Maybe if she got up from this table, threw on her clothes, and hurried out before the doctor could make any pronouncements, she would be safe.

And so would Makayla. That was the heart of her fear. Not for herself, but for her child. And at nine, Makayla was still a child.

The irony was that Nic sometimes entertained morbid fantasies about her daughter—Makayla coming down with leukemia or meningitis, Makayla hit by a car or bitten by a dog—just to insure her safety. Because if she worried about it, it would be too ironic for it to actually happen.

But Nic had never bothered to worry about herself.

She couldn't—she wouldn't—leave Makayla alone on this earth. Because who would raise her? Every redundant aspect of Nic's life was organized, except this one. She had never made a will, because she couldn't decide whom to name as her daughter's guardian. Nic's parents were good people, and they loved their granddaughter as much as Nic herself did, but they were growing frail. Her four brothers? They didn't always see eye to eye. But how would Makayla become a healthy adult without someone Nic trusted to guide her?

Nic put her hand on her belly and tried to take a breath that went all the way down.

There was a knock on the door. Dr. Magel came in and shook Nic's hand. She was slightly plump, with dark curls and light brown skin. Turning to wash her hands in the sink, she asked Nic questions over her shoulder.

"And you're—how old again?"

"Thirty-three."

"When did you first notice the lump?"

"About ten days ago."

"Any family history of breast cancer?"

"No." Nic then amended it to, "Not that I know of." Who knew what her parents' aunts and cousins and grandparents' sisters had died from? And she wasn't going to tip off her parents by inquiring. Not until she was sure there was something to worry about.

"Okay, lie back and I'll do a breast exam." Dr. Magel's gloved hands were warm. She looked, not down at Nic's breasts, but off into the distance. Nic tried to read her face, but it gave nothing away. Then her fingers stopped. "Is this it?"

"Yes."

She gently kneaded it. "Well, there's definitely something there, but your breasts are pretty fibrous, which at your age is more common than not. And nine out of ten lumps aren't cancerous. We're going to need an ultrasound and a mammogram to start. We can have those done down the hall, and then we'll talk again."

Nic had never had a mammogram before. It didn't hurt as much as she had heard. After imaging both breasts, the technician switched to smaller plates and only did her left breast, zeroing in, Nic imagined, on the spot. The lump.

The mammogram tech pressed the button for the X-rays and then checked out the digital images to make sure they were clear. When she did, Nic tried to read her face, but it revealed nothing. For the ultrasound, a different tech had her lie down, smeared cold lubricant on her breasts, then slid a handheld sensor over each one, lingering on the lump again as she peered at her screen. Nic watched this woman's face, too, but her intent expression gave away nothing.

Everything could go up in flames. Without any warning. Just when Nic was beginning to heal from what had happened a decade ago. After all this time, she was finally starting to feel safe around men. Well, around Leif anyway.

Was it a mistake to be here alone? In her head she had tried out telling people.

She couldn't bring that kind of cold fear to her mother. Or see the pain in her father's big sad eyes. No parent wanted to outlive a child.

And Leif? Once the doctor gave Nic the bad news, Leif would keep up a good front, sacrifice himself, pretend to still find her attractive, even after he secretly felt only pity. The Nic Leif was attracted to was strong, confident, professional, beautiful. Cancer could take all that away. Leif would support her unconditionally. Nic knew that in her gut. But whatever it was between them might not be strong enough to survive a life-or-death challenge.

Then there were Cassidy and Allison, her best friends. She knew she could count on them to support her, at least in their own ways. But either of them, when faced with something that might be bearing down on her like a freight train—how rational and lucid would they be?

Cassidy would move heaven and earth to help her, but she would also probably try to redecorate Nic's house according to feng shui, or beg her to go to some kind of alternative medicine provider who would prescribe coffee enemas and elder-flower root.

Allison knew what it was like to have your body betray you, to be consumed by something you had no control over. She would understand, at least a little, how Nic was feeling. But she would probably want to pray over Nic, or at least for her. Like that would help. It was like islanders thinking the weather gods were angry after a tsunami. You grasped at straws when you were desperate. Looked for symbols and portents, willing to sacrifice anything to save yourself. Once Nic had even found herself praying when she thought she was on the verge of death—and then had been ashamed of her weakness.

For now, she was saying nothing to them. She needed her friends to not treat her any differently. It allowed her to pretend that this wasn't happening.

She sat straight-backed in the waiting room, her notebook and pen on her lap, while she waited for her test results. Finally the nurse led her back to Dr. Magel's office. The doctor was sitting behind a wooden desk, looking at her computer screen. Nic took one of two seats opposite her.

Dr. Magel looked up. "Our radiologist says the mammogram is inconclusive. The ultrasound, though, shows a dense spot. In other words, it's not a fluid-filled cyst, but rather something else.

It could be a fibroma, which are fairly common and benign. Or it could be cancer. I'm going to refer you to a surgeon to discuss next steps. But we need to get this looked at."

Nic realized she hadn't written a word in her notebook. "Do you think it's cancer?"

"Nicole, it's too early to say."

But it seemed to Nic that Dr. Magel's eyes told a different story. One where she knew that the news was bad.

Allison was always telling her there was a God. But what kind of a God would give Nic everything and then just snatch it away?

CHAPTER 12

Portland Fitness Center

"That's Elizabeth," Cassidy whispered to Allison as they entered the exercise room. She had badgered Allison and Nicole until they had agreed to give boot camp a try. It was hard to claim a conflict when the class started at six a.m.

Elizabeth was as tall as Allison, with rich auburn hair cut in a swinging bob that showed off her high cheekbones. Her intense blue gaze seemed to weigh and measure Allison in a half second. A wave of dizziness passed over her, and she had to put her hand on Nicole's arm to steady herself.

"Are you all right?" Nicole's brow creased with concern.

Allison straightened up. "Just a touch of vertigo, that's all. The doctor says I'm a little anemic." She hoped that was the reason there were still times she felt flattened and empty. And why this woman's gaze had left her off balance.

The only three mats next to each other were in the last row. Cassidy looked disappointed, but Allison was relieved that they wouldn't be right in front of the instructor.

When the three of them had been at Catlin Gabel together, Allison had been a straight-A student. Except for PE. No matter how hard she tried, she was rewarded with a string of Cs. Allison's natural reaction when a ball of any type came in her direction was to duck. Even in sports without balls, her clumsiness was always on display. She twisted her knee on the pommel horse, knocked over rows of hurdles, and in archery bruised her arm from elbow to wrist with the bowstring. Even standing on top of a balance beam had seemed as daring as Icarus flying to the sun on wax wings. With each new sport, the only thing that changed was the location of Allison's bruises.

Coordinated people had always intimidated

her. She might be able to argue circles around them, but once she was on a dance floor they would best her, no problem.

Or in an exercise studio. By the time Allison got the hang of one move, Elizabeth was switching to the next. Longingly, Allison looked at the clock on the wall again, but the hands seemed not to have moved. She still had forty-five minutes to get through. Forty-five minutes of torture.

Next to her Cassidy gamely puffed along. If it had been Nicole who had been singing the praises of this class, Allison could have understood. But Cassidy? Cassidy and discipline did not belong in the same sentence. Unless it came to her job. Then Cassidy would willingly do the heavy lifting, if it meant she ended up with a great story.

Cassidy looked over with her brows pulled together, as if Allison's panting and poor form personally reflected on her. "Suck it in," she mouthed, patting her own hollowed-out stomach.

The problem was that Allison already *was* sucking it in. But no matter how hard she tried, a little shelf of flesh remained just below her navel. If she hadn't miscarried, it would have made a comfortable cradle for the baby. Lately she had tried to fill that empty space with eating. Everything from Cool Ranch Doritos from the office vending machine to olive-oil poached halibut and the spring vegetable medley at Paley's Place. At home, there were scalloped potatoes made with half-and-half and Tillamook cheddar cheese. Umpqua Dairy's almond mocha fudge ice cream.

And now that her sister was living with them, Lindsay seemed to be trying to bake her way into their hearts. Every night Allison came home to the smell of fresh-baked cookies or brownies. Just thinking about food made her want to stand up, walk out of class, and buy a slice of coffee cake from the snack bar they had passed on the way in.

Allison hadn't felt in touch with her physical self since she lost the baby. Her body had betrayed her. She had done everything right—or as right as one humanly could—and still it had turned on her.

After the miscarriage, she had thrown herself into her work, spending evenings at her desk, coming in early to try to catch people before they went out for the day on the East Coast. When she came home, she only had enough energy to eat and go to bed. Not to hit the treadmill.

Elizabeth barked out, "Second set of lunges."

Second set? Allison had only managed the last few repetitions by telling herself it was nearly over.

Cassidy was watching Elizabeth with something like awe. This was a side to her that Allison hadn't seen before. Cassidy seemed to long for this woman's approval, automatically doing everything a little bigger and better any time Elizabeth's gaze turned in her direction.

On the other hand, Cassidy had kind of an addictive personality, and exercise certainly beat her past problems with men, alcohol, and Somulex. If her friend was going to plunge headfirst into something new, Allison thought as she sneaked another glance at the clock, at least boot camp was a healthy choice.

CHAPTER 13

Portland Fitness Center

"And squat and press," the instructor said, demonstrating. "Focus on the ceiling to help keep your spine aligned." Nic obeyed, but instead of staring up at the ceiling, she found herself looking at the other women's breasts in the mirror. Small, big, bouncing, sagging. But they all seemed to have them. What if she went through this thing and she lost one or both of hers? She would gladly give them up. In a heartbeat.

But what if she lost her life?

It was the thought she kept circling back to, like a tongue probing a sore tooth until it flares into agony.

There were so many things—like her breasts and her hair—that would have seemed so important a few days ago. Now she was ready to sacrifice them without a second thought.

The instructor, Elizabeth, had perfect breasts. Perfect everything. Her arms and legs were as taut and smooth as if they belonged to one of Makayla's dolls. Nic wondered how much upkeep was required to look so flawless. If her hair was highlighted, then it must take her stylist hours to achieve those dozens of shades of cinnamon, paprika, and red chile. Or maybe Elizabeth was just one of those genetic freaks who woke up every morning looking beautiful.

Elizabeth flashed her a hard look, and Nicole realized she was staring. She pulled her gaze away as Elizabeth said, "Okay, let's do some squats."

While she demonstrated the correct form, Nic bent over and wiped her forehead with the hem of her T-shirt. This class was proving to be something of a surprise. It took a lot to get her to sweat.

But now her body, which still appeared strong, held a rottenness at its core. Oh, she knew Dr. Magel would say that it was far too soon to know. But Nic knew. From the moment her fingers touched it, she had known that her body had turned on her in secret.

Scattered moans rippled through the group as

Elizabeth called out, "Nineteen and twenty!"

There was something about the instructor that turned Nic off. She didn't like jealousy, especially in herself, but that's clearly what it was. Five years ago, when Allison, Cassidy, and Nic had gotten reacquainted after their tenth reunion, Cassidy had been enthralled with the idea that Nic was an actual FBI agent, plied her with all kinds of questions. Now Cassidy was in the throes of a new enthusiasm. It wasn't pretty, but Nic had to admit that she must be feeling a little green-eyed.

These days everything went through the filter of knowing that she might be dying. And not a lot made it through. Most things simply turned into white noise. With just a portion of her brain, Nic interviewed witnesses and prepared the reams of documents for the Foley case. At home, she signed permission slips and homework logs for Makayla, pressed the phone to her ear as her mother worried about her older brother's impending divorce, put tasteless food in her mouth and automatically chewed. But her thoughts were elsewhere.

Where, she wasn't sure.

So the secret of the lump and all it might mean stayed inside. It didn't press up against her lips, begging to be released. Instead it was a small black hole in the pit of her stomach, sucking up her energy and time and emotions.

“Okay, let’s stretch out for the last five minutes,” Elizabeth said, and Nic followed her instructions automatically.

She was most afraid that she would be reduced to begging. Nic prided herself on never letting anything touch her. Never asking for anything. But she might turn into one of those people who desperately searched for new treatments, pleading to be enrolled in trials for some new drug that would prove to be no breakthrough. Until finally she ended up in a dirty clinic in Mexico paying the last of her retirement savings for some treatment that would turn out to be watered-down drain cleaner. Begging fate or the God she had decided long ago she didn’t believe in to spare her.

Nic wasn’t going to change her beliefs simply because her life was on the line. There were no atheists in foxholes, according to conventional wisdom. But even though she was ready to go to war, she wasn’t going to turn her back on her hard-won wisdom that the only one looking out for you was *you*. And when you died, you stayed dead.

Nic’s dark, raging fear was colored with bottomless grief when she thought of telling her parents. Mama was already beside herself at Darren’s divorce. But if she knew her daughter’s life—and soul—were on the line, Mama was sure to become even more frantic. And Daddy—

Daddy's huge sad eyes would fill up with pain. Telling her parents would only hurt them, and she wanted to spare them that as long as she could.

The class ended, and people began to put away their mats and exercise balls. Nic followed Cassidy and Allison as they carried their large plastic balls into an adjoining storage room.

And her daughter? Makayla was only nine. She hadn't even gotten her period yet. It had been only a few weeks since she'd learned the terrible truth about her father. Nic couldn't stand to think of how lonely her daughter would be, how the very foundation of her world would be just ripped out from under her. Couldn't stand to imagine how her daughter's green eyes would fill with tears as she realized her mother was leaving her.

And that was the thing that Nic feared most. Her life snuffed out. Gone forever. And the world would move on without her, inexorable and uncaring. Makayla would grow up without her guidance. Leif would find another woman.

Even her friends would eventually replace her.

CHAPTER 14
Portland Fitness Center

"And I say to all who complete a successful boot camp class—" Pressing her palms together, fingers pointing up, Elizabeth murmured, "Namaste" over and over as she bowed slightly and made eye contact with each woman in turn.

Now she stood in the corner, making sure, simply through her presence, that they all put away their equipment. As she looked at their reddened, sweating faces, she felt a surge of satisfaction. She had pushed most of them past their abilities. But finally Elizabeth had bested the one participant who had mattered to her at that moment. A wince had crossed the face of that black girl, one of the two friends Cassidy had brought.

The other one, with her milky skin and dark hair, had been doomed from the start. Her muscles had trembled as she struggled to do even the simplest things. Sure, there had been the pleasure of correcting her already poor form and hearing her fail to suppress a moan. But it had been nothing in comparison with proving that the fierce-looking black girl, with her slanted eyes and her powerfully muscled legs, was no match for Elizabeth.

As people put away mats and exercise balls and gathered their things, Cassidy brought the two women over. Elizabeth put on the right smile. Open, curious, friendly. She had practiced it many times in the mirror.

"Elizabeth, these are my friends, Allison Pierce"—Allison was the white girl, who at least was no longer breathing audibly—"and Nicole Hedges. This is Elizabeth Avery."

The black girl gave Elizabeth a cool nod.

Cassidy continued, "The three of us all went to the same high school—can you believe it?"

Elizabeth shook hands with them, nodding like she cared. If Cassidy thought who she had gone to high school with was impressive, what would she have thought of the kids from the Spurling Institute? Rapists, drug addicts, kids who heard voices but wouldn't take their meds. About half of Elizabeth's classmates had had their fees—6,000 dollars a month—paid for by their wealthy families, families who would pay anything in the hope that the school could make their child normal.

Elizabeth had been in the other group, the ones whose stays were paid for by the state. At Spurling, Elizabeth had figured out that she liked rich people better than poor people. Through careful mimicry, she had learned how to talk and act like them. And how to keep them in line.

Cassidy's smile was too big, and her eyes

darted from one face to the next. Elizabeth could tell she wanted them all to be friends with each other. Just one big happy family.

Right.

Like some gushing grandma, Cassidy said, "Allison edited the paper and got the highest SAT score at our high school."

"Second highest, actually," Allison said, acting embarrassed.

Elizabeth knew the type. The kind who bragged about themselves, but pretended not to. The kind who pointed out that they thought they were better than you by pretending they weren't doing any such thing.

She consoled herself with thinking about how Allison had struggled in boot camp. When her face went pale and she started biting her lip during a ninety-second plank, it had lightened Elizabeth's heart. So she had tacked on fifteen more seconds without telling anyone.

"And this is Nicole Hedges," Cassidy persisted. "She's an FBI special agent."

"It's good to meet you."

Nicole's smooth dark face didn't give anything away. She reminded Elizabeth of Grandma's cat, too good to come when you called it.

Twenty-five years earlier

Elizabeth didn't like to think about Grandma. Grandma belonged to another person, a girl with a different name. A girl with bad things in her past. But she had left the girl behind.

The girl who had been called Sissy Hewsom.

When she was seven, the first of the bad things happened to Sissy. Her parents were arguing, the way they always did. But then her dad stormed out of the house and came back with a small black gun. And her mother's eyes went wide and there was a *boom* and then there was a bloody hole where her right eye used to be. And then her dad slipped the gun into his own mouth, not even seeing Sissy. Not even seeing her! Just leaving her alone with two bloody things that used to be her parents.

At their funeral, everyone dressed in black and cried and cried. Sissy had cried. She had to go live with Grandma, who smelled like an ashtray and who made her drink milk out of yellow melamine cups stained brown inside from years of coffee.

As she got older, more bad things happened. They weren't Sissy's fault, no matter what anyone else said. But still, when Sissy was thirteen, she found herself in the Donald E. Long juvenile detention center awaiting trial.

Grandma visited just once.

Sissy ran to her, threw her arms around her. She knew she only had one chance to get this right. One chance to sway Grandma to do anything she could to get her only grandchild out of this awful place. Because Sissy couldn't stay there one minute longer. Where you ate your food with a plastic spork and the lights never went off, not even at night.

But instead of hugging her, Grandma pushed her away. She didn't even sit down at one of the tables. Around them, other kids met their family members, who hugged and kissed and cried and bought ice-cream sandwiches from the vending machine.

"I'm only going to say this once, Sissy." Grandma's mean little eyes narrowed. She looked like a snake. "They say it's possible you might get out before you're eighteen. If so, don't come crying to me. I never want to see you again."

She was forced to make her pitch in a hurried low voice. "But, Grandma, what happened was like a mistake. It's not like they said. They're making up lies about me. They think just because Daddy was bad that I am too. But I'm not."

Grandma didn't blink. "You can lie to whoever you want. But don't bother trying it with me." Her jaw clenched like a bulldog's. "I found Snowball."

"But I didn't—"

"Stop. Just stop. I saw what you did to him."

Sissy made her eyes wide. "What are you talking about?"

"The twine around his legs. You did it to him.

Whatever you did. Did you make him suffer?" She lunged for Sissy, her fingers hooked in front of her like claws. Like she was determined to do what the cat had not been able to.

"No!" Sissy got up and started backing into the corner.

One of the guards grabbed Grandma and took her away.

And that was the last Sissy ever saw of her grandmother.

Her second day in the detention center—which was a jail, no matter what they called it—they gave Sissy an attorney pro bono, which meant free. But when they brought her in to meet him in one of the private conference rooms, Mr. Dowell wasn't anything like the lawyers she had seen on TV, with their beautiful dark clothes and their expensive sleek cars. His suit jacket didn't even match his pants. There was a patch of silvery stubble under his left ear. And Sissy didn't need to be able to see into the parking lot to know that his car was an old junker.

He looked at her like he was weighing her too. His lips firmed, pressing together for an instant. In that one movement, Sissy could see that he wished he were anywhere but with her.

Mr. Dowell started to speak, stopped, coughed, cleared his throat wetly. She was more disgusted by him than ever.

"Elizabeth—"

"It's Sissy," she interrupted him. "Everyone calls me Sissy. That's what Mikey called me. He couldn't pronounce Elizabeth."

He tilted his head as if he were surprised to hear her use her cousin's name. "Okay. Sissy. You need to know that the state of Oregon is considering charging you as an adult."

Her attention snapped back to her plight. "But I'm not an adult." She couldn't go to prison. Live in a place like this forever? "I'm only thirteen."

"And I'm fighting it. The one thing you have in your favor is your age. If you were sixteen or even fifteen, it would be much harder. With adults, there is often an emphasis on deterrence or punishment, but the laws for juveniles are focused on rehabilitation. Do you understand what I'm saying?"

Of course Sissy understood. The question was, should she let him know that she understood? Would he do a better job of defending her if he thought she was some half-wit mouth breather who was too stupid to understand what she had done? Or would it be better to reveal to him how smart she was, how clever? Or was sympathy the real angle that would get him to work his tail off for her, a poor girl who had never had a chance?

When they learned about chameleons in third grade, Sissy had felt a spark of recognition. Chameleons were lizards that could change their skin color. They were like magic.

Mr. Dowell spoke before Sissy could decide what he needed her to be.

"I think we will succeed in keeping you in the juvenile system. But there are still many decisions we need to make. Later today, you're going to have to plead guilty or innocent. It might be possible for me to get the court to agree to you pleading guilty to a lesser charge."

Sissy did not plan to admit anything. "And what would happen if I did that? Would I still go to jail?"

"Well, not jail, not if I succeed in keeping you in the juvenile system. You might have to go to a reform school. It's not a bad solution."

Sissy had to get out of there. Out of any place like this. Where you were never alone, and eyes watched everything you did.

"No. I'm innocent. I was lying when I said those things to that FBI agent. I just wanted to get away from my grandmother. She's really the one who did it." This was one approach she had been considering, but she spit it out too soon, without a chance to add the details that might sell it.

"Sissy." He held up one hand wearily. "Please."

She couldn't give up, not that easily. "But I'm not guilty. I'm not going to plead guilty. I won't."

"Okay." Mr. Dowell sighed. "The next step is deciding whether we go before a judge or a jury.

With a jury, we might be able to persuade people that you had a reason to do what you did. With a judge, it all depends on the luck of the draw."

Sissy imagined twelve pairs of cold eyes on her. She was good at making herself be what one person wanted. But it was impossible to be what twelve people wanted, not all at the same time. "A judge."

He made a note. "Okay. We'll tell them you want to waive your right to a jury trial and go before a judge." He looked up. "Now are you sure that's what you want to do? Not plead to a lesser charge? Not request a jury? These are big decisions, Sissy, and I'm happy to discuss their ramifications with you."

Sissy assessed her odds. This old man was being paid to defend her. She needed him to care. She needed him to be willing to do anything, anything in the world, to make sure she didn't go to jail. While there was a window in the door, the guard outside hadn't looked in. Not once.

She leaned forward and put her hand on the inside of Mr. Dowell's thigh, above his knee.

His eyes went wide.

She slid her hand higher.

He gulped.

CHAPTER 15
Portland Fitness Center

The boot camp class had gone well. Cassidy imagined this becoming their new routine a few times a week. She thought she could talk Allison into joining, but Nicole was trickier. But then she gave Cassidy an unexpected opening.

"Do you know if they have swimming lessons here?" Nicole asked Elizabeth. The four of them were the last people in the exercise room. "When my daughter was three, we were at a family reunion, and she slipped into the lake when no one was watching. Luckily she was only there for a minute or two, but it left her terrified. She won't even go to the pool with her friends. I've tried to teach her, but she's picked up that I'm a little nervous around the water myself, and it just makes her more afraid."

Cassidy hadn't heard before about Makayla's accident. Nicole was always so vigilant about her daughter. It must have been horrible for her.

"Actually, I offer one-on-one instruction for reluctant learners." Elizabeth took a card from the top of the wooden console that held the stereo system and scribbled a phone number on the back. "Give her to me, and I'll guarantee that by this summer she'll be splashing and having fun."

Nicole took the card. "Hey, thanks. I'll be in touch."

Looking from her old friends to her new one, Cassidy said, "I've got an idea. Why don't we all go have coffee?"

Allison and Nicole nodded, but Elizabeth shook her head. "Oh, I wish I could, but I have a personal training session scheduled."

The news splashed cold water on Cassidy's vision of the four of them laughing around a table. Elizabeth would have told them about one of her amazing adventures—rock climbing in Nepal, working as an assistant to a famous novelist, a May–December affair with one of her father's rock star friends—and Allison and Nicole would have hung on every word. And Cassidy would have basked in Elizabeth's reflected glory.

Now she would be free to parse Elizabeth with her two old friends, but all they would have to go on was how Elizabeth had taught the class. And while Cassidy could try to repeat one of her stories, she didn't think she could do any of them justice.

"So what did you think?" Cassidy asked as they settled around a table at the gym's café.

She had gotten a mocha, Allison a nonfat latte, and Nicole had only asked for ice water. Nic could normally be counted on to order the largest size coffee available, but Cassidy was too focused on Elizabeth to inquire about the switch.

"Wasn't her class amazing?" As a nod to their habit of always splitting the richest dessert on the menu, Cassidy had gotten the closest thing, a chocolate chip scone, and was now trying to break it into crumbly thirds. "There's one woman in there who has gone from a size sixteen to a six. I didn't even know where my triceps were until Elizabeth showed me."

"It's a tough class," Nicole said. Grudgingly, if Cassidy was any judge.

"It's more than tough," Allison said. "It certainly showed me how out of shape I'm getting." She pinched her midsection.

"So will you think about joining?" Cassidy wheedled. "If you do, the first month's dues are free."

"Maybe I should." Allison took a sip of coffee. "Although I think I'd rather work out at my own pace on one of the ellipticals or an Exercycle, instead of trying to keep up with everyone else. I'm not coordinated enough to be in a class like that."

"It's only complicated the first couple of times. After you know what to expect, it's automatic."

"I'll think about it." Typical Allison, never saying what she really thought. Then she surprised

Cassidy by adding, "You know who I would really like to see join here? Lindsay."

Nicole, who hadn't even seemed to be listening to the conversation, raised her head. "Your sister?"

"She's living with us for a little while."

"With you?" Cassidy asked. "Why not your mom? Isn't that where she usually goes?"

"Mom actually said no. She's said no before, of course, but this time she meant it. I guess she got burnt out." Allison sighed. "But I couldn't turn Lindsay away. She won't stay in a shelter. If Marshall and I didn't take her in, she'd be out on the streets."

Even back in high school, Lindsay had been notorious for getting into scrapes.

Cassidy asked, "Do you feel comfortable having her at your house when you're both gone all day?" Then she wondered if she had gone too far. Lindsay was Allison's sister, after all.

"She says she's not using right now, and I believe her, because she looks terrible." Allison sighed. "She's trying to get back on her feet again. But I would like to find something healthy to keep her occupied. Otherwise she just might go running back to Chris."

Or steal all their stuff and pawn it, or party in their beautiful house with some new friends she had just met at the bus mall, or pass out in the bathroom in her own vomit. Over the years, those were the kinds of stories Cassidy had heard about Lindsay. But she admired Allison for never giving up on her sister.

Cassidy turned the conversation back to her new favorite topic. "It's too bad Elizabeth couldn't join us. She's amazing. She's done, like, everything. Her dad is—well, I can't really tell you who he is, she would kill me—but someone famous. She even helped him write that song about—oops, almost gave it away." Cassidy put her hand across her mouth, hoping they would urge her on. If she told them something was a secret, they wouldn't share it. Both Allison and Nicole were far better at that sort of thing, sometimes to Cassidy's chagrin.

But Elizabeth's stories, told secondhand, clearly weren't as engrossing as the real thing.

"She sounds . . . interesting," Allison said politely.

And in her head, Cassidy heard Elizabeth's comment the first time Cassidy had talked to her about Allison: *Sounds like that girl needs to let her hair down*.

Nicole didn't even bother to say anything. She was staring into her glass of water like the ice cubes held the answers to life's questions.

Giving up, Cassidy switched subjects. "So I'm going to do that interview with the Want Ad Killer tomorrow. He's going to call in, collect."

"I'm surprised his attorneys haven't put a

stop to it." Allison flipped open her cell phone. "What time is that going to air?"

"At five and six thirty."

"So it's prerecorded?"

"I'm not taking the chance of doing it live." Cassidy pinched the last of the scone crumbs. "Too many unknowns."

Allison closed her phone. "You'll tape the whole thing, right? Can you let us hear it—even what you don't air?"

"Sure," Cassidy said. Phone calls from the jail were always recorded, so Allison could have subpoenaed the conversation anyway.

Allison tapped her phone against her lips. "Maybe you could even go one step further."

"What are you thinking?" Cassidy asked.

"What if we leaked you some information that you could use with Foley?"

"Allison!" Nicole's brows drew together.

Allison touched the back of Nicole's hand. "I'm thinking we could give her some information that wasn't quite right—and see if he corrects it."

Cassidy caught on. "Because it would be something only the killer would know." She imagined taking the stand to testify. She wouldn't just be covering the news—she would be making it.

"Exactly." Allison nodded. "But whatever happens, you'd better ask all the questions you can—it might be the only chance you get."

"He's promised me an exclusive." Cassidy felt smug. It had taken an endless amount of cajoling to get it. But given the chance to tell his side of the story, Foley had overridden the objections of his attorney.

Nicole made a huffing noise, and the other two women turned to her.

"Sometimes it feels like your priorities are all out of whack. Don't forget, there are three dead women out there. And you'll be giving the guy who killed them a platform."

The words hit Cassidy like a blow. "Colton has a right to be heard as much as anyone else. And I've offered the same deal to the friends and family of the victims, but they won't go on camera."

"And this might help us, Nicole." Allison laid her hand on Nicole's arm, but she shook it off. "Cassidy could get him to say something that we could use against him in court."

"Do you really think that she'll trap Colton Foley into incriminating himself?" Nicole's laugh was devoid of humor. "She'll just give him a chance to be in the limelight. That's the kind of thing Foley craves, and you'll be handing it to him on a silver platter. And I just keep thinking that those three women never got a chance to speak." Nicole pressed her lips together before she spoke. "And now it's too late."

"Hey, Nic. This is just what Cassidy does. She

talks to people who you and I can't talk to—or won't. And sometimes that means she learns things before we do. We all have the same goal—making sure the bad guys get what's coming to them."

"Oh, really? Are you sure her goal isn't to get more air—" Suddenly Nicole put her hand over her mouth and closed her eyes.

Cassidy and Allison exchanged a shocked glance.

Finally Nicole said, "I'm sorry. I'm not feeling well today." And then she pushed back from the table and left without saying another word.

And as she did, Cassidy heard Elizabeth's voice in her head: *Why be such a killjoy?*

CHAPTER 16

Unincorporated Washington County

Teachers, counselors, and even a judge had lectured Joey about the dangers of playing with fire. By the time he was discharged from the Spurling Institute, he could reel off fire's "negative impact": property damage, fines, prison, injury, death, trauma. All of which he had seen firsthand.

But that denied the beauty and truth of fire. Fire changed things. It burned things clean. Fire was terrible and magical, warm and cruel, beautiful and ugly—all at once.

Joey had discovered fire when he was eleven. It started when he took a book of matches from a bowl on a restaurant counter. Just having them in his pocket had been like having a special secret. It had made him forget the new baby, who cried all the time, and his new stepdad, who didn't like Joey very much. Who sometimes called him Josephine. Called him a little girl.

That night, in the basement, Joey lit a match. The flame shimmered. He was mesmerized by how it moved, dancing like a sculpture in motion. Finally, he blew it out. He lit another match, for longer this time, only blowing it out when it singed his fingers. The end was black and curled. It crumbled away when he touched it with the tip of his finger.

Soon he was experimenting every day after school. His mom never asked what he did. She was just happy that he was entertaining himself. Joey learned how fire tested everything. Some things turned black and shriveled up. Some made red and orange flames, others blue and purple. Pens and plastic spoons melted and dripped.

Away from the basement, if his mom was busy upstairs with the baby, Joey put things in the toaster, laid them on top of the burners on the oven. Stuck them in electrical outlets.

So many things burned. Cleaning fluids.

Rubbing alcohol. Paint. Hair spray. Perfume. Spray deodorant. You could shoot a torch of fire if you had the right kind of spray can and a lighter. And by now Joey had stolen his stepdad's silver Zippo.

He taught himself some stunts and then impressed the heck out of other kids in vacant lots. Like curling his hand into a ball, filling it with gasoline, and lighting it.

Walking home from school one day, Joey pulled out the Zippo. He was alone. The other kids liked his tricks, they did. But when two or three would decide to play fort or soldiers after school, they never asked him. He told himself he didn't care.

A dead bush sat at the edge of an empty lot. No leaves, just gray brittle branches. Joey flicked the lighter, and the flame popped up obediently. He ran the orange-red wavering triangle underneath one of the branches until it began to smoke. As fast as water, the fire ran down the branch, streams of orange and red that hypnotized him. He could smell the smoke now, the good smell of a campfire.

Watching it come alive was a thrill, the way it always was.

But what happened next came as a shock.

The bush crackled as the fire leapt from one brittle twig to the next. It was moving much faster than he had expected. He had planned on stamping it out. But then suddenly the dead yellow grass underneath the bush was also on fire.

Joey turned and ran to his house, three blocks away.

And then was lured back by the sirens. Two red fire trucks. And from them spilled shouting men with fire hoses and high boots and heavy brown coats circled by orange reflective tape.

Joey had done this thing. Made all these adults rush around. They didn't know it, but they were dancing to his tune.

Fire was everything Joey wanted to be. Exciting. Dangerous. Beautiful. Destructive. And yet he controlled it. Other people were too boring, too afraid to do what he did.

So he conjured up fire more and more. Until one evening when he was fourteen, the fire again leapt out of his control. Only this time it was in his home. Wild flames raced along the floor of the basement, fed by the paint thinner he realized, only too late, that his stepdad must have spilled during his latest project. Then the blaze found the pile of newspapers in the corner.

Joey tried to trample it, but the fire was too fast for him. In less than a minute the flames had doubled, snapping, leaping, climbing to the wooden rafters supporting the oak floor above. Six minutes later the neighbors called 911. The firefighters were there in another three and a half minutes. By that time, everyone in the house but

Joey was dead. His mom and his stepdad and his little brother—they had been on the top floor of the old house.

Joey had always thought of fire as being synonymous with light. But trapped in the basement, he discovered that fire could also be dark, due to the smoke. Finding the door to the outside was like finding his way out of a maze, blindfolded. He had to crawl on the ground like a snake, because it was the only place where the air was cleaner and cooler. But to open the door, he had to stand up. Stand up into the fire. When he ran out, his clothes and hair were ablaze, and the hand that had turned the knob was ruined.

At the trial, they said that parts of the fire had reached a thousand degrees. His mother, stepdad, and his half brother had not died from the flames but from breathing superheated air that destroyed their lungs. When they found his stepdad, his body was wrapped around his son. The fire had melted their clothes onto their skin.

The juvenile judge sentenced him to the Spurling Institute. The first person Joey saw when he was driven through the barbed-wire-topped gate at Spurling was a guy wearing a five-foot-tall dunce cap. Around his neck were three or four homemade cardboard signs. The top one said in block letters WELCOME MAT, and Joey's first confused thought was that some guy named Mat was coming.

Like Joey, half the students had a criminal conviction, referred by state juvenile corrections systems with no place to put them. For the rest, Spurling was the end of a line that had begun with an exclusive boarding school, then devolved through a series of less-choosy schools, and finally a military academy or two. Most had exhibited bad behavior of some sort—taking drugs, stealing, vandalizing. Some were violent. A few had mental illnesses that either hadn't been diagnosed or that didn't respond to medications. But for everyone, Spurling was the school of last resort.

In fact, there was very little school going on at the school. During the day, the students provided much of the labor that kept Spurling running, as well as attended group therapy sessions and individual counseling. School was held for just a few hours after dinner, and it was easy enough to cheat. Spurling liked to brag that its students had a B average or better, but administrators never revealed that the tests were all open book.

At Spurling, Joey was told that he was a delinquent, irresponsible, oppositional, lacking judgment, and had poor interpersonal skills.

According to the lesson plan the school filed with the state, at Spurling Joey was supposed to develop self-esteem, insight, and self-awareness.

He was supposed to learn how to express anger "in an appropriate and verbal manner."

None of that was as beguiling as the sound of a Zippo.

Joey was not allowed to have lighters, matches, cigarettes, or magnifying glasses. He could not "accumulate combustibles."

He was searched, as was his room, every day. But it was like they thought he had no imagination. A single piece of paper, held against a lightbulb long enough, would catch on fire. A fire that had to be carefully shielded until it could be applied to something else.

And then there was Sissy, one of his few friends at Spurling. Which was far better than having her as an enemy. They were the same age, but by the time Joey was sentenced to Spurling, Sissy had already been there for a year. She liked being held up by the administrators as a success story, an example of how even someone who had committed the most terrible offenses could be rehabilitated. So at Spurling she was careful to cover her tracks. But she had a million sneaky ways of getting back at someone she didn't like.

And a few ways of helping you, if that's what she felt like. So sometimes Sissy would bring Joey a match. A single match, but he would do whatever she wanted for that match. Give extra food to her, do her chores, plant contraband in the room of an enemy. He knew she lied to him sometimes, but it didn't matter. Not when she was willing to be his friend. Not when she acted like she couldn't see the scars on his face and hand.

Once he got caught with a match in his room. But Joey never admitted where the match had come from, not even when he was forced to stand out in the stifling August sun for two days straight wearing shorts, no shirt, no sunscreen, and a sign that read BURN BABY BURN.

Sissy left Spurling six months before Joey. He got used to being alone, which was good, because it wasn't any different on the outside. People took one look at his patchwork face and then looked away. Even his dad winced when he looked at Joey's hand. Once he was in line for a slice of pizza, and a kid told him the workers should just put the toppings on his face. Younger kids would sometimes ask what had happened, but more than once before he could even answer, a mom would drag the child away, warning the kid not to talk to "those people."

Whenever things got to be too much, when someone yelled "Freak!" at Joey from a passing car, or he lost another job, well, there was always fire.

He stuck to small brush fires, out in the woods, along the edges of old highways. Sometimes an abandoned barn or house, falling in on itself. But never anyplace where people lived.

Then Sissy paid him to go one step further. It woke something in him, the desire to burn something bigger and better. Which was why Joey was standing with his gas can outside a half-constructed home in unincorporated Washington County, some McMansion that would sit in solitary splendor on five acres.

The phone rang in his pocket. Joey nearly jumped out of his skin.

"Hello?"

Sissy said, "I need to see you again."

"Why?" He liked the *idea* of Sissy, but the reality of her made him nervous. "That lady's house was a total loss, just like you wanted."

"Yeah, but that's just her house. Meanwhile, she's probably raking in thousands in insurance money. I ended up doing her a favor. Instead of messing up her life, I made it better."

Joey didn't like the way this was going. A nervous jolt went through him when he heard her next words.

"I've been thinking. You need to help me find a way to stop her. Permanently."

CHAPTER 17
Channel Four

"Channel Four," Jenna Banks said into the headset while underlining a passage in *Cash In: How to Make More Money and Get the Promotion You Deserve.* It was ridiculous that Channel Four's management still insisted she give the receptionist her lunch breaks. Jenna had been at the station for nine weeks now, finishing her degree in broadcasting and mass communications. Marcy, the receptionist, had been at the station for twenty-five years—longer than Jenna had been alive! It was clear that Marcy wasn't going anywhere. But Jenna? Jenna was destined to be a star.

"I need to talk to a reporter about a murder," a man's voice said. "A murder that might be committed."

Dropping her book, Jenna grabbed a piece of scratch paper. "I'm a reporter."

CHAPTER 18

Multnomah County Courthouse

Twenty years earlier

Mr. D—Sissy had taken to calling her lawyer, Mr. Dowell, that—said they got lucky when Judge Irvine was assigned to her trial. He said that the judge would be fair.

Even though Sissy wanted to dress in a way that showed off her figure, she regretfully decided that her best move was to appear younger than she was. Even though she was now thirteen—a teenager, nearly an adult—she put on a loose cardigan over a dress that hid her curves, wore no makeup, and pulled her hair into pigtails. She worried that the pigtails might be over the top, but a quick look in the mirror reassured her that they were the perfect touch.

She had thought the courtroom would be full, but instead there were just a handful of people. Mr. D whispered to her that, for her own good, the court was keeping the event from being a spectacle.

Sissy had dreamed of flashbulbs and shouted questions.

She quickly grew bored with the proceedings. When they were talking about her, it was interesting. When they were droning on about the law, it was totally *not* interesting.

"This is a child," Mr. D told the judge.

That was what Sissy had decided was her best move after he had leapt out of his chair when she touched his thigh, sputtering, eager to get away from her. She had begun to act younger and slower, sometimes even lapsing into baby talk or calling him "Mithter D."

"Elizabeth was easily led by investigators to agree with whatever they said. In fact, this girl has learned in her short, sad life that the safest thing to do is to please the adults around her."

When the witnesses testified, Sissy grew tired of their tears. *She* was the real victim. The best part was when she got to speak directly to the judge. Sissy could cry on demand. She was good at crying. Very good. She could say the right words and do the right things. And she was sure that all of it would add up to her going free.

She watched the smallest changes in the judge's expression, when his pupils constricted or dilated, or his nostrils flared, and adjusted her story accordingly. She made the tears fall from her eyes. But not too many. She didn't want her nose to run and ruin how pretty she looked. How dramatic.

She was so sure that the judge liked her that when he found her guilty it came as a horrible shock. The floor felt like it was falling away from beneath her. She put her head on the table.

That afternoon, Mr. D told her that everything was not lost. As part of sentencing, he would explain to the judge that there were mitigating circumstances and she deserved leniency. Sissy grasped at the idea and held on for dear life. She had already been in custody for weeks and weeks. That should be enough.

When they gathered again in front of the judge five weeks later, Mr. D said, "Judge Irvine, while we didn't plead 'not guilty by reason of insanity,' there are clearly mitigating circumstances. Not only does this child lack the intellectual or moral capacity to understand the consequences of her actions, but the records show that she has also been horribly damaged. The state failed to care for her, failed to protect her. Instead, it let her go from one terrible situation to the next. Even before she was born, Elizabeth was unwanted. Her parents married only under duress when her mother was six months pregnant. The marriage was so volatile and violent that her mother repeatedly abandoned Elizabeth at her grandmother's when she was a child. Her father beat her with a belt as well as his fists. She may well have brain damage. And then when Elizabeth was seven, she saw something no one should ever see, especially not a child. She saw her father kill her mother and then turn the gun on himself."

He paused to let the weight of his words settle in. Elizabeth wished she could stuff her fingers in her ears, close her eyes, and not have the images replay behind her lids.

"Then she was forced to live with her grandmother, who made it clear she saw Elizabeth as a burden. As a result, this girl was brought up in a toxic environment, one where lashing out before you yourself could be hurt was the norm. The court should not compound the wrongs the state has perpetuated against this girl by punishing her for acts that to this day she does not understand. She bears the burden of a tragic past and present—help her find the bright future she so deserves. If any child deserves leniency, Your Honor, it would be Elizabeth."

Next, the psychiatrist said that Sissy had not been able to tell right from wrong when the bad things happened, that she had been incapable of knowing the nature of her actions. Listening to him, Sissy felt a surge of pride. She had done a good job of letting him think that.

She could not—would not—be labeled crazy, any more than she would embrace being called retarded. But pleading temporary insanity seemed like the best of both worlds. Basically, it would prove that it wasn't her fault.

Mr. Whitlock, the prosecutor, seemed personally insulted by the psychiatrist's words. When he looked at Sissy, his upper lip curled. "We need to think of all the would-be Miss Hewsoms out there. Harsh sentencing acts as a deterrent to teens who are considering committing crimes. Light sentences don't teach teens the lesson they need to learn: if you commit a terrible crime, you will spend a considerable part of your life in jail. I'm confident that as the court looks at all of the facts and circumstances, Miss Hewsom will be held responsible for her actions.

"Judge Irvine," Mr. Whitlock continued, "in this state, we have a strict legal standard required to prove insanity at the time of the crime. Was Miss Hewsom unable, at the time of her crimes, to distinguish between right and wrong? No. The defense has not presented clear and convincing evidence to prove insanity was a mitigating circumstance. In fact, Miss Hewsom was capable of lying and covering up evidence of her crimes directly after committing them."

Judge Irvine steepled his fingers. "I have listened to the arguments. Mitigating circumstances were already taken into account in my initial ruling that Elizabeth Hewsom should be tried as a juvenile instead of as an adult. It is clear, however, that Miss Hewsom requires specialized care. She is a deeply, deeply troubled individual. But rehabilitation could give her a second chance to overcome both the wrongs that were done to her and the grievous wrongs she herself has done. In view of that, the court has decided to send Miss Hewsom to the Spurling Institute, a private institution that has had great success in treating people who lack values and morals to guide them."

It took a few seconds for the truth to settle in. Sissy had thought the trial would end with her going free. But instead she would be locked up for years. She realized she had made a mistake. Mr. D hadn't wanted to help her get free. He wanted to get her away from him.

Which wasn't the same thing.

CHAPTER 19
Channel Four

Cassidy looked into the camera. "Tonight, Channel Four offers you an exclusive interview with the accused Want Ad Killer, Colton Foley. And his fiancée, Zoe Barrett, opens up about her ordeal.

"Colton Foley is being held without bail in the Multnomah County Jail. Foley is twenty-three and a medical student at Oregon Health Sciences University. He is charged with robbing and killing three women who variously described themselves in want ads as masseuses, exotic dancers, or strippers. Two other women who were robbed, but not killed, have also come forward.

"He allegedly contacted women through the 'Meetings sought' section of the local alternative weekly." Cassidy held up a section of newsprint. "Here's how one ad he answered read: *If you'd like to spend some time with a sweet blonde, give me a call.*"

Brad Buffet, the anchor, asked, "Do authorities suspect that there are other victims out there, Cassidy?"

She nodded. "The assistant United States attorney has posted an ad in the weekly alternative paper—ironically, the same paper believed to have been used by the killer to hook up with the three dead women. The ad says something like *Please come forward if you were a victim*. But will they? It's quite possible they were doing something illegal. We may never know how many more victims are out there. But one young woman says that there is yet one more victim in this story: Colton Foley himself. She is Zoe Barrett, Foley's fiancée."

This part of the story was a "donut," with Cassidy speaking on either side of a piece of video that had been put together beforehand. In the video, she sat in an upholstered chair while Zoe Barrett, a blandly pretty woman with honey-blonde hair, faced her on a matching couch. With her big eyes and snub nose, Zoe looked younger than her twenty-three years. But her words were direct and her tone unwavering.

"Your fiancé, Colton Foley, is facing accusations that he is the man behind what have become known as the Want Ad Killings," Cassidy said. "How do you feel about that?"

"Unfortunately, Cassidy," Zoe said, "you were given wrong information, as were the rest of the press and the public. Colton is completely innocent of these trumped-up charges."

Cassidy offered her a patient smile. "Pardon me for saying this, but isn't that what anyone in your situation would say?"

"You think I wouldn't know?" Zoe straightened up. "I met this man three years ago when we volunteered at a food bank. We're both training to be doctors. We've lived together for the past eight months. I know Colton's character, inside and out. He is a kind, gentle, caring man, not some sick killer. The police have got the wrong man, but they don't want to admit it. Colton was set up."

"But why would they do that?" Cassidy persisted. "What would be their motive?"

"Cash," Zoe said bluntly. "We've heard that a Portland police officer has been making the rounds of the tabloids, trying to make big bucks off of selling Colton's story."

Was it possible? Sure, one cop might want to leak something to the media in the hopes of getting an under-the-table payment. But a whole task force focusing on the wrong man? The reasoning seemed thin, even specious. The girl was grasping at straws, but she was too close to see it.

"All of his friends and family would tell you the same thing: Colton is a kind, intelligent man," Zoe said. "We need to get this travesty of justice reversed as soon as possible. Colton and I still plan to marry in September and share a wonderful, meaningful life together."

Cassidy recognized a rote response when she heard one. The last thing she wanted was a well-rehearsed speech that might—and probably would—be given to every reporter who got close enough. Trying to build a bridge between them, she softened her voice. "It must be terrible for you."

Tears welled in the young woman's eyes. "My fiancé is in prison on some trumped-up charge, and I am being hounded everywhere I turn. The reporters, the shouting, the questions from the police . . . it's all been too much. The man who is being portrayed in the media is nothing like the man I know. The man I've known for three years."

"I know this is awkward," Cassidy said carefully, "but what about those plastic restraints found in your condo?"

Zoe colored and put her hands to her face. "My private life is private. All I can say is that those were part of my private life, the life I shared with Colton. The only woman those were used on was me. With my consent."

"Uh-huh," Cassidy said noncommittally. She made a mental note to point out the wording to Allison and Nicole. Despite what Zoe had said earlier at the press conference, it sounded like the restraints had been Colton's idea. Had he wanted to try them out on a more willing victim before he took them on the road? Or had he tried to spice up his home life by mingling in some of the elements of his acted-out fantasies?

Zoe sighed. "I really don't want to say anything further. Just that I love Colton, and I know he will be proven innocent of these charges. And that's up to the courts to decide. Not the media. Not the court of public opinion. The justice system. And that's all I'm going to say."

At that point, Cassidy had known she couldn't press the young woman any further. "We wish you the best of luck."

Back in the studio, she introduced the second segment, the one with the accused killer himself. The one that, to her at least, revealed the truth behind the mask.

"And finally tonight, in this exclusive interview with Channel Four, Colton Foley speaks out for the first time from inside the Multnomah County Jail. We spoke to him earlier this afternoon by telephone."

The screen switched to a graphic that read

Accused Want Ad Killer Speaks Out and had images of a gun, a high-heeled shoe on its side, a set of plastic restraints, and a piece of torn newsprint.

In a series of text messages, Cassidy, Allison, and Nicole had brainstormed about the best way to catch Foley in a lie. In the end they had decided that his vanity was his weak spot. From the outside, Foley looked perfect. And if he was a sociopath, as Nicole believed, then he could not stand to be thought of as anything less than perfect.

Now the video switched to a still photo of Cassidy on the left side of the screen and on the right a photo of Foley taken at his arraignment. In Cassidy's experience covering the crime beat, most first-time offenders looked terrible at their arraignments, with bruised eyes, uncombed hair, and rumpled clothes. Foley looked like a model —or a politician—in a dark suit, white shirt, and red tie.

Cassidy's voice began the segment. "First of all, Colton, is there anything you'd like to say to Channel Four's viewers?" On the bottom of the screen, the words appeared as they were spoken.

"My heart goes out to these women and their families. I pray that they will find the perpetrator."

"So you're saying you're innocent?"

"Of course." His tone was relaxed.

"Then why did the police arrest you?"

"I suspect it's on the basis of a faint resemblance between me and the real killer, whose image was caught on the hotel surveillance tape. You have to look at this logically, Cassidy. The police were desperate. The public was demanding that they solve this crime. So they brought me in and hoped that all the attention would scare the real killer off."

"Did you know you were the subject of a manhunt?" Cassidy asked.

"Like everyone else, I had been reading about the situation in the *Oregonian*. Of course, I didn't think anything of it at the time when the police said they were looking for a young man with dark hair who was about five foot eleven. I mean, that could be anyone! But then my family said the police had been by asking leading questions about me. So I knew. I orchestrated my own capture, for my family and fiancée's sake. They feared, with reason, that I would be killed. So I made sure that I was spotted in a public place where there were plenty of witnesses."

"Are you saying you were afraid the police would harm you?"

It seemed that Foley's theory was that if you threw enough dirt, some of it was bound to stick.

"I'm saying that there was a lot of pressure on them to solve the case. There's clearly been a rush to judgment. And if I were dead, it would save them having to put me on trial. It would save them having to admit that they got the wrong guy. Look, Cassidy, I can't say much more. I need to save it for my defense. But I can tell you this—I am completely innocent of these accusations."

Cassidy got ready to dangle the bait. "You know, Colton, I interviewed a well-known profiler today, and she said that the type of man who would commit these acts would feel powerless and afraid most of the time. Basically, she said the person who did this is a coward. The type of person with no real friends and no real relationships. The only way he could get love is to buy it."

"Then that clearly rules me out," Foley said evenly, but Cassidy thought she detected strain in his voice. "Anyone who looks at Zoe would know that I'm an extremely lucky man."

Nicole had said that sociopaths were all about the surface, all about appearances.

"The profiler also said," Cassidy continued, weaving the web that her friends had designed, "that the type of women the man sought out was very revealing. What kind of man would go out of his way to seek out grossly overweight women?" Photos of two of the victims had not yet been released to the public, but this was a flat lie. A lie designed to prick Foley's vanity.

"But—" Colton began, then cut himself off midsentence.

"But what?" Cassidy echoed, not letting her jubilation show. "Are you saying they weren't?"

"How would I know." It wasn't a question. "I never saw them." Foley's voice grew stronger as he found a lie to paper over the other lies. "But if they were making a living selling their bodies, I would imagine they would have to be attractive."

Cassidy tried one last time to knock Foley off balance. "Unless this man was so unattractive himself that he could only feel better about himself by paying women who were even less attractive than he was."

Foley's mocking tone was firmly back in place. "Interesting theory, Cassidy. But the facts are these: I have no idea what these women looked like because I never saw them. I was never there."

CHAPTER 20

Mark O. Hatfield Federal Courthouse

Allison had always known it was likely that Colton Foley had other victims. And her hunch had been confirmed when a woman answered the ad she and Nicole ran in the alternative paper. She called in to report that she had been robbed by a man who "looked like that guy on the TV."

Nicole and Allison arranged a meeting with her in Allison's office. Allison could never interview potential witnesses by herself. If they said something different on the witness stand, she couldn't take the stand herself to rebut them.

"So take us through what happened," Allison said to the woman, who was named Didi. Her face was a mask of makeup, and she had to throw her shoulders back to offset the weight of what had to be implants.

"He saw my ad and called me, said he'd like to come spend some time with me." Didi had a smoker's rough voice.

Allison said, "And the assumption was . . ."

"The assumption was that he would pay me for my time." Didi's tone was matter-of-fact. Allison had already reassured her that she wouldn't be prosecuted for prostitution. "My rate is $200 an hour. He called me when he got to my hotel. I met him by the elevator. I do that for security purposes. And if I'm not comfortable, I just walk away."

Nicole made a note. "And what did you see?"

"Just a regular good-looking guy."

"Do you recognize that man in any of these photos?" Allison slid a six-pack over to Didi. A six-pack was like a lineup, only with photos. They had chosen the other photos with care. If the other five looked too much like Foley, it might serve only to confuse the witness. At the same time, they couldn't salt the six-pack by using a black guy, an elderly nun, and the kid who starred in *The Wonder Years*. If Didi testified, the photo array would be part of the evidence. If the evidence seemed biased, the defense attorney would move to suppress it.

It took Didi only a second to pick out Foley's photo. "That's him," she said, tapping it with one long pink fingernail.

"So then what happened?" Allison asked.

"So I said hi, and he said hi, and I motioned for him to follow me. Because I didn't want to be talking about it in the hallway. As soon as we got to the room and I closed the door, he pointed the gun at me and told me to lie down on the ground." She put her hand to her chest. "My heart started beating so fast. And I was saying, 'You don't have to do this, I'll give you what you want, you don't have to do this.' But he just kept telling me to lie down, and that he wasn't going to hurt me. And when I lay down, he put the gun back in his pocket. He pulled on some black leather gloves. Then he knelt down with one knee between my legs and told me to put my hands behind my back. And he tied me up."

"Did you think he was going to hurt you?" Nicole asked. "Kill you?"

Didi shrugged, but Allison noticed how her hands twisted together. "I wasn't as nervous as before, because of him putting the gun away. He cut the phone line, and then he picked up my phone and erased his number out of the call log, then took out the battery and threw it behind the bed. Then he opened up my purse, put my money in his pocket, and took my credit cards, and he asked me the PIN number for my bank card. Which I told him. I was too rattled to make up a number."

Nicole asked, "Did he take anything else?"

Didi nodded. "My suitcase was in a corner, and he walked over to it and picked up a pair of my underwear and put them in his pocket."

Allison and Nicole exchanged a look.

It took another twenty minutes to finish interviewing Didi. Before she left, she shook her head and said, "I just don't understand how somebody that is obviously smart, has his own life ahead of him, has a beautiful fiancée, is getting married, is gonna, you know, live the life, could do something like this."

"That's what we're wondering too," Allison said. "But what about you, Didi? If you keep doing this, the next time the guy might not put the gun back in his pocket."

"Oh, don't worry, I've quit," Didi said quickly. Too quickly. "It's too dangerous. I'm probably going to go back to school."

"That's good!" Allison patted the back of her hand and tried not to think about how the girl hadn't met her eyes.

Nicole walked Didi out to the lobby. When she came back, she said a single word: "Souvenirs."

"Yeah. It sounds like it," Allison said.

Serial killers often took a little token with them before they left the scene of a crime. Sometimes it was something that would never be missed, like change from a victim's pocket. Sometimes it was a driver's license or a piece of jewelry. And sometimes it was something intimate, like underwear.

"But if he's got more, where are they?" Nicole asked. "Not at his house."

"They have to be someplace," Allison said. "We have to find them."

With a sigh, Allison put her key in the front door, only to find it was already unlocked. Even though Lindsay had been living with them for more than a week, Allison still wasn't used to the idea that just because Marshall's car wasn't in the driveway, it didn't mean no one was home.

Now, instead of coming home to silence or Marshall just coming back from a run, Allison always found Lindsay. Sometimes with Marshall, sometimes alone. But always talkative, bored, restless. Today her sister hurried around the corner carrying a bright turquoise box emblazoned with the word *Congratulations!*

"This came for you in the mail today. What is

it? Did you win a prize?" Usually Lindsay looked closer to fifty than thirty, but right now she looked about ten.

After setting down her briefcase, Allison took the package from Lindsay, slit the tape with her keys, and lifted the lid. Four identical smiling babies looked up at her. The package held four cans of baby formula and a sheaf of coupons.

Someone in some doctor's office somewhere had sold her name. Without speaking, Allison tried to jam the lid back on. Her hands were shaking. She couldn't line up the corners. As soon as she managed to close it up tight, the box would go straight into the trash.

"Why did they send you this?" After a long pause, Lindsay answered her own question. "Oh, Allison." She put her hands on Allison's shoulders. "Leave that alone. I'll get it in a minute."

Allison felt her sister's scrawny arms go around her waist as she hugged her from behind. Tears clogged her throat.

Lindsay whispered into her ear, "I didn't know."

"We hadn't told anyone yet. I didn't even make it to three months."

"What happened?"

"They don't know." Allison twisted away from her sister. This time she managed to get the lid back on. She took a deep breath. It would be wrong to throw it away. She would donate it to the Oregon Food Bank.

"Are you going to try again?" Lindsay asked.

Allison didn't answer. She had opened up her home to her sister, but she didn't have to open up her heart. Especially when the answer was one she didn't yet know herself.

"I would love to have a baby," Lindsay said slowly.

Allison gritted her teeth. Was that how Lindsay planned to fill her newly empty days, her lack of sober or stable friends? With a baby? When she could barely care for herself?

"But I can't," Lindsay continued. "A few years ago I got some kind of STD so bad that the doctor said my tubes are ruined."

"Oh, Linds." Allison was suddenly ashamed of her unkind thoughts. *Lord, give me a loving heart. Help me to see my sister through Your eyes.*

Now Allison was the one who hugged her sister, and it was Lindsay who tolerated the embrace for only a few seconds before moving away. She sat down on the couch.

"It's okay. I mean, what kind of life could I give it?" Lindsay picked up a throw pillow and pressed it against her chest. "I never went to college. I've never had a real job, at least not one that didn't involve me wearing a uniform and asking people if they wanted fries with their order. And who would want to hire me now, with my record?"

"The longer you stay clean, the more people will be interested in hiring you."

Lindsay's mouth twisted. "Do you really believe that? In today's economy? They'd rather get some sixteen-year-old cutie."

"Still, it would be good for you to find something to do, Lindsay. Maybe volunteer work. Something."

"I've been trying to keep busy." Lindsay crossed her arms over the pillow. "I go to NA meetings. I pick up the house. Today I gave myself a pedicure. I haven't thought about my toes in years. They were all raggedy. I found some polish in your bathroom—I hope that's okay." She looked up at Allison. "Did Mom know about the baby?"

"I hadn't told her yet. I knew she would be really excited. First grandchild and all that. We just wanted to be sure. I guess we were right to wait."

Lindsay dropped her head, so her next words were muffled by the pillow. "Have you talked to her about me?"

"Of course I told her you were staying with us. I didn't want her worrying about you."

Allison had done a little more than that. She had driven over to her mom's the day before. "Mom, won't you just talk to Lindsay?" she had said. "She's really trying."

"I can't," her mother had answered. "My counselor said I need to practice tough love. If your sister is really better, then I'll talk to her in a few months."

"But she's your daughter!"

"You think I don't know that?" Donna Mitchell's dark eyes, so like Allison't own, drilled into her. "But I don't do her any favors if I keep enabling her. I'm not going to rescue Lindsay from the consequences of her own self-destructive behavior anymore. The last time she was here, I told her if she left that was it. And she still did."

"That's why she needs to know you love her."

"I do love her. But it's not about love anymore, Allison. I know you think I'm being cold. I'm not. It's tearing me apart. You don't know how many times when you were in college I took her in, bailed her out, hung up the phone when one of her druggie friends called, drove to some terrible part of town and picked her up, held her head when she vomited, listened to her lie to me, and then realized after she left that she had—yet again—stolen from me. I've been doing it for years. And I just—I just can't anymore."

She ran her knuckles under one eye, and only then did Allison realize she was crying.

"Lindsay had every advantage you had—she was smart and pretty and had such a beautiful spirit. Now she's missing teeth! I don't even want to think about what she's done out there on the street to earn money."

"Mom," Allison said gently, "the one thing Lindsay didn't have is Dad. I got three more years of him than she did. She was only thirteen when he died. She had started pulling away from him, and then she never had a chance to come back."

She remembered Lindsay sobbing the morning their father had died, crying so hard she had thrown up. Weeping, gagging, and moaning, "Daddy, Daddy, Daddy," her face red and sweaty and indescribably bereft as she lay curled up on the bathroom floor.

"You think I don't know that? I grieve for her, too, Allison. For the Lindsay I used to know, the Lindsay I raised. But that was seventeen years ago. She's a different Lindsay now. If you give her a roof over her head and food on her table, then you're just giving her a little R&R before she goes back to what she always does." With a shaking hand, Donna pushed a piece of hair out of her eyes. "She'll end up going right back to her old life. She has no reason to change, because she knows that she'll have someone to pick up the pieces. Lindsay needs to suffer major consequences for her behavior. The more she gets rescued, the less reason she has to change."

"But she's trying, Mom. She's really trying. She just needs a little help."

"Help to what? Self-destruct? You're trusting her when she doesn't have the willpower of a gnat. Sooner or later Lindsay will go back to her old ways—and you'll be the one who learns why you can't say yes to her."

"But, Mom—" Allison said again.

Donna had held up her hand. "Let me finish. You know why I know that? Because it happened to me. For years and years, you covered up my drinking. But that didn't really help me. It just put off the inevitable. It's called codependency, Allison. And the more I helped your sister, the more I was helping her self-destruct. That's not helping. That's hurting."

Now Allison looked at Lindsay, at her hollow, lined face, and hoped that she was helping her sister more than she was hurting her. That she was making the right choice.

CHAPTER 21

Barbur Bargain Motel

Jenna was tired of how Cassidy Shaw, Channel Four's crime reporter, was always going on about how young Jenna was. Like that was a bad thing. Everyone knew that if you were young, you had more energy. You had more to prove. You worked harder. Jenna didn't sit around complaining about having already paid her dues. She was willing to do whatever it took to get ahead, even if it meant getting her hands dirty.

And it was paying off. If Marcy had taken that call, she probably would have only pretended to listen, writing the guy off as one of the crazies. But Jenna—Jenna knew a lead when she heard it.

The story that the caller—Joey—had told her was this: An old friend, a woman named Sissy, had hired him to burn down a woman's house. Which he did. And got paid five hundred dollars. But now Sissy had called Joey again. She wanted to meet to discuss a new "favor" he could do for her.

And Joey was afraid he knew what the favor was. "This time, I think Sissy wants me to kill this lady," he said as Jenna frantically scribbled everything down.

"Now who is this woman exactly?" Jenna asked. "Not Sissy, the other one. The one whose house Sissy had you burn down."

A beep sounded in her ear, meaning someone else was calling Channel Four, but she ignored it. Let it go to voice mail. This was a story! This was news!

And now it would be Jenna's big break.

"She's Sissy's boyfriend's ex. I guess Sissy doesn't like that he has to pay this lady alimony. Something like that."

"Has Sissy told you that's why she wants to meet?" Jenna asked. "Because she wants you to kill this woman?"

"She didn't come out and say it. But she didn't need to. Sissy, man—she's crazy. You wouldn't know it to look at her, but she's done some bad, bad things. That's why I need some protection. I need someone else knowing about this. And if she ends up asking me to do what I think she will, I need some insurance."

Jenna wrestled with her conscience for several long seconds before she said, "Why not go to the cops?"

"The cops? Look, lady, I just admitted to you that I've committed a crime. Arson. That's a Class 2 felony. And I already have a record. If I go to them now, they aren't going to care about what Sissy *might* want in the future. They're going to care about how I just admitted I burned down this real house in real life. But if you tape this thing, the way you said, then *you* can take it to the cops. And maybe I won't even have to talk to them at all. Maybe they won't even need to know about the other thing."

A Peabody. Maybe even an Emmy. Jenna's heart quickened as she imagined stepping to the podium to pick up the gold statuette of a winged woman holding an atom. She could almost hear the murmurings from the audience. "She's the youngest ever to . . ."

She realized Joey was still talking.

Two days later, Jenna pressed her ear against the wall of the Barbur Bargain Motel ("Rooms by the day or week") listening to the low murmur of voices in the next room. One voice was lower than the other. Joey and the woman he knew as Elizabeth—Sissy—Hewsom. A Google search had turned up nothing on her. Nothing. When even dead people and ghosts were on the Internet.

Jenna had only Joey's word about Sissy's previous crimes. He told her that Sissy had developed a plan at the Spurling Institute to have her records expunged once she reached adulthood. So was that what had happened? Had she gotten out of Spurling and changed her name? Or was Joey wrong about the crimes or even the woman herself? Until she heard the second voice, Jenna had even wondered if there actually *was* a Sissy.

As she listened to the murmur of their conversation, Jenna just hoped that Joey was making sure Sissy spoke plainly about what she wanted done.

Because every word, every gesture would be captured by the hidden camera and microphone disguised as a smoke detector that Jenna had bought at I Spy Shoppe and then installed herself last night. She had perched on the single rickety chair she dragged into the middle of the room to serve as a makeshift stepladder. When she was satisfied that it didn't look out of place, she went back to the second room where she slept restlessly.

Besides allowing her to be in place the day before, renting the second room let Jenna know when the conversation began and ended. Otherwise, she might have had to slouch down in a car in the parking lot, hiding behind dark glasses and a newspaper. Standing out like a unicorn in a herd of zebras.

Their conversation seemed to go on forever. But finally there was a silence. And then Jenna heard a car start up in the parking lot. A minute later, another engine coughed to life. Taking a risk, she twitched the curtain a half inch. Enough that she could see Joey's gold El Camino following another car out of the parking lot.

To be safe, Jenna gave it another ten minutes. She peeked outside. The coast was clear. Just a housekeeper's cart at the end of the row.

She used the second room key to slip inside. The room was empty. Jenna was dragging the chair back to the center of the room when a knock on the door made her jump.

"Housekeeping," a woman called in a heavy accent.

"It's okay. I don't need anything."

The knock came again. "Housekeeping!"

Jenna moved closer to the door. "I don't need anything."

"Housekeeping." The woman sounded like she had memorized a single English word.

"Nothing." Jenna tried again. "Nada."

A flurry of knocks. Frustrated, she looked out the peephole. All she could see was the pile of white towels the woman held in her arms.

With a sigh, she opened the door. "I told you, I don't need—"

A sudden push knocked her off balance. The towels tumbled to the floor like a soft white waterfall.

Jenna stumbled backward, her eyes on the woman who slammed the door behind her with one foot while both hands held a gun. A big gun.

Pointed right at Jenna.

CHAPTER 22

Bertie Lou's Café

Leif dug a fork into his omelet. Everything at Bertie Lou's could be accused of overkill. Did an omelet really need ham, bacon, cheddar cheese, green pepper, onion, garlic, *and* gravy? Except once you tasted it, you realized it did.

A smile spread across his face. Good food and a Saturday morning with Nicole—what more could he ask for? Well, maybe a whole weekend, instead of a few hours while Nic's parents took Makayla to her ballet lesson. Even so, Leif had looked forward to these two hours all week. Maybe afterward they would go for a walk along the river.

But when Leif looked across the table at Nicole, she hadn't touched her food. On Leif's recommendation she had ordered the Ranch Benedict, a mouthwatering—and artery-clogging—combination of poached eggs and crisp bacon served over biscuits and covered in gravy. Instead of picking up her fork, she still cradled her mug of coffee in front of her face, the rim resting against her lips so Leif couldn't see her expression.

"Are you okay?" He kept his voice low.

The tables were close together, but the clatter of silverware provided a kind of camouflage. Nicole didn't like to look vulnerable in front of anyone. Even strangers. Even friends. Even the guy who hoped that she might consider him her boyfriend.

"Hm?" She shook herself and focused on him. But only for a second. Then her gaze slid off to the side. "Just admiring the decor."

Leif turned to see what she was looking at. Was it the inflatable moose head or the glittering disco ball? Or maybe it was the old pinup calendar from back in the day when Miss May actually wore a one-piece bathing suit? Or maybe it was nothing at all, and Nicole was just looking for an excuse not to make eye contact.

Bertie Lou's in Portland's Sellwood neighborhood was a hole-in-the-wall, with room for maybe two dozen diners, tops. From the vintage movie posters to the menu that warned *Open 'til 2 p.m. or until the cook gets tired or quits,* the restaurant was one of a kind. Even the waitstaff was anything but generic. The waiter had the market cornered on mellow surfer dude, and the tattooed, pierced, and dyed waitress was all sassy post-punk.

Leif had thought Nicole would enjoy the restaurant's funkiness, but so far she had yet to crack a smile. "You've got to try this," he said, lifting his loaded fork toward her. Would she refuse? You never knew exactly how Nicole would react to an offer.

Instead she obediently opened her mouth, and he slid the fork between her lips. He wanted to kiss her in the worst way. With a small sigh, he ran his thumb over her top lip, wiping away a stray chip of garlic.

Nicole's lips finally relaxed into a smile, and her gaze met his—and then stayed put. Her look was as warm and intimate as any kiss. Leif forgot all about his food as he watched Nicole swallow, the long column of her throat moving, and then lick her lips.

Leif had worked alongside Nicole for months before he had seen her smile at a New Year's Eve party. But that smile had surprised him. Jolted him, even. Her whole face changed. Her eyes warmed, the skin at the corners of her eyes crinkled, and her expression relaxed from guarded to joyful.

The second he had seen that smile, Leif had decided he would go to whatever lengths were necessary to see it again. Nicole's smile let him catch a glimpse of the girl she must have been. Before she had learned to be cautious. Suspicious, more often than not.

That caution and suspicion made her a fine FBI agent. But were they so good for being a human being?

Her expression changed, as if she had remembered something she had left undone. She looked away again. Leif took the opportunity to shovel in another mouthful and look around the restaurant. Nicole's was the only black face. What was it like, he wondered, to so often be the only African American? At work, she was not infrequently the only woman, or the only black person, in a room. He figured it was just one more reason, although an unspoken one, why her face was always guarded. Her eyes observed but gave nothing away. In meetings, she often held her hand over her mouth whenever she wasn't speaking. And she said very little.

But when she did speak, everyone listened.

Over the past year Leif had watched agent after agent try to flirt with Nicole—most of the single men, even a few of the married ones. All of them capsizing on the icy shoals of her disregard. Her look and her tone said she couldn't be bothered.

As a result, there were rumors. Heath Robinson, another agent, was the worst. He wasn't used to rejections. He bragged that no woman ever turned him down. But Nicole had. In spades. So now Heath whispered behind her back that Nicole hated men and, if he felt he had a receptive audience, that she more than likely was a lesbian.

At work, Nicole kept to herself, a cipher who never talked about her personal life, never bothered to deflect rumors. She didn't even keep a picture of her daughter in a frame on her desk. But shortly after Leif had transferred to the Portland field office, he had seen a photo of the girl. Of Makayla. He had needed a paper clip, and had been standing next to Nic's cubicle. After a moment's hesitation, he slid her pencil drawer open a couple of inches and then caught a glimpse of the edge of a photograph. Knowing she would kill him if she caught him looking, he had inched the drawer open a little farther.

And found not the picture of a man he had half expected, but the picture of a little girl with neat braids. With green eyes and skin lighter than Nicole's.

That had been a surprise. And when, a few weeks ago, Nicole had told him the secret of who Makayla's father was and what he had done, it had set Leif back on his heels. It helped him understand why Nicole was always on guard. And made him fall even more in love.

Now he wondered if she had another secret. Bigger even than the one she had told him before. Whenever she saw him lately, her eyes would light up, but then the light would fade. He could actually see her tamping it down.

She looked guilty, that was it. Like something was bothering her but she didn't want to tell him.

"I love to see you smile," he said now. "I'd do anything to see that smile more often."

Apparently that was the wrong thing to say. Her face tightened up.

"I'm not like you," she said in a low voice. "I can't let down my guard and laugh and joke around. I am what I am, Leif. People like you, sometimes they spend all their time trying to get me to smile, to laugh, to loosen up."

People like you? Leif opened his mouth to interrupt, but she lifted her hand.

"And at first, you like the challenge. But

eventually you'll get tired of it. And meanwhile, I'm still me. And I didn't change. It'll be you who has changed." She pressed her right hand over her heart.

"I don't want to change you, Nicole," Leif protested. "I like you. And I want you to be happy."

"You know what I've been wondering lately?" Nicole said. "And please don't take this the wrong way."

Had those words ever been followed by anything good? Leif said evenly, "What's wrong?"

"Why are you dating a black woman, Leif? Aren't there any blue-eyed WASPs out there?"

A pit opened up in his stomach. "I'm not dating a black woman. I'm dating *you,* Nicole. Or at least I'm trying to."

"Are you thinking that I'll be easy?" Her eyes flashed. "Is that what you're looking for?"

Leif snorted. He couldn't help it. "There is nothing about you that is in any way easy, Nicole Hedges." In a way, it was a compliment. At least his version of one.

Her face closed up like a fist. She pushed her chair back and got up.

"Nic, no, don't."

His voice had risen. Her shoulders hunched, and she looked, not at him, but at the faces of the other diners staring at her.

And then she was gone, the door banging shut behind her.

CHAPTER 23

Barbur Bargain Motel

Elizabeth kicked the motel door closed behind her. There was already one witness too many.

"Don't make a sound." She pointed the gun—one of two that Donald Dunbar had given her—not at the stupid blonde twit's head, but at her chest. Center of mass. So many important organs and major arteries were located in the trunk of the body. Even if you didn't have a marksman's aim, you could still kill someone with a single shot. Don had taught Elizabeth that when he taught her how to shoot.

It was a million little things that had told Elizabeth that something might be up. The tight way Joey had held his body when she hugged him. The way he had enunciated each word so clearly. How he had practically demanded she spell out what she wanted. As if he knew he had a witness. But she hadn't felt any sign of a wire when she hugged him, running her hands up and down his back.

So afterward she had stayed in her car in the parking lot, pretended to flip through a magazine, looking up every few seconds. And ten minutes later she had looked up from an article on teeth whitening to see a blonde girl slipping inside the room Elizabeth and Joey had just left. She must have been listening on the other side of the wall.

"I'm a reporter for Channel Four," the stupid girl said, lifting her chin. As if that would stop her from being killed. As if Elizabeth was supposed to put down her gun and have an animated discussion about freedom of the press.

And then the words sank in. *Channel Four*? "Did Cassidy put you up to this?"

"What?" The girl's face changed as she did a rapid calculation. "Is she jealous? Is that what this is all about? I was going to give her this story, I was. I just wanted to find out more about it before I told her?" Her voice rose at the end of every sentence, turning even statements into questions. "Do the legwork for her? That's all? But I was going to turn it over, I swear. I'm not trying to steal her story. Where is she? This is all some kind of joke, right? A trick?"

She started to drop her hands, looking behind Elizabeth as if she expected someone to jump out and yell *Surprise!* or *You've been punked!*

Without giving any warning, without really knowing herself that she was going to do it, Elizabeth squeezed the trigger.

And then she let out a little sound that was nearly a laugh as the girl's body fell back across the still-made bed. That had worked out well. And it was much more satisfying than a paper target.

Except, Elizabeth realized as she heard a rustle, the stupid girl was still alive, twisting restlessly on the bed like a sleeper trying to wake.

Slowly, Elizabeth walked over to stare down at her. Keeping her distance, in case it was some kind of trick.

The bullet had caught her just below the hollow of her throat. The girl pressed her fingers to it, but the scarlet blood ran between them like water.

"It's so hot," the girl murmured, her eyes rolling back in her head. And then suddenly two lines of blood shiny as paint ran from her nose. More spilled out of her slack mouth. Her body shuddered and then was still.

She had to be dead. Still, Elizabeth touched her arm to make sure. A poke and then a pinch. Hard and sharp.

The girl didn't move.

Had anyone heard? Elizabeth stood still for a moment. She had read that most people who heard a single gunshot wrote it off as a car back-firing. The room was filled with the sound of the five lanes of traffic rushing by, horns and motors and squealing tires. No one went to this motel expecting peace and quiet. No one expected to sleep. When she looked through the peephole, she saw nothing out of the ordinary.

Elizabeth's mind was racing now. Part of her was jubilant. She had done this thing. Taken care of the threat. It had been years, but she still remembered how good it felt to do that.

Another part was thinking about what had to be done. Step by step. How had the girl known to come here? There could only be one answer. Joey. Joey had gone behind her back. Had turned on her. Rage burned in her veins, but she forced herself to think it through. If she herself killed Sara—and Elizabeth would like to, it would be a pleasure—it would be all too easy for the authorities to figure out who had done it. She still needed Joey. Needed him to do the thing she had paid him to do. And after that, all bets were off.

Working fast, Elizabeth wrapped the dead girl in the bedspread. Luckily it was made of some kind of cheap brown fabric that seemed closer to plastic than cotton. She dragged the body off the bed and across the floor and left it next to the door.

After putting a washcloth under the bathroom faucet, she wiped down anything she might have touched—the doorknob, the doorframe, the light switch, and the wall around the switch. The damp marks it left behind showed her any areas she missed.

The key card was still by the TV. Taking it, Elizabeth went outside, moved her car until it was just next to the door, and popped the trunk. Then she waited in her car, watching until the housekeeper pushed her cart a few steps closer to the room. She had to move fast. As soon as the housekeeper went into another unit, Elizabeth opened the door. It took all of her considerable strength to heave the girl's wrapped body into her arms, pivot, and let it thump into the trunk.

She didn't hesitate, she didn't look around, she didn't act nervous. Just closed the trunk. Act as if what you were doing was perfectly natural, Elizabeth had learned, and everyone around you saw it the same way. Furtive looks and nervous movements were for amateurs.

The housekeeper would notice the missing bedspread, but this seemed like the kind of place where they expected a certain amount of thievery. Everything was either bolted down or so cheap it wasn't worth stealing.

The wallpaper behind the bed was an ugly pattern of a dozen random colors. It had been specially designed to not show dirt or fingerprints. And as Elizabeth left the room, she didn't notice that one more color had been added to it. High-velocity impact splatter was not one of the things Don had taught her about.

CHAPTER 24

Downtown Portland

On Wednesday Cassidy had been hanging up her mat when Elizabeth said, "Nordstrom is having a sale this weekend. Want to go shopping Saturday?"

Cassidy tried hard to look like the offer was no big deal. She had dropped so many hints about how she would love to do something with Elizabeth besides take her class and occasionally drink coffee in the café. "Sure," she said lightly.

"Do you have a Nordstrom's card? Because you earn double points this weekend for anything you charge."

"Of course. A Nordstrom's, a Saks, a Macy's, and all the way down to Office Max. I always fall for that 'if you open an account today, you can save 10 percent on your purchases.' "

"Yeah, I'm a sucker for that too." Elizabeth had smiled, a private smile, but she left the room before Cassidy could ask what she was thinking.

Cassidy spent the next few days anticipating the weekend. Her friendship with Elizabeth was clearly going places. It took away some of the hurt of what had happened with Nicole. It wasn't even so much that Nicole had been rude.

It was that she had revealed what she really thought of Cassidy.

She had worked hard for that exclusive, and then Nicole threw all that hard work back in her face. How many times had she given Nicole and Allison tips? Since she didn't have to worry about whether something was admissible, sometimes Cassidy was even one or two steps ahead of them.

But she wasn't some ghoul. People had the right to know what had happened. And people —even suspects—had the right to be heard. And she *had* offered the dead women's relatives a chance to talk. It wasn't her fault that they declined.

As a reporter, Cassidy was good at compartmentalizing. It was that ability that had allowed her to report on a possible Sarin gas outbreak a few weeks earlier without being overwhelmed by the worry that she herself might be dying. And now, after a day or two, it allowed her to take Nicole's accusations and put them in a box.

On Saturday she was up early, even though Elizabeth had said the day before that she wouldn't be able to go until early afternoon. Cassidy made sure her makeup was flawless and her hair casually tousled—a look that took twenty minutes with a blow-dryer, two brushes, and three hairstyling products to achieve. Would Elizabeth want to stop by her condo afterward?

Just in case, Cassidy picked up magazines and newspapers, put dirty dishes in the dishwasher, and shoved everything else into her bedroom closet.

Finally she took the trolley to where Elizabeth lived in Northwest Portland. It was a five-story brick building that looked like it had been built at the turn of the last century.

After Cassidy knocked, Elizabeth called, "Come in!"

Cassidy pushed open the door to reveal oak floors, mahogany moldings, plaster walls, and ten-foot-high ceilings. The furniture was Mission style—dark slatted oak with brown leather cushions. Cassidy thought of her own condo, which usually seemed sleek and modern. Suddenly it seemed cheap and charmless.

Elizabeth came around the corner. Like Cassidy, she was wearing jeans and a sweater, but Cassidy knew the minute she saw them that Elizabeth's jeans probably cost three figures and had never been marketed as having a "secret slimming panel."

Elizabeth's feet were still bare, and she was towel drying her hair. "Sorry I'm running a little late. I've had a crazy morning!" She rolled her eyes.

"What happened?"

A frown darkened Elizabeth's face. "Just a problem I needed to take care of that took longer than I thought." Then she smiled at Cassidy and her face smoothed out. "Would you like me to read your tea leaves before we go?"

Cassidy's stomach did a little flip, but she ignored it. "Sure."

She followed Elizabeth into the kitchen, trying not to look like she was cataloging everything. The appliances were stainless steel. Gleaming copper pans dangled from the ceiling.

"Have a seat at the breakfast nook," Elizabeth said as she filled a kettle with water and put it on the stove. Then she set an empty china cup and saucer in front of Cassidy.

"They're so beautiful," Cassidy said, touching the delicate edge of the empty cup. The rim and handle were edged in what looked like real gold, and the widest part of the cup was encircled by a delicate band of pink, yellow, and blue flowers.

"That cup and saucer came across in a wagon train with my great-great-great grandparents. They abandoned everything along the way that they didn't absolutely have to have. But that cup and saucer—they held on to them." After opening a box of loose tea, Elizabeth set the cup aside and shook the dry leaves onto the saucer. "Now stir the leaves with your index finger and think about the questions you would like to ask."

Seeing her focused expression suddenly made

everything more serious. And Cassidy had so many questions. Should she leave Channel Four? Would she ever get married? Have a child? Be rich?

When the kettle whistled, Cassidy jumped. For some reason, she always felt a little nervous around Elizabeth. Anxious. It was just that Elizabeth exuded so much energy. Next to her, Cassidy felt both less and more. Less exciting. More clumsy. Heavier.

Elizabeth poured the water into a plain white ceramic teapot. "Okay, put the leaves in the pot with your fingers." After Cassidy sprinkled them on top of the water, Elizabeth replaced the lid. "Now we let it brew."

"Who taught you to do this?"

"My grandmother. She was a wise woman. Some of my ancestors were actually hanged for witchcraft."

Cassidy felt a moment's confusion. "But didn't you say both your grandmothers died before you were born?"

After the briefest hesitation, Elizabeth smiled. "Oh, I just meant the woman I called my grandmother. She was really my grandmother's sister. Now pour the tea."

Cassidy finished pouring, trying not to make a face as she looked at the murky tea with bits of leaves bobbing in it. As a child, she had been a picky eater. She used to worry that a bug had landed in her food without her noticing. The slightest strange texture on the back of her tongue had made her gag, as she imagined tiny struggling legs and wings disappearing down the back of her throat.

"Now we need to let it cool." Elizabeth leaned back in her chair. "You know, ever since I met you, I've been watching a lot more of Channel Four."

Cassidy's feelings of flattery were quickly dashed when Elizabeth added, "So who's that young woman reporter who works there? The one with the long blonde hair?"

Cassidy rolled her eyes. "That's Jenna. And first of all, she's not a reporter. She's just an intern. She's still finishing college. She's a total suck-up. But all the men just eat it up, like they can't get enough."

"So she doesn't report stories?"

"Sometimes," Cassidy admitted reluctantly. "She's talked her way into a couple of assignments, and she's always nosing around, looking for more. She's the kind of girl who practically sticks her chest in the station manager's face and says"—Cassidy made her voice breathy—" 'I would do absolutely *anything* to get ahead in TV news.' It's disgusting."

Sure, Cassidy herself had striven to get ahead when she was Jenna's age, but she was sure she had relied on a little more than her hair and cleavage.

"Sounds like she's the kind of person who tries so hard it backfires on them." Elizabeth touched the back of Cassidy's hand. "Okay. The tea should be ready. I want you to sip it while you concentrate on your question."

And what came into Cassidy's mind was: *Will I always be lonely?* And she realized she was. Lonely at her core. She had Allison and Nicole and now Elizabeth, she had her job, but she needed something more. She would have labeled it a man, but even when she was dating, she still sometimes felt empty. She lifted the cup to her lips.

"Try not to drink the tea leaves," Elizabeth cautioned.

"No worries!" Cassidy said, suppressing a shudder. Looking over the rim of the cup, she saw Elizabeth watching her, as dispassionate as a scientist. Cassidy felt queasy. Was she getting sick? Sieving the tea through her teeth and suppressing a shiver, she swallowed the last dregs.

"Okay, all done?" Elizabeth didn't seem to have noticed anything. She took the cup in her left hand, covered it with her right. Closing her eyes, she swirled it clockwise three times. Her lips moved, and even though Cassidy strained her ears, she did not hear any sound.

Elizabeth lifted her hand and peered into the cup. Cassidy got up to look over her shoulder. Tea leaves were scattered along the rim, sides, and bottom.

Elizabeth rolled the cup between her palms, her face intent. “Look, there you are, Cassidy, riding a wild horse!”

Cassidy followed her pointing finger and tried to see what Elizabeth saw. Obviously, reading tea leaves took training.

“And look! There’s a big wedding bell over your head—and you’re trying to get away from it.” She glanced up at Cassidy, her blue eyes sparkling. “It’s like you want to get married, but you really don’t. Because you’re too wild to marry. No man has ever been able to tame you.”

That was so true! Cassidy thought. And the way Elizabeth put it, it didn’t sound like a negative.

“Hm, that might be changing. I can see that you have recently gotten over a hard, emotional time in your life.”

Cassidy had told Elizabeth about it, at least some of it. But it was like the leaves were telling her friend even more.

“That’s interesting,” Elizabeth murmured.

“What?”

She pointed. “Look at that square. It means you need to be cautious.”

Cassidy looked past the tip of Elizabeth’s perfectly manicured finger. She didn’t see a square, but she nodded.

"But there's also this triangle, which means good karma."

Cassidy thought she could see the triangle. Maybe.

Elizabeth rotated the cup, peered closer. "This arrow next to the broken necklace means that you work hard for people to like you, then push away the people you love, because you don't love yourself."

That was true. Cassidy did work hard on her friendships. But lately it seemed like it was Allison and especially Nicole who were pushing her away, not the other way around.

Elizabeth's eyes narrowed. "Oh, that's not good."

"What?" Cassidy scooted closer and squinted at the blobby bits of leaves.

"It's a cat. That means a false friend. And it's so close to the rim. That means it's big. Life changing."

"Does it tell you who?"

Elizabeth gave her a long look. Cassidy had the feeling that she really knew the answer but was holding back for some reason.

She patted Cassidy's hand. "I guess the best I can tell you is to watch your back."

CHAPTER 25
Northwest Portland

Nic would not let herself think of the pain and bewilderment on Leif's face as she had pushed him away. She still had a couple of hours before she picked Makayla up at her folks' house. The best way to fill the time was to keep busy. So she got on I-405 and headed in the direction of Foley's condo. There had to be more evidence —but where? There was no sense in searching his place again. They had already been over it with a fine-tooth comb, even looked for hiding places built into the walls, floor, or ceiling. But they had found nothing.

She had to keep busy. Keep her mind off Leif. Breaking things off had had to be done, for his sake. If he found out that she had cancer—and Nic knew in her bones that she did—then he would have stayed with her. No matter what. Even as his love changed to pity, his desire to distance, his joy to a burden. Because that was the kind of man Leif was. Honorable. Dedicated. Nic had worked side by side with him long enough to know that he would never give up once he had committed himself.

If Nic let him embark on this terrible journey with her, she would never know how he really felt. She wouldn't be able to trust him. For the best of reasons, but still. Nic needed to know that if Leif ever said he loved her, he meant it. A pure, uncomplicated love, not one with an asterisk after it that meant *because you might be dying and I know you need to feel loved.* Besides, she told herself as she cruised by Foley's condo, even in the twenty-first century, it wouldn't have been easy. A black woman and a white man still made some people look twice. Even in Portland.

Staring at Foley's condo, Nic drove in ever wider circles. Here was his gym, but they had already checked out his locker there and found little more than a bottle of dandruff shampoo.

She was doing Leif a favor, really. Aside from the cancer, in some sense Nic was damaged goods—because how could anyone have gone through what she had and *not* be damaged? Leif was the first outsider Nic had told about what happened, how two cute guys offering to buy her a drink after she got off work at a restaurant had led to a night she still didn't remember, a court case, and the birth of her daughter. She hadn't dated since. Ten long years of relying on no one but herself. And until Leif had come along, she had been perfectly happy with that.

Nic passed a storage rental place that was only a mile from Foley's condo building. But they had already checked the records of every storage rental place in the city, and neither Foley nor his fiancée had rented a unit.

Nic had Makayla, and that had to be enough. And there were hard times ahead. Even a nine-year-old knew what the word *cancer* meant. Her daughter didn't need to deal with all the changes the treatment would bring *and* a new, strange man in her life. Nic and Makayla were a team. The two of them against the world.

And Leif? Ending this thing now was best for him, too, Nic told herself, as she automatically stopped at a red light. Before it had put down roots. Before he yoked himself to a woman who would need more and more and could give less and less.

Leif would say otherwise, but how could he not need things from her? He would want closeness and honesty and communication. He would want her to bare her heart, share her soul. If she were unhappy, he would try to cajole her, prop her up, until she felt she had to pretend. How long would it be before he became just one more demand among the many that already overcrowded her day?

Nic shook her head. What was she doing, driving aimlessly through Northwest Portland as if she might just stumble over a clue? She obviously wasn't accomplishing anything, other than wasting government gas.

She put on her blinker and started to make her

way back to the freeway. On the way she passed Good Samaritan Medical Center. Two men walked out of the main doors, both of them wearing white coats, loops of stethoscopes sticking out of their pockets.

And Nic realized there was one place she hadn't looked.

Two hours later Allison and Nic were in front of the magistrate judge on call, asking him to sign off on a warrant to search Foley's medical school locker. And before another hour had gone by, Nic was using a bolt cutter to snip the combination lock in a hallway gone weekend-quiet, with Allison looking over her shoulder.

But when Nic swung open the metal door, her heart sank. A pile of textbooks and nothing more. With gloved hands, she lifted them to make sure there wasn't anything underneath. When she did, something shifted *within* the stack, making a soft clunk.

"Did you hear that?" she asked Allison, who nodded. "Something's off."

Nic set the pile of books back down and then lifted each one, giving it a little shake before rifling the pages. In addition to dense prose, she caught quick glimpses of a line drawing of a spine and a photograph of a chest cracked open to reveal the heart. The last book, the one on the bottom, was a copy of the 1,500-page *Gray's*

Anatomy. The weight was all wrong in her hands. She opened the cover, revealing a space hollowed out with surgical precision.

Allison looked over Nic's shoulder. Inside were a Sig Sauer pistol, a dozen plastic restraints, and several pairs of women's underwear. Underneath those was a stack of money, at least a dozen credit cards, and a gift card that read *Happy Birthday*. Nic flipped the last over with the tip of her gloved finger. On the back someone had filled out the *To* line with the first name of one of the dead women. And on the *From* line was the word *Mom*.

CHAPTER 26

Southwest Portland

Even though Allison never set her alarm for Saturday morning, she still found herself waking at six. For the next twenty minutes she tried to persuade herself to go back to sleep. But some orders the body simply disobeyed.

She had shifted positions for the dozenth time when Marshall rolled over, gathered her into his arms, and gave her a kiss.

"Mmm," he said, his eyes still closed. Marshall was not a morning person.

Maybe the kiss would have led to something

more, but now that Lindsay lived with them, they had begun sneaking around like teenagers.

So instead Marshall let his head flop back on his pillow.

Allison tried to go back to sleep, but with Marshall's muscled arm now under her neck, it was even more out of the question. She sighed and swung her legs over the edge of the bed.

With a muffled groan, Marshall propped himself on one elbow. His tousled black hair fell across his still-closed eyes. "What's the matter?"

"Don't you want to sleep?"

He smiled and opened one blue eye. "Not if you're going to sigh like that. What's wrong?"

"Oh, everything just feels unsettled. Nicole was really snappy at Cassidy on Monday. After that exercise class we took together."

"Why?" He patted the bed beside him, and she lay back down with another sigh.

"For giving airtime to the Want Ad Killer. Nicole had a point, but she didn't need to come down so hard. Especially when Cassidy tried to help us by letting that guy trip himself up. Cassidy has a lot more freedom than either of us does. Sometimes that means she does things—both good and bad—that we couldn't. Or wouldn't."

"Uh-huh." Marshall curled his knees up.

Allison draped her legs over his. "I don't understand why Nicole acted the way she did. She's been really prickly lately."

Marshall kissed her ear. She wasn't even sure he was listening. But talking out loud, even to herself, helped clarify her thoughts.

"I think something's up with Leif," she continued. "Nic says she wants to take it slow, but by the time she's ready to admit how much she likes Leif, they'll both be in a nursing home. I don't know. I can't see him giving her any grief. He's a good guy. It feels like something else is bugging her. But I've tried talking to her about it, and she says it's nothing."

"Really?" He kissed her shoulder.

"Even Cassidy is acting kind of weird. She's always going on and on about that instructor. You know, the one who taught the boot camp class. According to Cassidy, Elizabeth walks on water. I don't like her nearly as much as Cassidy does, but I have to admit she is pretty amazing looking."

"I know someone else who is pretty amazing looking," Marshall whispered. After his lips found hers, Allison forgot about her worries about her friends.

And after that, they were very, very quiet.

When Lindsay finally got up a couple of hours later, Allison waited until she had drunk half her coffee before she said, "I'm going to check out that gym Cassidy took me to. You should come with me. I'm thinking about getting a family membership."

Marshall was a runner, but if they had a gym membership it was possible he might use it as well. He had gone into work for a few hours, so she and Lindsay had the house to themselves.

"Just go on without me." Lindsay didn't look up. Her gaze was fastened on the table. Not even on a newspaper. Just a blank stretch of polished wood. "That's okay."

"Is this the same Lindsay who was the star of the volleyball team?"

Lindsay made a *pfff* sound. "In eighth grade. And in case you hadn't noticed, that was seventeen years ago. If you want to go to the gym, great. But I don't. I think I'll make snickerdoodles while you're gone."

Snickerdoodles? Even though her mouth watered at the thought of their soft sugar-cinnamon sweetness, snickerdoodles were the last thing Allison—or Lindsay, for that matter—needed.

"I'll make you a deal, Linds. I need your help. Between"—Allison hesitated, still having trouble saying it out loud—"between losing the baby and all the treats you make, I'm beginning to blow up like a house. I figured if you started going to the gym with me, you could keep baking and I could keep eating—only without gaining weight."

"But I don't want to go a gym." Lindsay took another sip of coffee.

"Why not?" Allison felt a prickle of irritation. This was the first thing she had asked of Lindsay. What would it hurt her to say yes?

"No one is going to want to see me in the dressing room. Trust me. *I* don't even want to see me in the dressing room. Look at me, Allison. I mean, really look." Lindsay lifted her puffy face. Her eyes were shiny with tears. "I used to be pretty. Now nobody is going to want to watch me take off my clothes. Take it from me. I got laughed out of the last strip club I tried out at. I've got that divot on my leg from when I fell off Chris's motorcycle. I've got scars on my arms from when meth made me feel like bugs were crawling under my skin. I'm all lumps and bumps."

"But that's why people go to the gym. To get in better shape."

Lindsay smiled wanly. "Yeah, and then maybe the other people can point me out to their kids as a cautionary tale. 'See, honey, that's what happens when you take drugs and end up living on the street.' "

Inside, Allison winced. Lindsay sounded like she was ready to give up. Like her life was over at thirty.

But Allison was her big sister. And big sisters didn't take no for an answer.

"How about this? We can put on our workout clothes before we go, and afterward come back and shower here. No dressing rooms."

Lindsay finally agreed, reluctantly. But once they were at the gym, she warmed up as one of the front desk employees toured them around and she saw all the options. It wasn't the room full of exercise equipment, the basketball court, or the Olympic-sized pool and the smaller heated pool that made Lindsay's eyes light up. Instead, she was interested in the sauna, the Jacuzzi, the massage rooms, and the café.

Allison ending up spending only twenty minutes on the treadmill, while Lindsay flopped down on various pieces of equipment—moving only when someone actually wanted to use whatever she was sitting on—to watch one of the half dozen closed-captioned, large-screen TVs. Still, Allison thought, if they made coming here a regular habit, maybe Lindsay would start taking advantage.

As they were leaving, they passed a line of framed photos of the various instructors.

"Hey," Lindsay said, pointing at a picture of a red-haired woman and then leaning forward to look at the gold nameplate screwed into the frame. "Elizabeth Avery. She looks familiar. Did she go to high school with us?"

Elizabeth, the instructor that Cassidy admired so much. "I don't think so. In fact, I'm sure she didn't, or Cassidy would have brought it up. She really likes Elizabeth's classes and talks about her all the time."

Lindsay shrugged. "Maybe I've just seen her downtown or something."

Allison had an uncomfortable image of a wasted Lindsay panhandling Elizabeth.

Compared to that, she thought, today was an unqualified success.

CHAPTER 27

Nordstrom

As they took the trolley to Nordstrom, Elizabeth said, "So, like I said, I've been watching Channel Four news lately."

Cassidy wanted to ask what she had thought of her but knew it would come across as needy. So she settled for humor. "You probably just doubled our number of viewers in the twenty-five to thirty-four age bracket."

Elizabeth grinned, a flash of white teeth. "I did notice the commercials were all for old people's products."

"Yeah, it's all bladder control drugs and electric scooters." The joke—that wasn't quite a joke—around Channel Four was that soon the news wouldn't have any viewers because they all would have died. "If it weren't for seniors and their maladies, we probably wouldn't have any sponsors." Cassidy sighed. "It's all changing so fast. I got into this business to be a reporter. Now they want me to blog, answer viewers' e-mails, Twitter, and do person-on-the-street interviews when half the time the average person doesn't actually know anything. And I have to stand there holding the mike and nodding like they're some genius. It's starting to feel kind of desperate."

"I'll tell you what one of the problems was. You were the only good one on the broadcast." Elizabeth rolled her eyes. "I mean, take that Brad Buffet."

"What do you mean?" Cassidy straightened up, a grin already tugging at the corners of her lips.

Elizabeth snorted. "He's so stiff. It's like they reanimated him and stuck him on camera. But when I listen to you, I feel like you're talking right to me."

"Thank you. Thank you," Cassidy repeated, as the words settled in and a glow spread through her.

TV people were always thinking about themselves. It was a self-obsessed business. But the problem was that she hardly ever got any unbiased feedback.

"That's something I really work on. See, when you're on TV or the radio, you don't want people to be able to tell you're reading. So some people, like Brad, make an arbitrary decision to stress every third word or maybe every noun or whatever. Listening to him just drives me crazy. *Because* he just *ends* up talking *like* this. Singsong." Cassidy warmed to her topic. "You don't want to rip and read your copy. Instead, you go through it beforehand and find the words that really count."

Elizabeth turned in her seat to face Cassidy. "What do you mean?"

"When you get home tonight, go into your living room and switch on the TV. Then go into the kitchen and start dinner. You won't be able to hear every word, but you should be able to hear the important words. Maybe you'll hear *accident* and *Northwest Portland* and *two killed,* and that will be enough to pique your interest because you live in Northwest Portland, so you'll go back into the living room to see what happened. But if you were listening to Brad, he might accent completely random words—and no one will ever leave their kitchen for that."

"So why aren't *you* the anchor instead of Brad or that other girl, the one they said just came to Portland from—Delaware?"

Cassidy suppressed a wince. "Connecticut. Her name's Alissa Fontaine. And even though they've made a big deal about bringing her in, they still give Brad all the important stories. If it's a political story or a natural disaster, they have a guy cover it. Women get the fluffy stuff. I had to fight for the crime beat. Sometimes I think TV is still a man's business. Just because you're young and pretty doesn't mean you're not a serious journalist."

"But since you're the crime reporter," Elizabeth said, "that must mean they believe in you."

"I *made* that beat. It wasn't there before I came along." Cassidy thought of Jenna. "And I still have to fight for it."

"You mean like with that intern you told me about?" Elizabeth asked. "Because she might try to get to a story before you?"

Cassidy felt listened to. "Exactly. Instead of making her own beat, it's like Jenna wants to take over from me."

"Like that's going to happen." Elizabeth shook her head. "You're twice the reporter she could ever hope to be."

The train pulled up at the stop closest to Nordstrom. As soon as they walked through the glass doors, Elizabeth lit up, obviously in her element. She was so self-confident and strong.

Cassidy felt a pang of envy. Why was she always filled with self doubt, hanging back, not committed enough? Why didn't she go for it?

Elizabeth chose a half dozen outfits—most of them not even on sale—and encouraged Cassidy to pick up this and that. She obviously thought Cassidy made a lot more than she really did.

TV only looked glamorous. It was all fake. Up close, the studio carpet was stained, and the decal that showed the city skyline was peeling on the bottom corners. The chairs didn't even have backs, so that if someone was off camera, the viewers didn't see an empty chair.

But that fake glamour attracted so many people who were willing to work for crummy wages. Even, as in Jenna's case, for free.

Cassidy picked up a few things, but Elizabeth's arms were soon full. A saleslady hurried up to relieve her of her burden. "Do you want to share a dressing room?"

Cassidy most certainly did not. Elizabeth looked stunning in her clothes. How much better would she look out of them?

But before she could say anything, Elizabeth smiled and said, "That's a great idea!"

As they tried things on, Cassidy used all her tricks to keep most of herself covered, while Elizabeth spent a good deal of her time wearing only a pair of panties.

Shoot, Cassidy thought sourly as she surreptitiously eyed Elizabeth's mile-long legs, *if I looked that good, I would charge admission.*

And make a million bucks.

Feeling short and stubby, Cassidy tried on the "vintage matchstick cords" that the saleslady had suggested and Elizabeth enthusiastically seconded. With both of them watching, Cassidy had been forced to pick a size smaller than the one she normally wore. The pants were so narrow it was hard to get her feet through them, let alone her thighs. Finally, she got them pulled up and—ugh—buttoned. With her stomach sucked in, she took a few experimental steps around the dressing room.

Wiff, wiff, wiff.

At the sound, Elizabeth stopped zipping up her dress and turned her head. With horror Cassidy realized the sound came from her thighs rubbing together. She sat down on the narrow bench and began to extricate herself from them, hiding her struggle whenever Elizabeth looked her way.

By contrast, even things that looked terrible on the hanger looked great on Elizabeth. A short silver silk dress with a cascade of ruffles at the neckline showed off her long, slender legs. A delicate lavender cashmere cardigan exposed her elegant collarbone. A sea-foam zippered jacket from Nike emphasized her narrow waist. And this being Portland, it would fit in at the gym as well as at any Pearl District restaurant.

The saleslady outdid herself, going to other floors and other departments and then knocking softly on the dressing room door to make yet another offering to Elizabeth. A brown skinny suede belt. A pink crystal necklace that tied with ribbons. A pair of gray high-heeled fringed moccasins that seemed ridiculous when the saleslady held them out, and which suddenly looked cutting-edge glamorous once they were on Elizabeth's slender feet.

Cassidy ended up with just a cardigan, twin to Elizabeth's, only in a shade described as heather hydrangea. One hundred fifty-eight dollars she knew she shouldn't be spending, but she couldn't just go to the counter empty-handed. She would look cheap.

Elizabeth had the saleslady ring up everything she had tried on. For a total of $1059.78.

She opened her purse and began to rummage through it, leisurely at first, then with more agitation. "Oh no, I must have left my wallet at home." She sighed. "I guess I'll just have to come back. Although I don't know when I'll have time again. My schedule is packed."

"The sale ends tomorrow," the clerk put in.

Cassidy found herself taking out her Nordstrom card. "I'll get it."

The saleswoman nodded and reached for the card just as Elizabeth put her hand over it.

"You most certainly will not. That's too much."

A nagging voice inside Cassidy agreed, but instead she said, "Don't worry. Besides, I'll be getting *your* double points. Anyway, I know you're good for it. Don't forget I see you pretty much every weekday."

CHAPTER 28

Ruth's Chris Steak House

Elizabeth felt all eyes on her as she followed the waiter through Ruth's Chris Steak House. She wore the silver silk dress, gray spike-heeled moccasins, and pink crystal necklace that tied with ribbons. The cashmere cardigan was loose around her shoulders. The admiring (from the men) or jealous (from the women) looks just confirmed what she had seen in her mirror earlier when she was getting ready. And she hadn't paid a dime for any of it! Cassidy had even been eager to offer to pay.

Elizabeth knew that Cassidy would eventually start hinting about getting her money back. And then she might switch to demands. But that was theoretical and in the future. And Elizabeth was all about right now. She had seen an opportunity and taken it.

There were three types of people in the world, Elizabeth believed. Some, like Cassidy, were naïve and full of ridiculous scruples that held them back from ever enjoying life. Others, like that Allison and Nicole, were phonies who pretended to care about others. And some—only a few—were like her. Strong enough to take what they could. And smart enough not to get caught.

Smart enough to play The Game.

And Ian? Ian fell into his own special category. He looked good, and they looked good together. He had money and power and influence.

He also wasn't stupid. He had caught her in a few lies, luckily only minor ones. She had gotten out of them by lying some more, lies designed to cajole and flatter.

To Elizabeth, lying came as easy as inhaling and exhaling. Just as she didn't need to think about breathing, didn't need to consciously slow her breathing down when she went to sleep or speed it up during boot camp class, the lies came out of her mouth as she needed them.

There was often a lot of truth in Elizabeth's lies, because those were the best kind. Once people heard something they knew to be true, they tended to believe the rest. Occasionally, she even found herself saying something bad about herself. Sometimes it was true, or sort of true. Sometimes the very warp and woof of it was spun from lies. But the listener thought that if Elizabeth "admitted" to something bad, she must be telling the truth about the rest.

As they walked through the restaurant, Ian was a half step behind her, his hand on the small of her back. By the way heads turned to follow them, she knew they made the perfect couple. Even when Elizabeth wore heels, Ian had two inches on her. Tonight he was dressed in a charcoal two-button suit and an ivory shirt, open at the throat. With his dark hair going silver at the temples and a tan face that set off his pale blue eyes, he had the kind of looks that made women look twice.

And now he was all hers. Or he would be, as soon as Joey took care of Ian's moneygrubbing ex.

Elizabeth had called Joey while the girl's body was still in the trunk.

"Hello?"

Joey sounded nervous, Elizabeth had thought. Well, he was about to get a lot more nervous.

"I took care of your stupid girl." She was driving on a narrow road somewhere next to the Columbia River. Somewhere out in the boonies. "The one you told about me." She couldn't believe that she had gone out of her way to make Joey some of her famous pasta salad. Tried to butter him up.

"What?" Joey's voice cracked.

"Don't tell me you didn't know about it."

In her ear, silence. She turned onto an even less used road.

Finally Joey said, "What did you do to her?"

A laugh spurted from Elizabeth's mouth. "What do you think? She's dead."

"But Jenna was only a kid!"

"You're the one who brought her into this. Not me. Does anyone else know?"

"No! No! I swear it! I just wanted a little insurance." He hesitated. "I just don't know if I can kill anyone."

"Don't give me that. Remember your whole family?"

"You know that was an accident. I never meant for it to happen. But this—this is looking someone in the face and pulling the trigger. And what if her kid is there? I just don't know if I can do it."

"But I can." The car jounced over the road, which by this point was nothing but potholes and gravel. As soon as she had taken care of the body, Elizabeth was going to have to go to the car wash, clean the car inside and out. It was one hassle after another. And she would have to hurry if she wanted to be back in time to meet Cassidy for their shopping trip to Nordstrom. "And you know what? If you don't take care of this problem, then I will."

"You'll shoot her?" Joey's voice was filled with something like relief.

"No, dummy. I'll shoot *you*. So you had better take care of business." Elizabeth would gladly kill Sara herself, and take pleasure in doing it, but only an amateur would think that the police wouldn't figure that out in a minute. But no one would tie Elizabeth to Joey. On paper, the girl who had gone to school with him a decade and a half ago didn't even exist.

"Okay, okay." Joey's voice rose in panic. "I will. I promise."

By this time, Elizabeth was next to the river, and there was no one in sight. She pulled over, getting as close as she could. After killing Jenna, she had stopped at A-Boy hardware and bought some cement blocks and rope.

Now she leaned into the car and trussed the body, in its bedspread wrapper, into a neat package, tying the ropes around the body's feet and shoulders. Then she carried the blocks one at a time to the edge of the riverbank. She had to haul and drag on the ropes to pull the body to the lip of the trunk. She let it tumble to the ground, and then, muttering curses under her breath, dragged it to the edge of the steep bank. After tying the blocks to the ropes—now a little looser from being tugged and pulled on—she rolled and shoved the whole thing until it fell into the river with a splash. Sure, the girl would probably be found sometime. But the only person who could tie Elizabeth to Jenna was Joey.

And she would take care of Joey soon. As soon as he did what she was paying him to do.

The rest of the day had gone more or less as planned. Elizabeth acquired a new wardrobe without paying a cent. And she sowed enough hints in Cassidy's fertile imagination that the silly twit was sure to begin doubting her friends. It had been so fun to mess with her head.

And after she parted ways with Cassidy, she had found a pay phone a few blocks away and looked up Channel Four's number.

"This is Jenna?" Elizabeth told the woman who answered, trying to imitate the girl's annoying way of making even a statement sound like a question. "I'm really sick? Some kind of flu? Can you tell them I won't be in this week?"

And when the receptionist transferred her, Elizabeth simply hung up.

Now the waiter stopped in front of a table. Pink rose petals were scattered over the white cloth.

"What's this?" Elizabeth said as the waiter pulled out her chair.

"I told them I was taking a special girl out to dinner." Ian smiled as he sat down opposite her and settled his napkin onto his lap. "So I asked if they could make the table special too."

Elizabeth leaned forward and squeezed his hand. Could he be thinking of asking her to marry him? That was part of her plan, even though they had only been dating for two months. But Ian loved it when Elizabeth was impulsive. Maybe he was just trying to match her spontaneity.

The menu was eye-poppingly expensive. Everything was à la carte, meaning that to assemble a meal you had to order six or seven individual items. Elizabeth let Ian do the ordering for her —he loved to pamper her, and she loved to be pampered—but as the crab-stuffed mushroom caps were followed by lobster bisque, she wondered where she would put everything.

While they were waiting for their steaks, he put his hand over hers. "There's something I need to talk to you about."

She tilted her head to the most flattering angle and gave him a smile she had practiced a dozen times in the mirror until she got it just right. "Yes?" *He* does *want to get married,* she thought with mounting excitement.

"Sara and Noah are going to be moving in with me. Temporarily."

Elizabeth pulled her hand back. "What?" Giving him a look she had most definitely not practiced in the mirror.

Just then the waiter arrived. "Now be careful, these are about 500 degrees," he said, setting down the heavy white plates.

The steaks sizzled and sang. Each was topped with a large pat of butter, which melted and ran down the sides, hissing when it hit the plates. The baked potato was so big it commanded its own dinner plate. Smothered in sour cream, butter, and bacon crumbles, it was the biggest potato Elizabeth had ever seen. But she wasn't in the mood to be distracted.

"I told you about our new house burning

down," Ian said. "It's a total loss. Sara and Noah have been staying at a hotel, but it looks like it's going to take a long time to rebuild. She called to tell me she needed more money so she could pay for a place to stay while the house is being rebuilt. There's insurance money, of course, but the company is dragging its heels because it looks like it was arson. I certainly don't want to pay her any more. And then there's Noah. I never see him enough as it is. There's really only one solution."

"Um-hum." Elizabeth narrowed her eyes, forgetting for a moment to keep her mask firmly in place.

"They're moving back in tomorrow afternoon. Temporarily. They're only going to live with me until the house is finished. I know it might make things a little awkward for us, but I need to make this as easy as possible on Noah."

Right. Like the kid who lived a cushy life at Ian's expense couldn't stand to be camped out in a hotel with maid service. Elizabeth had looked it up. The hotel Sara and her brat were staying at cost easily three times as much as the dump where she had met Joey. This would not do. This would not do at all!

From now on, Ian would be lavishing his money and time and attention on a spoiled five-year-old brat who wouldn't even appreciate it. And what incentive would Sara have for leaving? None at all. They would be back to being the perfect family.

Unless Elizabeth figured out a different way to play The Game. She put her hand to her heart, not incidentally drawing attention to her décolletage. “Of course, Ian. He’s your son. You have to put him first.”

Ian nodded and then cut another piece of his steak.

Before he could bring it to his mouth, Elizabeth said, “That looks wonderful. Can I have a bite?”

He turned his fork upside down and offered it to her. She took it delicately, then licked her lips.

“Let’s leave,” she said impulsively.

“What? You’ve hardly touched your steak.”

“That’s not what I’m hungry for.”

Ian gave her a delighted grin, then caught the waiter’s eye. “Can we have the check and the food boxed to go?”

The waiter frowned. “Is everything all right?”

“It’s fine—we just realized we needed to be someplace else,” Ian said.

As the waiter whisked their plates back to the kitchen, Elizabeth watched Ian open his wallet without looking like that was what she was doing. The fat sheaf of money gave her a thrill. He counted out enough for the bill and then added a fifty-dollar bill as a tip and closed the black folder.

She felt a pinch of irritation. What had the waiter done to deserve that? They had barely had time to settle in. Slipping her sweater from her shoulders, Elizabeth let it fall to the floor.

"Ready to go?" Ian asked.

She answered with a sly smile.

As soon as they got to the front door, she put her hands to her shoulders. "Uh-oh! I left my sweater," she said, and ran back inside before he could offer to retrieve it for her.

She grabbed the sweater at the same time as she slipped one of the fifty-dollar bills from the black leather folder. When she turned, the waiter was watching her, his mouth pursed. Had he seen? Elizabeth shrugged. It didn't matter. Ian had paid for the food. And a tip was a reward for great service, and there hadn't been any service to speak of.

But Elizabeth, now, she gave great service.

CHAPTER 29

Southwest Portland

"Two pints of the IPA," Marshall said to the waitress at the Old Market Pub.

IPA stood for India Pale Ale, but in Portland, which had the most craft breweries per capita in the United States, it was always shorthanded to IPA. This pub was one large room filled with several dozen high-backed pine benches and tables. Big-screen TVs mounted on the walls made it easy to watch whatever sport was in season.

"And I'll have a bacon cheeseburger, and my wife will have the Caesar salad with chicken."

It was just the two of them at the table. Lindsay had stayed home. She was engrossed in a TV marathon of *Dawson's Creek* reruns, fantasizing about a teenage life she'd never had.

"I don't know," Allison said as the waitress walked away. "Maybe I should have ordered a milk or a soda."

"What?" Marshall took his eyes off the baseball game. "Why? Is there a reason?"

Allison realized he thought she might be pregnant again. They weren't trying, but they weren't *not* trying, either.

"No. Sorry. It's just that I don't want Lindsay to smell beer on me."

When Lindsay had first moved in, they had locked all their alcohol—which wasn't much, maybe a half dozen bottles, mostly wine—in Marshall's trunk. Just to keep from tempting Lindsay. Although, as Marshall had pointed out, the nearest 7 Eleven, which basically sold only cigarettes, Slurpees, and beer, was only a few blocks away.

"Allison." Marshall took her hand. His palm was cool and a little rough. "Your sister has to live in the real world at some point. And in the real world, most people drink beer. Some people can't, or won't. But those two groups don't live in separate worlds. They figure out how to live in the same world."

"But she's still recovering. I don't want to be the one to set her off." Allison pulled her hand back and began to toy with the saltshaker, which was a repurposed empty beer bottle with holes poked in the metal cap.

"Lindsay is an adult. She's thirty years old." Marshall touched the back of her hand again, and she looked into his blue eyes, the color of gas flames. "Thirty," he repeated. "She's not a kid anymore."

"But sometimes I feel like she got stuck. She was only thirteen when Dad died, and part of her never got any older. Sometimes I feel like our family let her down." Allison's eyes felt wet. "It's not like we meant to, but first Dad died and left her behind. Then Mom basically checked out. And I was so busy trying to prove that everything was okay with me that I left Lindsay to fend for herself."

"Lindsay had choices, the same as you did," Marshall said with a hint of impatience. "Only she made bad ones. Lindsay alone is responsible for her behavior. Not you."

The waitress appeared with two glasses of beer. "Here we go. Two IPAs."

Despite her half-formed idea not to drink, Allison pulled her glass toward her and took a sip. "But it's too simple to say it's all Lindsay's fault. Maybe part of it is my parents' fault for babying her when she was growing up, so that she fell apart when Dad died. Maybe it's society's fault for not finding a way to help her when she started to get into trouble. Or the school's for letting her cut so many classes before they even told us." Allison set her glass back down on the coaster. "Sometimes . . ." She hesitated. "Sometimes I even think it's God's fault. He took Dad away and left us all alone. And all of us fell apart, in one way or another. Even if we all didn't show it."

Allison thought of the last two years of high school, of how she had lost sleep and lost weight, increasingly frantic to keep her grades up, keep the house picked up, keep appearances up. To convince the world—and herself—that they were all still okay. "Back then, I was so angry with Lindsay for skipping class and getting in trouble. It felt like she was doing it to embarrass me. I acted like the surface was the only thing that mattered. When it's what's underneath that counts." She thought of Colton Foley, whose perfect exterior hid the horrible black hole of his heart.

"Allison, listen to yourself," Marshall said. "Every day you prosecute guys that scare even me. And you don't let their lawyers make excuses for their bad childhoods and poor upbringings. But when it comes to your sister, you're willing to give her so much rope she could hang herself. There comes a point where Lindsay has to take responsibility for her own choices."

"I'm just afraid she's not strong enough."

To her surprise Marshall said, "You might be right. Lindsay probably isn't strong enough."

"But then—" Allison started.

Marshall raised his hand. "What I'm saying is that there are times when nobody is strong enough. Nobody. But with God, all things are possible. Look at Paul. He asked God three times to take away his weakness, but God said to him, 'My power is made perfect in weakness.' There comes a time when you have to let go."

Allison completed the thought for him. "Let go, and let God."

"Exactly."

CHAPTER 30
Southeast Portland

Buzzing. Something was buzzing. Joey swam out of a dream. It was morning. Barely. The slanted light hurt his eyes. He had spent the last twenty-four hours drinking. Ever since Sissy had told him that Jenna was dead.

And it was all Joey's fault.

Jenna, with her long blonde hair and her exuberance. She had seemed awfully young for a reporter. The first time they met, she had actually hugged him. It had been a long time since a woman who didn't expect to get paid afterward had touched Joey.

Jenna, who had been so impressed with herself for coming up with the smoke detector/hidden camera.

Jenna. All broken and bloody.

Joey had tried to drink enough that he wouldn't dream about her, but it hadn't worked. In his dreams Jenna had been trying to tell him something, her soft lips moving, her blue eyes wide, but when he leaned close to hear, dark blood flowed like a waterfall from her parted lips.

The buzzing was growing more annoying. It was coming from his phone, sitting on the floor next to his mattress. Which was also on the floor. The phone was the one Sissy had bought him at Target. Paying cash.

So there was no point in wondering who it was.

Or in trying to avoid her. He couldn't forever. He fumbled the phone to his ear. "Hello?"

"Why haven't you done it yet?" Sissy demanded. If you could demand anything while speaking in a whisper.

When Joey heard her voice a month ago, he should have hung up. When he saw her face, he should have turned on his heel and walked away.

Instead he had let her play him for a fool.

And now Jenna was dead. And this Sara soon would be.

Joey sat up. Mistake. A headache bloomed behind his right eye.

Pressing the heel of his hand against his eye socket, he said, "I've been thinking. I don't even know her."

The fire had been pure pleasure. But to shoot some lady, even from twenty feet away? No. He couldn't do that. Which was why he had called the TV station and talked to Jenna. And it had all been downhill from there.

"Well, thanks to your *thinking,* thanks to your foot-dragging, she's not even going to be at the hotel anymore. She and that brat of hers are moving in with someone. Today."

"Shacking up already?" Joey was surprised. "That was fast."

Sissy's tone sharpened. "It's not like that. It's her ex-husband—*my* boyfriend. Sara called him up and was all 'Boohoo, my house burned down.' Tell me, is that fair? No matter what I do, she just finds a way to suck more and more from him. And she'll never stop. Ever. So you need to take care of her, now. And that kid too. I definitely need you to do both of them."

Joey shivered. "Wait—now you want me to kill the kid too? A little kid?"

Crap, he should have done the lady yesterday. Then it would have just been her. But now—now both she and the kid would die. One way or another. Because Sissy didn't take no for an answer.

"Hey," Sissy said matter-of-factly, "you'll be doing the brat a favor. His mom will already be dead. This way, they'll be together." Her voice was flat, emotionless. "But you can't do it at my boyfriend's house. Because I don't want him getting dragged into it." Her voice turned thoughtful. "Of course, if he was at work with a half dozen witnesses, he'd have a perfect alibi."

"Maybe you could just talk to your boyfriend?" Joey ventured. "Maybe he could just get the whole alimony thing adjusted or something."

"How many times do I have to point out that I'm not paying you to think?" she snapped.

He had a flashback of Sissy at Spurling. Of what an angry Sissy would do.

Shortly after this girl named Ruby arrived at Spurling, Sissy had targeted her. Joey had liked Ruby, who was little but spunky. But Sissy had developed an immediate hatred toward her. Maybe because so many people had liked Ruby —unlike Sissy. Joey didn't know. All he knew was that when he and Sissy were on kitchen duty together, she would spit in Ruby's food. At other times she whispered behind Ruby's back, turning the other kids against her. And she hid cigarettes in Ruby's cubby and then told one of the counselors. This earned Sissy extra privileges and Ruby an especially confrontational group session when she refused to admit her guilt. Eventually Ruby tried to kill herself.

When she heard the news, Sissy had laughed and clapped her hands.

Why hadn't Joey thought of Ruby when Sissy first got back in touch with him? Why hadn't he remembered Ruby until it was too late?

He couldn't drink his problems away. He couldn't think his problems away. If he went to the cops, it would be his word against Sissy's. That was, if she let him live long enough to talk to them. The only way out was to do what Sissy demanded —go out and kill this woman and her little boy. And then try to forget he had ever done it.

"Okay, okay. I'll need the address. And if you've got it, the times she'll be there—and the guy she's staying with won't be."

Sissy gave him what he asked for. Joey scribbled it down on a paper bag from the liquor store.

"I'll give you three days. And that's it. Or I'll just have to start taking care of things myself. Do you understand what I'm saying, Joey?"

He understood, all right. If he didn't do this thing, then Sissy would put *him* on her list of things that needed to be taken care of.

CHAPTER 31

Northwest Portland

Elizabeth stared down at her cell phone, thinking. Would Joey chicken out? Or would he finally take care of business?

She jumped when she heard Ian calling from the bedroom. He had spent the night. Too impatient to wait for him to leave, she had sneaked out to the living room to make the call.

"I'm out here."

Wearing just a pair of black briefs, he came into the living room and kissed her forehead. "Who were you talking to on the phone, sweetie?"

Elizabeth's expression was guileless. "The gym."

His eyebrows drew together. "You sounded kind of firm."

She tried to replay her last words. At least she had been keeping her voice low. People were sometimes more afraid of calm than they were of shouting. And Joey already knew what she was capable of. She found an explanation that should fit anything Ian had overheard.

"Georgia, the girl who works behind the desk, has been scheduling personal training sessions without giving me enough warning. They're supposed to give me three days' notice. If you let them take an inch, they'll take a mile." She put her hands on Ian's shoulders and pressed her body against him, enjoying his firmly muscled chest under her palms, his height that allowed her to feel small and girlish. "And I want to make sure I have as much time as possible with you."

Rising to her toes, she kissed him. Her goal was to make Ian forget whatever words he had overheard, her tone. She pressed her hips against his. He groaned.

Mission accomplished.

So where do you want to take me for brunch?" Elizabeth purred as she towel-dried her hair.

Ian was still sprawled in the tangled sheets.

He hadn't showered, but Elizabeth couldn't stand to have someone else's smell clinging to her.

"Remember? Sara and Noah are moving back in today. I need to go home and get things ready."

Elizabeth put on a fake pout to cover the much stronger emotions she was feeling. "If I didn't know better, I'd be jealous."

"I'm doing this for Noah," Ian said. "Not Sara." But then he had to spoil it by saying, "Not that we're not friends."

Once Joey had finally taken care of Ian's ex-wife and kid, then Ian's money and attention could be put to better use. For Elizabeth.

Ian left not long afterward, but Elizabeth couldn't stop thinking about him. She deserved to be the one moving into his house. She deserved to be the one he put first.

As the day moved toward evening, Elizabeth drove past Ian's house. Through the window she caught a quick glimpse of a dark-haired woman standing in his living room, a small figure by her side. The very sight of them left Elizabeth shaking. She had only spent the night at Ian's house twice. But now, unless Joey did something, these freeloaders would probably stay there for weeks and weeks. Ian would hurry home to them. They would eat together, talk about their day, laugh. They would be like a little family.

And Elizabeth would be left on the outside,

looking in. The way she had been so many times before.

She drove aimlessly until she finally realized what she needed. A pick-me-up. Someone who would look at her with adoration—and *mean* it. Someone who would not believe his luck. Someone who had no ties, no entanglements. No eyes for anyone but her.

She pulled over and parked to redo her makeup. Elizabeth tilted her head, regarding her image in the mirror critically, trying on a variety of expressions. She widened her eyes slightly. There. That was better. She tucked her lower lip in so that just the edge of her white teeth showed. Blew out a stream of air between her pursed lips. And when Elizabeth thought of how Sara now had everything *she* should, she was able to make her eyes sparkle with tears.

"Ma'am, I can help you," the woman checker at New Seasons called out. "There's no one in line over here."

"That's okay," Elizabeth answered. "I'd rather stay in this line."

At the sound of her voice, Clark looked up. She gave him one of the smiles she had practiced, and he returned it. His mouth was a disgusting jumble of teeth.

When it was finally her turn, he said, "Hello, Korena."

"You remembered!"

"You would be a hard woman to forget." Putting his hand over his name badge, he said, "Do you remember my name?" He looked surprised by his own daring.

"It's Clark," she said. "Do you ever go into phone booths and spin around?"

"I'm not sure what Clark Kent does now that everyone has cell phones, but no, I don't." His expression darkened. "I'm always just me."

One of the things she had put on the black rubber conveyor belt was a six-dollar bar of sandalwood soap. Now she picked it up and sighed. "Do you think someone could put this back for me?"

"Did you want a different bar?"

"No." She looked down, bit her lower lip again. Knowing it emphasized how plump her lips were, like pillows. "It's just that right now it's a bit too expensive for me. After the day I had today, I was just wanting a little treat. But once I got up here, I realized I shouldn't have picked it up."

Clark set it next to the register and continued to ring up her items, bagging them as he went. Then he told her the total. Elizabeth wrote the check—another from the checks she had taken from Korena—and handed it over.

As he took it, his other hand slipped the bar of soap into one of her bags. "Let me give this to you. As a present."

She smiled, but only inside. Outside, she let her mouth twist. "I really couldn't."

"No," he insisted grandly. "My treat. To help make your day better."

"Well, if you insist . . ."

"I do. Now, can I help you out with your bags?"

They ended up spending fifteen minutes next to her car, talking. Clark told her about how he had graduated from high school the year before. The night, which cloaked his features, seemed to inspire a new confidence in him. He wanted to be an artist. His blue-collar parents worked in a factory in eastern Oregon and hunted whatever was in season. They didn't understand him. They had refused to help him pay for school unless he majored in something that might actually provide him with a paying job, so he was taking a year off and working at New Seasons to make some money.

It was easy to figure out what to say in return. Elizabeth carefully watched his reaction to every sentence she said and adjusted the next accordingly. And with every word of Clark's, every glance, every change of expression, she accumulated a small hoard of facts about who he was and what he longed for.

Then it was simple enough to become the woman he wanted.

When Clark said for the third time that he had

to go back inside, Elizabeth kissed him on the cheek. “Thank you again. Talking to you has completely turned my day around.”

He raised his hand to his face, looking dazed. “Would it be possible—I mean—could I talk to you again?” He looked down at his shoes. “I mean, not at work?”

She grinned. “What time does your shift end?”

They ended up at his place, the most dreary apartment imaginable. Worse even than the tacky motel where she had been forced to kill that stupid girl. She had told Clark it wasn’t a good idea to go back to her place, that her ex might be watching her house. The minute he got her inside the door, he started kissing her. It was a relief to close her eyes so she didn’t have to see the threadbare couch, the scarred coffee table, the tiny rooms that hadn’t been painted in this century.

Sex didn’t mean anything to Elizabeth. It was a tool, just like a smile or a compliment or a lie or a threat. Each had its place.

“Can I draw you?” Clark said afterward.

It was such an odd request that she laughed a little, then stopped cold when she saw the hurt in his eyes. This boy was like a puppy.

“Sure.” She pushed herself up on one elbow. “Sheet on or off?”

“Off?” he said, making it sound more like a

question. He got up and, after a moment's hesitation, pulled on the pair of boxer shorts he had discarded so eagerly only a few minutes before. From a small table, he took a pencil and sketch pad.

She enjoyed watching his eyes trace her curves as he sketched in her long legs with sure strokes, then slowed a bit as he came to the middle.

When he set down his pencil, she asked, "Can I come look?"

He reflexively clutched the sketchbook to his chest. "Sure. But I'm not very good."

Elizabeth got to her feet and came around behind him as he slowly lowered the sketch. Her breasts, she thought critically, were too small. Maybe she should rethink implants? But the rest of her looked good—taut belly, strong but slender legs.

"Do you like it?" He looked up at her and bit his lip.

Right. He meant the drawing. Well, everything looked in proportion. Only a few lines suggested her hands and feet, which Elizabeth had heard were hard to draw, but at least he hadn't bungled them. And her face was even fairly recognizable.

"It's beautiful. Can I have it?" There. That should make him feel better.

But instead of handing it over, he put it close to his chest again. "Can I hold on to it for a while? Because I'm sure that when I come home from work tomorrow, this will feel like the most amazing dream. I'll need proof."

"Proof?" Her tone was playful.

"Yeah. Something I can see and touch."

She pulled the sketch pad out of his fingers and gave him a sly smile. "How about this?"

"What's this?" Clark asked later, tracing a bruise on the inside of her upper arm.

She had bumped into the corner of the pec fly machine.

She gave him the sad little smile that she had practiced for moments such as these. "I don't really want to say."

"You can tell me." He puffed up his scrawny chest. "You can tell me anything."

"I had a little argument with my ex-husband. That's why I was having such a bad day."

His eyes widened. "He *hurt* you?"

"It's not like you think. He doesn't usually leave bruises." She looked away, like she was lying. Well, she was, but not in the way Clark would think.

He pushed himself up on one elbow. "*He doesn't usually leave bruises?* Can you hear what you're saying? You need someone who can take care of you and make sure nobody hurts you."

Elizabeth made herself relax as he covered her face with his eager, slobbery kisses.

She had only been with Clark for a few hours, but she could tell that he would be willing to do anything she wanted. He already appeared to believe that she was the one true love of his life.

There was always a use for people like that.

At two in the morning she told him she had to go, that she couldn't risk enraging her ex if he drove by her house and saw that her car was still gone. Elizabeth just wanted to get back to her house, to her own things, to her 600-thread-count cotton sheets, not the scratchy polyester blend on Clark's bed, even if they had been, thankfully, clean. It took another thousand kisses before he would let her go. Fifteen minutes later, she was showering his smell from her skin.

When her alarm rang at five, Elizabeth turned it off with a groan. Her head ached. She wanted to lie in bed and luxuriate in her memories of last night. How easy it had been to make Clark fall in love with her.

And now that he had, what would be the next stage of The Game? What would Clark give her willingly? And then what would she take? Elizabeth knew in her bones that he was going to be useful. And for more than a six-dollar bar of sandalwood soap. She just didn't know for what. Not yet.

Her hand reached for the phone to call in sick

to work. But then she remembered. Boot camp. Boot camp and her new best friend, Cassidy Shaw. Cassidy Shaw, who could also give Elizabeth so much.

Unless those stupid friends of Cassidy's interfered.

CHAPTER 32

Mark O. Hatfield Federal Courthouse

"You can't hide your head in the sand anymore," Nic said to Zoe Barrett. They had called Colton Foley's fiancée in for a meeting in Allison's office, without telling her what it was for.

"Zoe, what we have to tell you is difficult," Allison added, naturally falling into the good cop role. "But we got a search warrant for your fiancé's student locker. And this is what we found."

Nic slid the photographs out from a manila envelope and began to put them down one at a time, as if she were dealing a deck of cards.

The first photo was of the hollowed-out textbook. Zoe glanced at it and then back up at Nic, her face blank. The next was a fan of money. These weren't crisp notes from a bank, but wrinkled bills rifled from victims' purses.

Zoe's expression didn't change. Nic slapped down the next photo, which showed a bundle of plastic restraints. The same kind that had been found in their condo. The kind that had supposedly been Zoe's idea. Her face still showed nothing. A credit card. The girl's expression was still blank, but then Nic tapped on the photo. Slowly, Zoe leaned closer, and Nic could hear her suck in her breath when she read the name on the card. It was the name of one of the victims. The next photo showed six pairs of panties, one torn at the side. Zoe's eyes widened. And then Nic slapped down the trump card. A gun. Zoe put her fingers to her lips.

"Ballistics says this is the gun that killed those three women."

Zoe pushed back from the table. Her face was clammy and pale. "Someone could have put that stuff in his locker. It must be a mistake."

"I know this is hard," Allison said, "but think it through. The only one who could have all these things is the man who committed these crimes. And the evidence shows that it's Colton."

Zoe took a shaky breath and squeezed her hands together in her lap. "It can't be true. This is not the man I know. It's just—not. It can't be."

Nic said nothing. Allison patted the back of Zoe's hand. After a moment, the young woman took a shaky breath.

"Did you know he had a gun?" Nic said.

"No." Her head hung down so that now she spoke to her hands, twisting on her lap.

"Those plastic restraints. Do you know who brought those into your apartment?"

Nothing but silence.

"Who brought those into your apartment?" Nic repeated, her voice so soft it was nearly a whisper.

The girl was broken now. No point in playing bad cop.

"Colton did. He said it would be fun." She raised her wet, splotchy face. "And it was. And now I have to think of what that meant. What he did to those women. Did he want to do it to me?"

Nic and Allison were silent.

"All I know is that I loved what I saw of Colton. This man—the man who had these things—is not the same man. Now you're saying he had another side, one that I never saw." Zoe's voice wobbled. "But what I don't know is which version is true."

"Maybe they're both true," Nic said into the silence. "Some people have two sides. And one they keep hidden."

By the time Zoe left, she had agreed to help them. But Nic knew that that could change. Colton Foley had his hooks in the girl. Give him a few minutes on the other end of a telephone and he could probably convince Zoe that black was white, up was down, and that there was a perfectly good explanation for how those items had ended up in his medical school locker. It all depended on what you chose to believe.

Look at Makayla. For years she had been deathly afraid of the water, and Nic had aided and abetted in that belief, babying her, letting her daughter make excuses for not even dipping her toes into a pool. But then she had brought her to Elizabeth at Cassidy's gym.

Instead of acting like she expected Makayla to be frightened, Elizabeth had taken a hands-off approach, not asking if she was okay, not checking in with her over and over. Instead, she had simply expected Makayla to do what she said. Nic had watched part of the first lesson, but then Elizabeth said it would work better if it were just the two of them.

Driving home after the lesson, Makayla had chattered about how she had even ducked her head under the water. Before, getting her to put her head under water would have been like dunking a cat. In a way, it made sense. Without Nic observing, without Nic reaffirming her fear, Makayla could let go of being the kid who was scared of water.

After Zoe left, Allison went to the bathroom and Nic grabbed her coffee cup and went into the kitchen. She was trying to cut back on coffee

—she had read on the Internet conflicting reports about its relationship with lumpy breasts—but she figured a half cup wouldn't hurt her. Too late, she saw that Leif was there before her. At the FBI field office she could wear her armor and keep her distance. Here at the courthouse, seeing him unexpectedly, her defenses were down. She hoped her expression was neutral.

"Good morning." Leif gave Nic a nod. Completely professional.

So why did it feel like someone had reached into her chest and given her heart a twist?

He hefted the pot. "Do you want some?"

This was harder than she had thought. Why had she ever given in to him in the first place? She should have kept her private life separate from her work life. She had lived by that principle for ten years. Every night when Nic left work, she tried to really leave it, putting it out of her mind as soon as she put her key in her car's ignition. And at work, she made no mention of her home life. But Leif had slipped past her defenses.

"Want some?" he repeated, and Nic realized she hadn't answered. Her eyes met his for a minute. He held her gaze without a flicker, but she saw how much it cost him to keep his words light. She had pushed him away with every weapon at her disposal, except the truth.

Now she wanted to fall to her knees, lean her

forehead against his thighs, and weep. Tell him how afraid she was that her life was already lost, that she was walking around like a living woman who was soon destined to be bones moldering in a coffin.

Instead she just said “sure” and held out her cup. Careful not to meet his eyes again.

CHAPTER 33

Channel Four

“Cassidy Shaw,” Cassidy said in a distracted tone. She was working on a story about a man who had conned dozens of Portland-area women into giving him money, clothes, cars, credit cards, and worst of all—love.

“Someone for Jenna on line one,” Marcy, the receptionist, said. “I told them she wasn’t here, and they asked to speak to one of her coworkers.”

“Who is it?” Cassidy felt a twist of annoyance. *Coworker* sounded like peer. Really, Marcy was far more Jenna’s coworker than Cassidy was. The girl had called in sick over the weekend, but no one knew when she would be back. Supposedly she had some kind of flu. With Cassidy’s luck, Jenna would show up in a day or two with a pretty flush and looking even thinner.

"A motel in Southwest Portland. The Barbur Bargain Motel."

A motel? Cassidy had wondered if Jenna was really off enjoying the spring sunshine. But maybe she was carrying on some kind of torrid affair.

"Put it through," she said with considerably less annoyance and more interest.

"Hello?" A man's voice.

"This is Cassidy Shaw. I understand you're trying to get hold of Jenna. Unfortunately, she's out today, and I don't know when she'll be back. Can I help you?"

"Hm . . . are you a friend of hers?"

"Jenna?" Sensing it would be worth her while, she said, "We're very close. We're practically like sisters." Well, they *were,* Cassidy thought. Jenna could be the younger sister who was always jealous of her older sister's poise and success.

"We have something of hers that she left here."

Cassidy imagined a sexy black teddy, a pair of fur-lined handcuffs. There had to be a way she could use whatever it was as a weapon. "What is it?"

"Her purse and car keys. The housekeeper found them in one of our rooms. We got this number from her business card."

Purse and car keys? The little matter of Jenna having business cards Cassidy would address later. "When were they found?"

"Sunday around noon."

Today was Tuesday. "Why didn't you call yesterday then?"

He sighed noisily. "Look, lady, a lot of people don't come here because they just need a room for the night. They come here because their house just got foreclosed on and this is the only place they can afford. Or they're here to see someone at the hospital. Or they come here because they fell in lust with someone who's not their spouse and they need someplace private. We're more for emergency situations, like. I would never have tried to get hold of this Jenna lady at her house—but I figured her work would be okay."

The reality of what he was saying began to sink in. Cassidy would never be more than five feet from her purse. Every woman she knew was the same way. So how could Jenna have simply left it behind? And her keys? That made even less sense. She tried to remember what Jenna drove.

"Let me ask you something. Is there a black Honda in your parking lot? I think it's an Accord."

"Parked at the far end of the lot. Is that her car?"

"It sounds like it. And it's hard to imagine Jenna leaving her purse and keys. Why didn't you turn her things over to the police?"

"We figured she had to leave suddenly. It happens."

Cassidy imagined irate spouses recognizing certain vehicles as they drove past. "And you've heard nothing from her since she rented the room," she said, thinking out loud.

"It was actually two rooms."

"What?"

"She rented two rooms," he said. "Right next to each other."

"You mean one of those suites where there's a door in between and you can lock it or not?"

"No. They're adjacent, but there's no interior connection."

This was making less and less sense. "Okay, you said you found her purse and keys," Cassidy said. "What about the other room? Was anything found in it?"

"No. But there was something missing. The bedspread."

Cassidy had a bad feeling about this. "Could you hold on to her keys and purse for a little while? I need to do some checking."

After she hung up, Cassidy made a few phone calls, but hit nothing but dead ends. Then she called Allison. "What are you working on today?"

"Nicole and I are prepping for a grand jury presentation tomorrow. Why?"

"Do you think the three of us could grab a quick lunch? Because I think something's wrong, but I'm not sure. I need your advice."

"What's wrong?"

Cassidy looked around to make sure no one was listening. It was second nature, making sure her stories stayed hers. Then she realized who she was subconsciously trying to hide from. *Jenna.*

"Something bad might have happened to our intern."

"That Jenna person?"

"That Jenna person," Cassidy echoed. "I can't decide if I should keep my nose out of it or call the police. That's why I want to run it past you guys."

Allison conferred with Nicole, and the three of them agreed to meet in an hour at one of the many dedicated food cart areas scattered throughout the city. The carts were a popular addition to the Portland food scene. Even if you could only cook one thing, if you did it really, really well, with a cart you might be able to scratch out a living making it. And without the expense and overhead of opening a real restaurant.

This area was only a few blocks from Portland State, so it was popular with students as well as office workers. It was within walking distance for Allison and Nicole, and only about a mile from Channel Four. But Cassidy's four-inch heels made the distance prohibitive, so she drove. The day was overcast, but it wasn't raining, which made it a fine spring day by Portland standards.

They met up on the corner and began debating what to get. It seemed like new carts had sprung up overnight. Cassidy ended up with a pulled pork waffle from Parkers Waffles. Allison ordered a sandwich stuffed with handmade mozzarella and sun-dried tomatoes from the Portland Soup Company. And Nicole gravitated toward Asaase, a brightly painted green, yellow, and red cart. The man who served her wore a tall blue turban that nearly touched the ceiling of his tiny trailer.

"So what kind of food is that?" Cassidy asked Nicole as they walked across Fourth Avenue to the little park tucked behind an office building. It all looked fried, which in Cassidy's mind was a good thing.

Nicole popped a round orange-yellow slice of something into her mouth. "Afro-Caribbean. The people are from Trinidad. The husband's a reggae musician."

Cassidy tried to remember where Trinidad was, but she was more intrigued by Nicole's food. Pulled pork on a waffle had sounded exotic, but now she wished she had ordered something different. "What are those?"

"Fried plantains." Anticipating Cassidy's next question, Nicole held out her paper plate. "Want to try one?"

Cassidy picked up one of the circles. It was cut like a coin, yellow with crispy black edges from its time in the fryer. She popped it into her mouth. It was hot and sweet and soft. And irresistible. "Is this some kind of sauce?" she said, generously dipping another coin into the bright red sauce squiggled on the edge of Nicole's plate.

"Actually," Nicole started, "I think that's pretty ho—"

Too late. Cassidy's tongue was already on fire. Tears sprang to her eyes as she waved her hand in front of her mouth.

Allison shoved an open carton of milk into her hand. "Quick. Drink this. The milk fat will help wash away the oils."

Cassidy followed orders. Blessed coolness spread across her tongue. Allison *should* be a mother. She already knew all the tricks.

Nicole pointed at another of the goodies on her plate, a folded triangle of fried pastry. "That sauce was for the samosa. It's kind of bland without it. They told me they make the sauce themselves from Scotch bonnets. That's one of the hottest peppers in the world." She wagged her finger. "So will that teach you not to eat off someone else's plate?"

Cassidy chugged the last of the milk and grinned through her tears. "What do you think?"

Sharing a laugh, the three of them settled on a bench.

Allison turned serious. “So what’s up with Jenna?”

Cassidy explained about the phone call from the hotel. “I’ve called her cell. Straight to voice mail, like it’s turned off. And the answering machine at her apartment just has one of those really long beeps, you know, like when someone already has a million messages. I even managed to get in touch with her college advisor and got her parents’ number in Florida, but Jenna wasn’t there, and they didn’t know anything. I tried to make it sound like it was my mistake in case it was nothing.”

Nicole looked serious. “And she left her purse and keys?”

“That’s not all.” Cassidy blew air out of her pursed lips. “Her car is still parked in the lot.”

“Does she have a roommate?” Allison asked. “Or a boyfriend?”

“No roommate. And a boyfriend back home. Jenna flirts with anyone in pants, but never more than that. That I know of.” Cassidy had often wondered if the whole boyfriend thing was an act, designed to make Jenna a little more valuable.

“So what do you think of the idea of her meeting someone at a motel?” Nicole tossed her now empty plate into the garbage can next to her. “I know where the Barbur Bargain is. That place is a dive. From what you’ve said about

Jenna, she'd be more likely to end up at a hotel with turndown service and a gourmet chocolate on the pillow."

"You're right. It doesn't seem like her. The only reason I can think she would be out there was that maybe she was meeting a source for a story. She's always looking for anything that will make her stand out when she graduates. Although I have no idea why she would rent two rooms."

"I have a buddy at the Portland police," Nicole said. "I'll ask him to have someone on patrol look at the rooms. See if the hotel manager missed anything."

Allison touched Cassidy's arm. "And you should ask around and find out what story Jenna was working on."

"Sure," Cassidy agreed, taking the last bite of her waffle.

Although she knew there was no point in asking. If Jenna had been working on a story, she wouldn't have shared it with anyone else for fear it would be assigned to a more veteran reporter. She would have waited until she was so deeply woven into the story that it would have been impossible to tease her out.

Cassidy had taken the same approach herself.

Back when she had been a Jenna.

CHAPTER 34

Bridgetown Medical Specialists

The human body, when confronted with a threat, naturally responded with fight or flight. It wasn't designed to sit patiently with a two-year-old copy of *Better Homes & Gardens*.

Nic was beginning to realize just how much waiting there would be in her future. Waiting for the day of an appointment to arrive. Waiting to see the doctor. Waiting for test results.

The universe certainly had a sense of humor. Nic hated waiting. She hated pills, doctors, and needles. And most of all, she hated being forced to admit she needed help.

Today, she had come prepared for the wait with her BlackBerry and a thick stack of files. But when she checked in for her one thirty appointment, all that happened was that they drew some blood. Then it was back to the waiting room while the minutes ticked by and a succession of people filed in to join in the waiting or eventually have their names called to go back. Some of those who left later came back, walking toward the lobby with red-rimmed, unseeing eyes.

Propped up next to Nic's chair was a huge brown envelope—24 x 36 inches—looped twice with a thin cord and containing her films. Dr. Magel had given them to Nic and asked her to hand-carry them to the breast surgeon. When she took them, she had felt like she was carrying her future. But it turned out to be written in a language she couldn't read. In the privacy of her garage, out of Makayla's sight, she had undone the cord and sneaked a peek at the images, but they had meant nothing to her.

Soon, though, the surgeon would look at them. Today would mark another turning point. Just like the day she found the lump. The day she told Leif to leave her alone. And now the day she became the patient of a surgeon who specialized in breast cancer patients.

Nic desperately wanted off the conveyor belt that had been set in motion. Her foot jigged faster and faster.

"That's it," she finally said out loud but to no one in particular. "I'm not going to wait any longer." Nic picked up the envelope, gathered up the rest of her things, and stopped by the front desk. "I've been here nearly two hours without anyone saying boo to me. I need to go."

"Now just wait a minute, honey," said the receptionist. She was an older black woman with cornrows.

Nic pressed her lips together. "I think I'm done waiting. My office was expecting me back an hour ago."

"Look—is it Nicole?—you're new here, right?"

Like it would be a good thing to be a regular at a breast cancer surgeon's office. Nic gave the slightest of nods.

"We try to keep Dr. Adler to a schedule, but he takes the time he feels he needs for each patient. And what that means is that he runs late." She sighed, her ample bosom rising and falling. "But when it's your turn in there, you'll be glad of it."

"I just don't think I can wait any longer." Nic made a show of looking at her watch. "I'm missing an important meeting right now."

It was only half a lie. She *was* missing a meeting. It just wasn't important.

"Just give me a second, and I'll check with his nurse."

Two minutes later Nic repeated her threat to the nurse, the nurse got the doctor, and Nic got ushered back. Feeling like she had jumped the line. Feeling like she hadn't had any choice.

"I'm Dr. Adler. I'm sorry we're running behind." He was a fit-looking man in his mid-thirties, sinewy and tan, with a narrow face dominated by a beaked nose. He took the envelope from Nic and went out of the room while his nurse told Nic to get undressed from the waist up.

Nic waited. Again. But this time she couldn't think at all. It wasn't that her mind was blank. It was that it was filled with too many thoughts.

When Dr. Adler returned, he gave no hint of what he had seen in her films. He had her lie back and then did another breast exam, spending what seemed an endless amount of time. But finally he told her to sit up.

"What I want to do today is a core needle biopsy of the lump. Our radiologist will put a hollow needle into your breast several times so that we can pull out different samples of the growth for pathology to look at the cells. He uses a machine with an automated needle to make sure it's targeting the area."

"Sounds like fun," Nic said.

Dr. Adler didn't crack a smile, just walked her down the hall to where the radiologist was waiting for her. As she lay facedown and maneuvered her breast into the round hole on the special table, Nic felt more than a little ridiculous.

She was glad her face was turned to the wall so that she could try to put out of her mind that the male radiologist was eye level with her dangling breast. Only it really wasn't a breast anymore, just an anonymous piece of meat that needed to be cleaned and then injected with a local anesthetic, all accompanied by a murmuring commentary that was oddly soothing. It needed to be compressed and X-rayed and have its skin nicked. It needed to have a needle inserted through the nick. And then there needed to be a new X-ray to make sure the sampling needle would be properly repositioned. And then a second sample. And the whole process needed to be repeated a half dozen times.

Nic had been warned to lie absolutely still, but it was hard not to jump at the clacking sounds the machine made as it vacuumed various spots in a clockwise movement all around what the radiologist called "the target region." Around the lump. Each felt like a small electric shock.

After about thirty minutes the radiologist taped a gauze bandage over the spot and gave her a Barbie-size ice pack to slip into her bra. And then it was back to the exam room to wait for Dr. Adler.

"Okay, we're done now, so you can go ahead and get dressed," he said, once she was back in his office. "Your tissue samples are being sent to pathology, and they'll let me know as soon as they have the results. It's possible they might be here tomorrow, although it will probably be the day after. In my practice, I've come to believe that it's better to give patients the news as soon as I know it, so I'll call as soon as the results are in."

"Could you tell by looking at my films if it was cancer?"

"No," Dr. Adler said.

Nic heard the lie in his voice.

CHAPTER 35
Mark O. Hatfield Federal Courthouse

Allison walked into the grand jury room, set her briefcase and purse on the prosecutor's table, and turned toward the jurors' expectant faces. This was one of two federal grand juries, each serving two days every other week for eighteen months. During that time they might be asked to investigate everything from bank robbery to bankruptcy fraud, from radical animal rights groups to sex traffickers. This grand jury had already served about two-thirds of a term, so the members had developed relationships with each other and with all of the federal prosecutors—including Allison.

"Good morning," she said, and was met with smiles and nods. "Today I'm going to bring you information about the case we are building against Colton Foley, the man we believe robbed and murdered three women, as well as assaulting and robbing several others. In the press he has been dubbed 'The Want Ad Killer.' "

Her words made the jurors straighten up. A few nodded or murmured. The Want Ad Killer had been front-page news for days. Because grand jurors served for so many months, they weren't sequestered or forbidden from watching the news in general. But now that they knew they would be considering this particular case, they would have to avoid watching, reading, or hearing anything more about it.

Unlike a trial jury, a grand jury never saw a single case through until the end. Once they had voted to indict a given individual—or declined to—their job was over. Because they weren't asked to determine guilt or innocence, only decide whether charges should be officially filed, their standards were looser than those of a trial jury. Their decision didn't even need to be unanimous: only eighteen of the twenty-three needed to agree.

Inside the grand jury room it was only the prosecutor, the jurors, and sometimes a single witness. Allison could have skipped the grand jury and gone right to a probable cause hearing in front of a judge. But in that case, Colton Foley and Michael Stone would have been on hand to hear every word of her argument—and then the balance of power would have tipped the other way. A probable cause hearing gave the defense an early crack at the case, and an opportunity to cross-examine the FBI agent—in this case, Nicole—who testified to the evidence.

"We've been able to collect quite a lot of evidence. To help us understand it, I'd like to call to the stand FBI Special Agent Nicole Hedges."

After coming in from the anteroom and being sworn in by the court reporter, Nicole explained to the grand jurors what she and Allison had learned. She showed the jury the photographs from the hotels' surveillance cameras and talked about tracing an e-mail sent to one victim back to Foley's address. Nicole also told them about the locker and the secrets it had contained.

Nic had a good speaking voice, low and lively, that would make her an interesting witness even if she had been describing tax law. Hearing about the hollowed-out textbook, the gun, the panties, and the gift and credit cards left the jurors hanging on her every word.

"We believe," Nicole said, "that Foley kept some of these items as souvenirs. He may have intended to use the cash and even the credit cards. The gun and the plastic restraints were probably to be used on future victims. But the women's underwear are more than likely mementos."

"What do you mean by mementos?" Allison asked, not for herself, but for the grand jury.

"Many serial killers keep souvenirs from their victims. They're usually personal items that allow them to enjoy the memory of the crime. For a comparable situation, you might think of a woman who keeps a pressed flower or a ticket stub to remind her of a special evening."

Several of the jurors winced.

After Nicole finished her testimony, Allison asked them, "Do you have any questions for Special Agent Hedges?" She liked to hear what they were interested in, something she would never be able to ask at the jury trial. The grand jurors' questions could help shape her approach to any future trial. And sometimes they thought of angles she had missed.

The foreman, a retired hardware store owner, was the first to speak. Allison knew she could always count on Gus Leonard to ask a question. And then another. And another.

"When my boy was in high school, he shared a locker." Gus tilted his head. "Did this Foley share a locker at the medical school?"

"That's a good question," Nicole said. "I believe he did not, but I'll need to check on that." She made a note. It was the kind of thing that might have tripped them up at trial but would remain secret in the grand jury room.

Gus and a few of the other jurors asked a half dozen more questions. Once they had satisfied their curiosity, Allison excused Nicole and asked her to tell Foley to come on in.

Although they would have rehearsed Foley's testimony a dozen times, Michael Stone would not be allowed to accompany his client into the grand jury room. Instead he would be forced to sit in the hall, twiddling his thumbs and hoping that his client didn't open his mouth and hang himself. Foley could always ask for a break to confer with his lawyer, but Allison was betting that he wouldn't want to seem weak by asking for advice, or guilty by taking the Fifth.

If Foley was a sociopath, as they suspected, then he would probably use charm and chutzpah to try to twist the truth to his own dark ends, pile lie upon lie. But what worked well with an individual person—say his fiancée—would more than likely falter under the cold eyes of twenty-three grand jurors and one federal prosecutor.

Foley walked to the witness stand with the faintest of swaggers in his step. He wasn't conventionally handsome—his face still looked a bit unfinished, and his dark hair needed a trim—but he carried himself as if he knew he deserved for all eyes to be fastened upon him. As he took his seat, his expression was oddly cheerful.

Allison said, "Mr. Foley, we are here today to talk to you about the three women found robbed and murdered in downtown hotels, as well as additional women who have come forward to say that you robbed them."

He shook his head emphatically. "I had nothing to do with what happened to these poor unfortunate women. In fact, I myself am the victim of shoddy police work."

Allison ignored his innuendo. "First of all, Mr. Foley, e-mails sent to one of the victims arranging for her to go to the hotel where she was murdered were traced back to your IP address."

He shrugged. "I live in a condo, and I have a wireless router. That means any of my neighbors can and do leech off my Internet. Some of those units are rentals—people are moving in and out all the time. There's even a coffee shop on the ground floor where you can piggyback on my signal if you sit in the right corner."

It might have been a good argument—if they didn't have an entire web of evidence. Allison picked up a photograph from the prosecutor's table. "Mr. Foley, let me show you what's been marked as Grand Jury Exhibit 36." It was one of the photos they had shown the grand jury earlier. "It's a photo taken by a surveillance camera in the hotel an hour before one of the victims was found. Tell me what you see."

He glanced at it. "A man wearing a baseball cap."

"What color is his hair?"

"Dark brown." He squinted. "Maybe black. It's hard to tell. The lighting is dim."

She handed him three more photos. "These are Grand Jury Exhibits 37, 38, and 39. Do they appear to show the same person?"

Foley shrugged. "I guess. They're not very good photos."

"And what about the jacket the man in those photos is wearing. Does it look familiar?"

He looked from one picture to another. "I'm not sure."

She handed him another photo. "This is Grand Jury Exhibit 40. It's an enlargement of the first photo, but focused on his jacket. Can you tell me what brand it is?"

"Columbia."

"And do you yourself own a similar jacket, Mr. Foley?" It had been seized in the search of his apartment.

"It's possible. Columbia Sportswear is headquartered here; there are at least four Columbia stores within five miles of my house. I would guess every other person in Portland owns something made by Columbia." Foley seemed to grow a little bit taller.

His strategy seemed to be to cast doubt on every connection between him and the victims. Allison was sure it wouldn't work for the grand jury. Unlike a trial jury, they only had to decide if there was *prima facie*—Latin for "at first glance" —evidence that crimes had been committed and that the accused had done the committing. But a trial jury might look at Colton Foley and see an upstanding medical student who had been caught in a web of unfortunate coincidences.

Allison took a deep breath. "I want to remind you, Mr. Foley, that you are under oath." She handed him the stack of photos that had shattered Zoe. "These are grand jury exhibits 41 through 49—items that were found in your medical school locker. They include plastic restraints, six pairs of women's panties, a gun, a gift card belonging to one victim, and a credit card in the name of another. Do you want to explain that all away, or do you want to tell the truth?"

"The truth?" He leaned forward, pointedly making brief eye contact with every grand juror. "The truth is that we all know that the Portland police have been battling a public relations nightmare. In the past year, one Portland cop has been convicted of sexually harassing women. Other officers have been charged with using excessive force. When the media began to blame the police for not finding this so-called Want Ad Killer, they were frantic to find someone to pin this on. I am the victim of a discredited police department desperate to put an end to a media disaster. I superficially fit a few of the characteristics of the real killer, so they planted evidence in my medical school locker to take the heat off. They came to the place that's the most sacred to me"—Foley's voice actually broke—"the place where I am learning to be a healer, and they took evidence that was already in their possession from the crime scenes and used it to frame me."

His words rang out with an intensity that was nearly mesmerizing. Allison glanced at their jurors' faces. They seemed to be listening.

A chill ran down her back. Colton Foley wouldn't walk—would he?

CHAPTER 36

Mark O. Hatfield Federal Courthouse

Twenty minutes before she was scheduled to go into the grand jury room, Nic had called Dr. Adler's office. She knew she was being stupid. The pathology report would take as long as it would take, and trying to hurry it along would accomplish nothing. And he had said he would call her. Still, she wanted to remind Dr. Adler that she was in suspended animation. That she couldn't move forward until she knew.

"We don't have results yet." Dr. Adler sounded as though he had said the same words many times before. "As soon as we do, Nicole, I'll call you. But at this point I wouldn't expect to get the report today."

At 2:12 Nic had been in the middle of a sentence when her phone vibrated on her hip. She kept testifying to the grand jury, but her mind split in two. Her mouth continued to speak, not hesitating over a single word. Her eyes looked at each of the jurors in turn, not at the BlackBerry's display.

But the other part of her?

It already knew who was calling.

Once she was out of the grand jury room, Nic called her voice mail. As she had known, it was the doctor's office with the biopsy results. Should she wait to call them back? But she had to know. Now. She couldn't stand waiting any-more. She pulled back the heavy door and went into the empty stairwell of the federal courthouse.

The last time she had been here, the whole downtown core was being evacuated and the stairwell had been filled with a panicked mob. Just thinking about it made her breath come fast and shallow. But, she reminded herself, even then, when things had looked so dark, the terror had eventually passed and the city had survived.

As she tapped in the number for the doctor's office, Nic was oddly proud to see that her finger was not shaking. The nurse put her on hold for five minutes, ten. Nic leaned her back against the cool wall while she waited. She thought about the elderly juror she had helped to survive the pandemonium on the stairs. But in the end, Mrs. Lofland had helped Nic just as much.

Finally the music—a never-ending loop of something sprightly—was replaced by Dr. Adler's voice. "The biopsy report did end up coming back today, and I knew you would want to know right away."

"And?" Nic said. Knowing he would have led with it if it were good news.

"Unfortunately, cancer cells were found."

The former English major in Nicole noted how Dr. Adler chose to use the passive voice.

How he distanced himself from the bad news. No one was really responsible for finding the cancer cells. The cancer cells had just appeared, all by themselves.

Nic's thoughts were oddly detached from her. *Yes. I knew it. Does this mean I'm going to die? Is this the beginning of the end?* It was as if they were floating above her head like cartoon speech bubbles.

Shock, Nic diagnosed. She was in shock. That was why everything felt surreal. Her legs were boneless. Only the wall was holding her up, and it wasn't doing a very good job.

"Is the test always correct?" She knew she was grasping at straws. "Is there any chance it's a false positive?"

"I'm afraid there's no doubt about it, Nicole. You do have cancer. Invasive ductal carcinoma."

"Invasive?" Somehow she gathered herself to ask a question. "Does that mean it's spread?"

"We'll need to run some more tests. IDC does have the potential to invade your blood and lymph systems. That means it can spread cancer cells to other parts of your body. We need to set up an appointment to discuss what surgical approach you want to take, but you're going to need at least a lumpectomy." Dr. Adler's voice hardened. "I want this out and in a jar." He was a general, talking about the enemy. "You'll also need to schedule an appointment with an oncologist. He or she will help you decide on other treatments, but you are probably looking at radiation, and possibly chemotherapy."

"What are my chances of survival?" If she could just make it until Makayla was in college, Nic thought, not sure whom she was begging. Just live long enough to see her baby turn eighteen. She couldn't leave Makayla now, not when her daughter was still so young.

"Well, the lump is fairly small, so that's good, but we don't know enough to say much more than that. We need to get that lump out and take a look at the nearest lymph nodes to see if it's spread. You'll need to speak to my scheduler."

After promising she would call back when she had her calendar in front of her, Nic said good-bye and then slid down the wall, her jacket rucking up in the back. She sat on the cold concrete, her legs splayed in front of her.

And she bit her hand to keep from crying out.

CHAPTER 37

Channel Four

Cassidy had been drawn to the crime beat because of its guaranteed drama. It offered murders, kidnappings, armed robbery, and the occasional hostage situation.

But predictable it wasn't. It wasn't like covering city council meetings, where you got a schedule for the whole year. Sometimes it was feast, others famine. But day after day, Channel Four had the same size news hole to fill.

Today Cassidy was working on a piece about a mom who had embezzled $2,000 from her kid's Little League team. A sad story to be sure, and a crime, but nothing that made Cassidy's heart beat faster.

And then she answered her phone late in the day, and everything changed.

"Hey, it's Nicole. I just heard back from the Portland PD. They sent out a uniformed officer to look at the rooms Jenna had at Barbur Bargain."

"And?"

"They weren't able to get a criminalist out until late last night, but they found blood at the scene."

Cassidy lifted her fingers from the keyboard. "You mean like Jenna cut herself, or was in some kind of fight?"

"The criminalist said it was high-velocity impact splatter. And there're only two things that make that. Getting a body part caught in high-speed machinery. Or getting shot."

"What? Do you mean she's dead?" Cassidy's stomach did a slow flip. How many bad things had she said and thought about Jenna? Sure, she hadn't liked her. Hadn't trusted her. But that didn't mean she had wanted her to die.

"I honestly don't know, Cassidy."

Nicole's voice sounded tired. Tired to the bone.

"It's not so much the blood that proves Jenna would have to be dead. But getting shot is obviously not a good thing. Someone wiped the room clear of fingerprints, but they missed the blood. The wallpaper behind the bed has this crazy pattern. The Vancouver PD said you could have Jackson Pollock throw paint on it and never notice the difference. But when their criminalist sprayed it with luminol, the whole wall lit up. Of course, they don't know if it's her blood. Now they need something with Jenna's DNA to see if it's a match. Does she keep a hairbrush at the office? Or a toothbrush?"

"I'll see if I can find something," Cassidy said, squeezing the phone between her ear and her shoulder. She had already opened up a new document and was taking notes.

"Even a water bottle would work. We could probably get a touch of DNA off her purse, but that's a much harder process than working off saliva or hair. They're getting a trap and trace on Jenna's cell, work, and home numbers. An officer will be by Channel Four around five to pick up anything that might give them a DNA sample. And of course he'll want to ask around to see if anyone at the station knows why Jenna went to the motel in the first place."

"I'll see what I can find out."

After she hung up, Cassidy slipped into Jenna's cubicle. Nicole hadn't told her to keep out of Jenna's stuff. In fact, she had asked for Cassidy's help in finding a DNA sample. So Cassidy wasn't snooping. She was *helping*.

But she knew she could also be helping herself to a story. In her head, it was already taking shape. The story of a beautiful missing girl who had left only her blood behind. Viewers ate that kind of thing up. A few months earlier, Cassidy's coverage of another missing girl had landed her in the national spotlight. *Someone* was going to own Jenna's story. Someone had to help find her —alive or dead—and bring closure to her friends and family. And help bring whoever had done it to justice.

And that person should be—would be—Cassidy.

The intern's cubicle, located at the end of a dimly lit hall next to the bathrooms, was the place where things no one at Channel Four wanted came to die.

Old binders, miscellaneous office supplies, and discarded phone books, some of them dating back a decade, were piled on the far edge of the credenza. Jenna's cast-off purple desk chair, with its coffee-stained seat and torn armrest, sat next to a battered burnt-orange visitor's chair. Looking at them, Cassidy was forced to admit that maybe Jenna's blue exercise ball, which she used in lieu of a chair, made sense.

In addition to the ball, Jenna had tried to add some of her own touches, such as pinning a few photos on the nubby blue head-high wall. Cassidy had never paid attention to them before, but now she studied them.

Jenna with a dark-haired guy sporting a Van Dyke beard. Must be her boyfriend. Jenna with a smiling middle-aged couple. They looked so much like her that they had to be her parents. And there was also, a bit oddly, a photo of just Jenna herself, dressed in a blue bikini and lounging on some tropical beach with a drink in her hand.

Cassidy bet that every man who worked at the station had salivated over that photo.

Yesterday, the photo of a nearly naked Jenna would have been annoying. But now just one phone call from Nicole had made these photos, even the bikini shot, unbelievably sad.

After taking out the thumbtacks, Cassidy slipped the photos into her jacket pocket. The cop would surely want them for any canvass, but before that, Cassidy would scan them.

When Jenna was here in the flesh, flaunting her perfect body and perky enthusiasm, Cassidy had been barely able to hold her jealousy in check. Now she felt a twinge of guilt as she realized that, in her own mind, Jenna was already morphing from a person into a project. Cassidy told herself it was like what Nicole had said over tacos. In order to do their jobs, certain professions couldn't afford to make emotional connections with the people they dealt with. Cassidy was no different from a surgeon, focusing on the problem, not the patient.

In an odd way, she was the person closest to Jenna at Channel Four. Not because she had bonded with her. Far from it. Cassidy had tried hard not to pay any attention to Jenna. As a result she had always been hyper-aware of the girl, of how she swung her blonde curtain of hair back from her dewy fresh face, of how all conversation stopped when she leaned down in one of her teeny-tiny skirts to pick up a dropped paper clip.

To figure out what had happened to Jenna, Cassidy had to think like her. Well, that shouldn't be so hard. Jenna was Cassidy minus ten years. Eleven, if you wanted to be picky.

Okay. She made herself think back to her first job, in Medford, where she had been a glorified gofer, minus the glory. She would have done anything to get on camera. To get a story.

So something must have been happening in that motel room that Jenna thought would become a story. But what could the story have been about?

In Jenna's desk drawer Cassidy found spare change, pens and pencils, a Starbucks card, and a Valentine's Day card signed *Love, Vince*. But nothing that seemed like it was labeled "clue." As she sorted through the items, Cassidy noticed the blinking message light on Jenna's phone.

Channel Four had a default voice mail password: 111111. When you started work at the station you were supposed to change it, but the steps to reprogram it were so complicated that hardly anyone did. Brad Buffet, the anchor, hadn't. Neither had Jerry Vanek, the station manager. Only Eric Reyna, the assignment editor, had. Cassidy had figured all this out one week when rumors had swept the station that layoffs were looming.

Now she cradled the phone with her shoulder, hit the voice mail button, and pressed the *1* key over and over. When it was time to choose among options, she selected *Play all*.

On Friday afternoon a man had left a message. His voice had the roughness of a smoker's. "Okay, get a room at the Barbur Bargain Motel and let me know the room number. And I'll see you tomorrow morning."

A chill went down Cassidy's back. Was she listening to the voice of Jenna's killer?

The only other message had been left earlier that very morning. It was a younger guy, his voice sounded strained. "Jen—where are you?

Why aren't you answering your cell? Are you mad? I'm sorry I said that about your story. Of course it's going to be big."

A big story, just as Cassidy had suspected. Whom did Jenna confide in? She giggled and flirted with Eric, Jerry, and Brad. But she wouldn't have gone to any of them to discuss a story, or to ask their advice. Jenna would have feared—with reason—that they would take it from her. It was called bigfooting, and it happened all the time. A junior reporter would get a lead, do all the work, and then before it could go to air, the more senior reporter would take the story and claim it as his own. In this case, probably *her* own. Because Jenna had probably been worried about Cassidy bigfooting her.

Even Cassidy wasn't immune from bigfooting. When she had wrangled a televised interview with a senator suspected of murdering a senate page, the network had flown out one of their marquee national talents to take over from Cassidy. Only some last-minute maneuvering had allowed Cassidy to continue.

As Cassidy was cogitating, one of the station's cameramen, Andy Oken, walked by on his way to the bathroom. Andy had no love for the on-air talent—she'd once overheard him referring to them as "blow-dried meat puppets"—but he could be counted on to put the story first.

"Andy, Jenna's out sick, and I'm playing catch-up. Has she talked to you about any stories she's been working on lately?"

He pursed his lips. "Last week she was asking about the lipstick cam we gave her for that undercover piece during sweeps month."

About as big as a tube of lipstick, a lipstick camera was great for undercover videos. And in extreme sports, it could be stuck to a helmet to give viewers a "you are there" feeling.

Hiding her wince, Cassidy remembered the story meeting where the segment had been proposed. It was the kind of stunt trotted out during sweeps month, when the news was taken over by the cute stories of kids who gave their hamsters mouth-to-mouth or anything else deemed moving or "aww"-inspiring. These, alternated with salacious eye candy masquerading as some kind of moral lesson.

This particular story had required a female reporter to dress up in red vinyl hot pants and high-heeled boots and troll for unsuspecting johns. The men would be directed to a seedy hotel room, where Brad Buffet was waiting with Andy to record their pathetic rationalizations. The station could pretend it was reducing crime, while viewers got to enjoy watching their fellow Portlanders end up in the twenty-first century video version of the stocks.

When the idea was first broached, Cassidy had

protested that the assignment would be demeaning. And then she had waited for them to beg her. Her plan had been to eventually give in, in exchange for some extra vacation days. Instead, Eric had smirkingly informed her that Jenna had already been picked for the piece—the unspoken implication being that Cassidy was getting a little long in the tooth to play the part.

"What did she want a lipstick cam for?" she asked Andy now.

He shrugged. "She didn't say. I told her we rented them. We don't have enough call for undercover cameras, and the technology changes too often."

So Jenna had been thinking of going undercover. But to do what? What?

Hadn't Cassidy seen Jenna talking to Barney, Channel Four's archivist, last week?

She tracked him down in his basement lair. Surrounded by stacks of tapes that needed to be cataloged, he was sitting at his desk, engrossed in the newspaper.

The representative of one dying form of the media reading another, Cassidy thought sourly. Working as a print or TV reporter used to be a good job. Now Cassidy felt like a dodo bird. A single video on YouTube of a bunch of ugly guys lip-synching a Shakira song could attract more viewers than the local news did—sometimes millions more. Eric reminded them every day that TV's slice of the ad pie had already shrunk 25 percent.

Barney still hadn't looked up. Maybe he was getting a little deaf. He was a Vietnam vet with a graying ponytail and a belly so round and high it looked like he might be strapping it on every morning.

Cassidy cleared her throat.

"You can't trust the government." Barney stabbed the newspaper as he got to his feet. "It's all a conspiracy."

Cassidy had learned long ago not to ask any questions when Barney started muttering. The administration might change in Washington, but Barney's suspicions did not.

"Barney, didn't I see you talking to Jenna last week?"

His expression eased into a smile. "Yeah. I wish all the interns were as cute as her. She wanted a digie for a story she was working on."

A digie was a digital recording. Barney's job mostly involved cataloging and filing film, but sometimes events made his services far more important. Had a politician been caught with a call girl? Had a celebrity had a car accident? Had a famous politician died? In less than five minutes Barney would be able to pull archived footage to run as B-roll under the story. The B-roll would be what viewers saw while Brad droned on about the deeper meaning of the event.

"Do you remember what it was of?"

"Yeah, she wanted . . . hm, what was it?" He scratched behind his ear. "Oh yeah, some footage of an arson that happened a couple weeks ago."

"Did they have any suspects?"

He looked up at the ceiling. "Not when it was shot, anyway."

Cassidy remembered the man's message on Jenna's voice mail. Had she figured out something the cops hadn't?

CHAPTER 38

Portland Fitness Center

As Elizabeth got ready for boot camp Wednesday morning, she thought about how Joey would soon take care of Sara and Noah.

He wouldn't want to. But he would. Because he was more afraid of her than he was of anything else.

After that, the next step would be to take care of Joey. He had served his purpose.

But Elizabeth didn't want to get her hands dirty. She hadn't worked this hard to end up in some prison that would make the Spurling Institute look like a picnic. What she needed was someone who would be eager to help her. And she already had someone in mind.

The teakettle whistled. After pouring the steaming water over the paper filter holding freshly ground coffee beans, Elizabeth set the kettle back down on the stove.

Without hesitation, she made a fist and hit herself in the right eye, her knuckles making contact with the top of her cheekbone. And then she poured milk into her coffee.

Twenty minutes later, just before she walked out the door, she checked her face in the bathroom mirror. The corner of her eye was already puffing up. It wasn't much of a bruise, but it would continue to darken. And there were ways to make it look much worse. A little purple eye shadow and a few tears could go a long way, Elizabeth knew.

She had done it before.

"Let my face be a lesson to you," Elizabeth said at the beginning of class. "Never turn your back on the lat pulldown machine. That bar can be vicious."

Cassidy was actually early to boot camp, and her form wasn't half bad. For once.

"You look like you're in a good mood," Elizabeth said at the end of class.

Cassidy attempted to blot the sweat off her forehead with one of the thin white hand towels the gym provided. "Actually, something terrible is happening at work. Remember the intern we were talking about? Jenna? She's gone missing —and it looks like something bad happened to her."

Elizabeth flattened her palm across her chest. "Oh, no! What happened?" She had been dying to bring up Jenna with Cassidy—*dying*—but there had been no good way to work her into the conversation. But Cassidy's next words shocked her.

"She was going to meet someone in this run-down motel on Barbur, probably for a story. Now she's missing. But she left her purse and car keys behind."

Elizabeth nodded, inwardly cursing herself. She had seen the girl slip out of one room and into the one where she had met Joey. Why hadn't she searched it? But no, she had been too eager to act. So eager to take care of one problem that she had only replaced it with another.

"The motel called me about it, and then I had my friend Nicole —you remember, the FBI agent? —look into it. And they found blood *sprayed* on the wall. It looks like Jenna was shot."

Elizabeth stiffened, barely managing to keep her expression unchanged. Worse and worse. Nicole was involved in this? The woman whose kid she was now giving swimming lessons? Elizabeth didn't know how it had come to this.

She just knew she had to put a stop to it.

CHAPTER 39

Northwest Portland

Today was the day. The day Joey had to kill Sara McCloud. Or Sissy would kill him.

Put like that, it wasn't much of a choice.

Joey's first stop was a 7 Eleven where he bought a newspaper and a liter bottle of Coke. The newspaper he could hide behind. The caffeine in the Coke would keep him awake. And lukewarm Coke tasted better than lukewarm coffee.

He parked the El Camino down the street from the house where Sara was staying. It was a neighborhood for people with money. The houses were set back from the street and spaced well apart. There was even a small park across the street, more green in an oasis of green.

About twenty minutes after he arrived, the garage door rose and a dark blue Lexus backed down the driveway. The guy driving was so busy texting on his phone that he didn't even notice Joey when he drove past. Joey had a feeling he wouldn't have noticed an entire herd of elephants. He seemed Sissy's type—rich, good-looking, and arrogant. And maybe not smart enough to see how he was being used.

A few minutes later the front door opened. A woman and a little boy walked out.

Joey panicked, wondering how he could follow them. If he drove behind them at a speed only a notch over idle, they would surely notice. But if he got out of the car to follow them on foot, and they took a bus or taxi or got picked up by someone, he would be up the creek.

His palms sweated and his breath came faster as his fingers hovered over the ignition key. Should he take it out? Or turn it?

But then they crossed the street to the park. It wasn't much of a park, just a swing set and some kind of colorful structure with a ladder, a slide, and a couple of plastic tubes. But the kid was young enough that he probably didn't know any different. Joey remembered the parks of his youth. Fifteen-foot slides, monkey bars where you could clamber to the top and defy death by hanging by your knees. Those things were probably illegal now.

Joey gave it a few minutes, then he slipped on some sunglasses, got out of the car, and walked to the park bench, carrying his newspaper and Coke. The gun was heavy in the small of his back, and he had to keep resisting the urge to hike up his pants. He sat down, angling his body away from the woman and the boy. She was pushing the kid on the swing.

The woman took one look at him, then looked away. Even with the sunglasses, the scars were still visible. Most people did that. Didn't let their gaze linger. Embarrassed that they had looked at him at all. And then they might try to sneak little peeks when they thought he couldn't see them. In a way, it was good that the scars threw her off. She would be too caught up in hiding her own reactions to his face to wonder why he was there in the first place.

The park, Joey decided, was also a good thing. It was right across the street from the house, but it was so small it was likely to be empty most of the time. So when they went back to the house, and he followed and killed them, there wouldn't be any witnesses here. And the houses on either side looked like no one was at home. Everyone at work, and no one the wiser.

Joey turned another page of the newspaper, pretending to read. It had been years since he had opened a newspaper. He was surprised at how thin it was. Didn't newspapers used to be more, well, substantial? All the sections seemed to have collapsed into one another. Only sports was still separate.

As he read about a baseball game, he watched Sara out of the corner of his eye.

"Give me an underdog, Mommy!" the boy demanded, and with a little huff she pushed him up high enough that she was able to duck and run underneath him as he reached the top.

Sara turned, laughing, brushing her dark wavy

hair out of her eyes. She was maybe five foot two, a little plump.

Nothing like Sissy.

Which was good. In Joey's opinion. The world didn't need another Sissy. It didn't even need one Sissy. He never should have agreed to this. When his dad had called and said someone named Sissy was looking for him, he never should have written down the phone number. He never should have called her, his heart knocking in his chest.

He should have remembered that the real reason Sissy made his heart beat faster was that he was afraid of her.

Joey spared a thought for Jenna. Another thing he never should have done was to call the TV station. That Jenna had been so excited, saying it was her big break.

Only it had broken her.

"Okay, honey," Sara said to the kid after she had gamely crawled through the plastic tubes after him and slid down the short plastic slide over and over. "It's time to go back."

"I don't want to." The kid stamped his foot.

Joey could sympathize. He wished they could stay here forever.

"I'll make you a snack." Sara held out her hand.

The boy hesitated, then grabbed her hand. Joey realized it was now or never. He had to do this thing. Even if it terrified him.

He waited until they had crossed the quiet street. Then he hurried up behind them, his feet silent in his Nikes. Sara didn't even know he was there until she put her key in the lock and he pressed the gun into her ribs.

"Don't say a word or I'll kill you."

She let out a gasp and pulled her son in close.

Later Joey would wonder about it. What if she had pushed him away, screamed at her kid to run, to not look back, to get the neighbors to call 911—what would he have done?

But she didn't.

Twenty minutes later Joey hurried back to his car. It was done. There was no going back now.

In the car, he flipped open his cell phone and looked at the photo. His stomach rose and pressed against the bottom of his throat. The woman with her arm around the boy. Their empty eyes and slack mouths as they lay on the hardwood floor in a spreading pool of red.

He had done what he had to do, he told himself. There hadn't been any other choice.

Joey keyed in Elizabeth's number and pressed the Send key. And then he began to drive. Not even knowing where he was going.

Less than three minutes later Elizabeth called. He could hear the smile in her voice.

"Good job. Let's get together tomorrow morning, and I'll give you the rest of the money."

CHAPTER 40

Portland Fitness Center

In an empty corner of the locker room, Elizabeth took one last look at the photo on her cell phone.

It didn't move her in the slightest. Not even the sight of Sara's limp arm around her dead child's shoulders. As if, even in death, she had been protecting her kid.

Because who had ever protected Elizabeth?

She stared at their slack faces one second longer, then hit the delete key. The photo blinked out of existence. She flipped the phone closed. Those two would have been a problem as long as they lived, she thought as she changed into her swimsuit. An endless sinkhole for Ian's money. But now they would no longer drain his checking account, demand his time. She tucked her hair into a silver silicone cap. She didn't want her highlights turning green.

Ian would be coming home sometime in the next few hours, depending on whether he came home straight from work or went out to blow off some steam. He would find their bodies and call the police. Elizabeth wondered how long it would be before he would think to call her with the news.

Before he did, she wanted to take care of the

one person who could tie all the loose threads together. She closed the locker and spun the lock. The person who could connect Elizabeth with Jenna. Who could connect Elizabeth with Sara and—what had that kid's name been again? Oh, yes. With Noah.

But she had a plan for Joey. Sure, it would still leave her with one loose end, but Clark didn't even know her name.

As soon as the six thirty lesson with Makayla Hedges was over, she would put the next step of her plan into action.

Elizabeth was sitting on the edge of the warm-water pool when the FBI agent walked in with her kid. Her navy blue pantsuit, worn with a peach-colored silk blouse, looked out of place in a room where everyone else was wearing scraps of Lycra and nylon.

Nicole Hedges looked, in Elizabeth's opinion, terrible. Her shadowed eyes were unfocused, her greeting perfunctory. It was clear that her thoughts were elsewhere.

And, thanks to Cassidy, Elizabeth knew where they were. On Jenna.

It was an incomparable rush, knowing that she was only two feet from the woman who was hunting her down. Elizabeth suppressed a grin. The FBI agent would never guess that her daughter's swimming teacher was behind the TV intern's disappearance.

And to make sure that Nicole never guessed, it was definitely time to snip the last remaining thread that tied Elizabeth to that stupid wannabe reporter.

Nicole's eyes focused on Elizabeth's face. "What happened?" she asked, raising her eyebrow and touching her own eye.

A lie hovered on Elizabeth's lips—lies were never far from her, just waiting to be plucked from the air—but she resisted the urge to pretend that someone had hit her or to spin a tale about a car crash. Instead, she stuck to the same lie she had been repeating all day. "I bumped into the bar on the lat pulldown machine. It looks worse than it feels."

"Ouch!" Nicole said, but her eyes still seemed to be weighing Elizabeth's words, her expression.

Elizabeth didn't need this chick looking at her like that. It reminded her too much of another FBI agent, one who had interviewed her twenty years ago. The one who had encouraged her to confide in him.

She turned to the kid and asked brightly, "Ready for your lesson, M?"

After a pause, the girl nodded, but didn't move away from her mother. She was all long skinny arms and legs, which was one reason swimming was hard for her. No body fat to buoy her up. The brief confidence that had filled her after her last lesson seemed to have disappeared.

"Bye, sweetie," Nicole said, kissing her daughter's forehead. "I'll be back in thirty minutes." She turned and walked toward the door.

Her kid watched her go and didn't make a move toward the pool.

"Okay, let's get in." Elizabeth continued to use a cheerful voice in case Nicole was still within earshot. The heated pool didn't have a lifeguard on duty, but if there was any potential for witnesses, Elizabeth was always careful to behave the way she should. You never knew when someone might wander in from the Olympic-size pool next door. While there were floor-to-ceiling windows, they just looked onto a green stretch of lawn and then a parking lot.

The warm-water pool was ideal for old people with joint problems. And for people who were afraid of swimming. Not having to face the shock of ice-cold water helped dial their fear back a notch. And because the pool was only ten yards long, and no deeper than five feet at any spot, it was not as intimidating.

It also tasted like pee. The gym ran groups of toddlers through here on weekends, and no matter how many chemicals they dumped in the pool after one of the baby swim classes, there was still no mistaking the taste of the water whenever Elizabeth was forced to put her face in.

She jumped into the water, but Makayla came down the steps agonizingly slowly, holding on to the stainless steel handrail with both hands.

Elizabeth pretended not to notice, although inside she squirmed with impatience. “Okay, the first thing we have to do is wash our face.” She closed her eyes and splashed water on her face. She opened her eyes. “Now you do it.”

Reluctantly letting go of the handrail, Makayla did a halfhearted job, only getting water on the lower half of her face. Even so, she gasped and blinked.

“Perfect!” Elizabeth lied. “Now let’s play the elevator game. What does an elevator do?”

“It goes up.”

“And down.” Elizabeth gripped the lip of the gutter. “So it’s like this.” She lowered herself straight down into the water until it was just over her head, blowing bubbles the whole time. Then she popped up.

“Now you do it.”

But the girl didn’t move. Just stared at Elizabeth with her huge green eyes.

“It’s easy, Makayla,” Elizabeth urged in a perky voice. “Just take a deep breath, put your head under the water, and blow! Like this!” Demonstrating, she pushed air out through her lips until they flapped comically.

Kids like this Makayla were old enough that they had learned they could get away with not always doing what they were told. They didn't know how good they had it. If Elizabeth had talked back to Grandma when she was growing up, if she hadn't jumped the second her grandma said "Jump," she would have earned a slap across the face or a trip to the closet, or both. But now, just because a kid didn't like something, they expected to be able to get out of it.

And it was clear that Makayla didn't like putting her face in the water. Even if it was one of the skills they touted in the brochure: *Participants with water-related anxiety will learn how to be comfortable and confident in water, to enter and exit safely, submerge face, exhale underwater, float, tread water, swim basic strokes, and more.*

At the rate Makayla was going, she wasn't going to achieve a single one of the goals. Then again, the girl wasn't exactly an official participant. Elizabeth had told Nicole to write the check directly to her. What the front office didn't know about, they couldn't take a cut of, nor withhold money from for taxes.

If challenged, Elizabeth would explain that Nicole was an old friend, and the lessons were only a favor. She would make no mention of payment.

But so far, no one had challenged her.

Meanwhile, Makayla's fingers were gripping the gutter so tight that her fingertips were white. Elizabeth put one hand on her shoulder.

"It's okay, Makayla. Nothing can happen to you," she said for the thousandth time. Like the girl was capable of listening. Gently, she put her palm on the top of Makayla's head and pressed it down toward the water. "Now blow!"

But the girl stiffened, throwing her head back. The feel of her tangled wet curls brought back a memory. A memory of when Elizabeth wasn't Elizabeth, but Sissy.

CHAPTER 41

Barbur Bargain Motel

With five lanes of traffic rushing by, it was unbelievably noisy. It would be easy to start shouting. Easy—and wrong. Cassidy's mike was only six inches from her mouth. Which meant it was in essence only six inches away from the listener's ear.

Any time a reporter started shouting, it made her look insecure and unsure. Which Cassidy definitely didn't want anyone thinking.

In her IFB earpiece she heard Brad Buffet's voice.

"Tonight—the mystery of the missing reporter. All of us here at Channel Four have a very personal stake in our top story, because it concerns one of our own: Channel Four's intern, Jenna Banks. We now go out to crime reporter, Cassidy Shaw, to fill us in."

Cassidy took a deep breath. "This is Cassidy Shaw, reporting to you live from the Barbur Bargain Motel in Southwest Portland." She gestured at the yellow crime-scene tape that crossed the doors of the two rooms Jenna had rented. Further setting the scene were the three police cars parked in the lot behind her.

"Portland police say they found personal items belonging to Channel Four's own intern, Jenna Banks, in a bloodstained room here at the Barbur Bargain Motel." Nicole had asked Cassidy not to publicly disclose that Jenna had rented two rooms. "Jenna is missing, and police suspect foul play and are asking for your help.

"About all we know, Brad, is that Jenna Banks came to this run-down motel on Friday evening. We believe she was planning to meet someone about a story she hoped to cover. She checked in Friday night, but she never checked out."

The last line had sounded good when Cassidy wrote it, but now *never checked out* sounded like something from an ad for a cheesy horror movie. Cassidy made her face sterner.

"Managers at this motel, which has been the scene of several prostitution busts, found Jenna's purse and keys in a room. Her car was in the parking lot. Police have towed it to see if it contains any clues. They also found other evidence in the room. There was blood on one wall, and they say the pattern is consistent with a gunshot wound."

"Now the police haven't been able to tell us definitively that this is Jenna's blood, have they?" Brad asked. His voice cut in and out.

With one finger Cassidy pressed the IFB more tightly to her ear. The earpiece allowed her to hear questions from the anchor, instructions from the producer, and all the other sounds of the newscast. The curly cord—a tan color that was more or less her skin tone—ran down from Cassidy's ear and was clipped to her back.

"Well, Brad, the information from the crime lab as to whether the blood matches Jenna's DNA will not be available for a few more days. But as you can imagine, this is terrible news for all of us at Channel Four. We are hoping and praying that Jenna will be found alive. Her parents are flying in from Florida today to be closer to the search.

"This is where you, our viewers, can help us. Have you seen Jenna Banks? Police are looking to talk to anyone who might have seen her Friday or Saturday."

Cassidy knew that folks at home were now seeing the photo of Jenna with her boyfriend, who had been cropped out. A few of the men had seriously argued for the cheesecake shot of Jenna in the bikini, but the women in the story meeting had overruled them in no uncertain terms.

"Jenna is twenty-two years old, five foot seven, and 125 pounds." This last was Cassidy's best, envy-tinged, guess. "She has blue eyes and long blonde hair.

"Police also want to know if you drove past the Barbur Bargain Motel on Friday or Saturday. Did you see anything suspicious? Did you hear a gunshot? Did you see someone being forced or carried into a car? All of us at Channel Four ask that you think back. And if you go to our website, you'll find more photos and more information about Jenna and her disappearance.

"Jenna is a college senior, majoring in broadcasting, who has been interning with us for a few weeks and helping us with stories. In fact, we have some footage of her."

This part had been prerecorded to be used within a live shot. Cassidy should have heard Jenna's voice saying "Hi, there," in a seductive voice as she leaned into some poor sap's Honda Accord. But in her IFB, there was only silence. With her free hand, she pressed the earpiece deeper into her ear.

Nothing. The IFB had just gone from being crucial to being a useless piece of plastic. She had to get them to order her a new one. Cassidy resisted the urge to swear. It was never safe to assume you were off-mike.

Dead air was lost money. Eric had drilled that into them.

"Well, it seems we're having a technical glitch," she said, crossing her fingers that it wasn't just on her end. Whenever she had a live shot, Cassidy made sure she had her exit line memorized so she could go to it immediately if she needed to. This seemed like one of those times.

"All of us at Channel Four are hoping for Jenna's safe return. Again, authorities ask that if you have seen Jenna, please call the number on your screen or call 911. This is Cassidy Shaw, reporting live from the Barbur Bargain Motel. Back to you, Brad."

CHAPTER 42

New Seasons

Sunday night with the woman Clark knew as Korena had been like a dream. He spent the next three days reliving it over and over. In the middle of ringing up a customer's order, he would imagine kissing her soft lips again. Biking to work, he saw her manicured hands on his body.

Clark barely ate, and slept in snatches. The

sheets still held her smell. He was lost. All nerve endings. Aroused, flushed, sweating, skin tingling. He didn't know where his memories left off and his fantasies began.

"Sweet dreams," she had said before leaving Clark's apartment.

"I'll dream about you," he had told her. And he did. Asleep and awake.

All he could see was Korena's face. Her body. Had he been too quick? Had he kissed her enough? Had he done everything right?

He didn't know where she lived, although it must be in the neighborhood. Why hadn't he written down the information on her check? Before he went to work on Tuesday, he biked blocks and blocks, looking for her car, but he never saw it. She must be at work, but he didn't know where that was, or what she did. It was embarrassing when he thought of how he had monopolized the conversation. He didn't even have her phone number.

Clark wanted nothing more than to kiss her again, undress her, touch her. To lie with her head on his shoulder while she haltingly told him her problems.

Sure, Korena was a little older than he was. It just meant that she wasn't a silly girl. That she was old enough to look past his face—and his zits *were* only temporary, the way Korena said—and see him for who he really was.

And even though she was twenty-five, she didn't know what real love was. It was clear that her ex-husband had used and abused her. It was a miracle that the girl could still smile, still laugh. That her heart hadn't shrunk down into a hard little ball.

Every time Clark thought of the bruise on the soft inside of Korena's upper arm, he wanted to find her ex-husband and punch him. Hard. When he remembered her sad voice saying that the creep didn't usually leave bruises, he felt sick.

What *did* he do then? Slap her? Punch her in the gut? Force her to have sex? Clark tried to ask, but Korena had refused to say much. But he was pretty sure it was something awful. And if this guy was her ex-husband, then why wasn't he leaving her alone?

"Hey. You rang that up twice!"

Clark blinked. He was standing behind the register, although he barely remembered coming to work or the after-work rush. An old woman wearing a clear plastic rain bonnet over her brown plastic wig was practically snarling at him.

"Sorry." He voided the second entry and then went back on automatic pilot.

The next person in his line had only a blue-and-white tube of arnica ointment. She was wearing a gray hoodie, and her head was down. Clark had been fantasizing about Korena so much that later he was ashamed he hadn't instantly recognized the shape of her shoulders, the curve of her hips. But he didn't. So it was a shock when she raised her head. The skin around her left eye was puffed and purple.

He gasped. "What happened?"

Korena's mouth opened. Her lips worked, but not a sound came out. She looked like she was ready to fly apart.

"Hey, Linda," Clark called to the other checker, "I'm taking a quick break." Not even asking for permission. Just telling her how it was going to be.

Clark stepped out from behind the counter and picked up the tube of arnica, even though he hadn't rung it up yet. He put his other arm around Korena's trembling shoulders and guided her to the back of the store and out past the loading dock until they were hidden between two stacks of empty wooden pallets. She opened her mouth to speak, but again, no words came out.

"Sh, sh." Clark reached out his finger to wipe the tears from her cheek. At the sight of his approaching hand, she flinched. His heart broke.

Someone had defiled her. Had *hurt* her. He couldn't fathom it. It would be like kicking a kitten. Gently, Clark put his hands on her shoulders and pulled her to him. She crumpled against his chest.

"He says he's going to kill me," she whispered

when she could finally draw a breath. "Oh, Clark, what can I do? What can I do?"

"Who said that? Who did this to you?"

"Who do you think?" Her voice was tinged with bitterness. She stepped back and wiped her face with the edge of her sleeve. "Joey Decicco. My ex. He knows I've been with someone. He says if I don't come back to him, he'll kill me."

Clark yanked his cell phone from his pocket.

"What are you doing?" Her voice rose.

"Calling the police." He flipped it open.

Korena wrenched the phone from his hand.

"You don't get it, do you?" Her lips were pulled back to expose her white teeth. "Do you think I haven't been to the police before? Joey's best friend is a police sergeant. If you call them, the only one who will get in trouble is me."

"But this is domestic violence."

"So? The cops don't care. They just think I'm airing my dirty laundry in public. They want it to stay behind closed doors." She let out a shaky sigh. "The only reason I came here was to tell you that I can't see you anymore. I can't see you ever again. Because if I do, Joey will kill both of us for sure."

"No." The word was torn from Clark's throat.

"He's killed people before. His whole family died in a fire. Joey was pretty badly burned. I used to feel so sad for him, losing his family like that. But after we got married, I learned the truth." Her red-rimmed eyes drilled into Clark's. "Joey set the fire on purpose. He was jealous of how his baby brother got all the attention, and he didn't like his stepfather. He *wanted* his family to die." She shivered. "I married a murderer. And since then, there've been other, other . . . incidents. I've already put you in far too much danger, Clark. I can never see you again. Or you'll be next."

"You don't really think he would kill me?" Clark was still having trouble believing the idea that her ex-husband would kill anyone.

"I'm serious. He guessed that I had been with someone. I was too slow to answer a question. And then he knew. *He knew*. He wanted me to tell him who it was. And when I wouldn't, he hit me." Gingerly, Korena touched her face. "I'm lucky that all he did was give me this black eye."

"So that's it?" Clark couldn't believe this. "You're just going to walk away from what we have? You're just going to let him keep hitting you? You're not, you're not a slave."

She sniffed back tears. "You don't understand, Clark. I don't have any other choice. I divorced Joey, but it doesn't make any difference. He still thinks I belong to him. And he won't let me get away. Ever." She managed something close to a laugh. "In his twisted way, Joey loves me."

"That's a load of . . . horse manure. He doesn't

love you." Clark was sure of it. "He wants to own you. That's not how you show you love someone. By hitting them?"

"He says he can't help himself. That I make him act the way he does. And he's right. I knew he would go crazy if I spent time with you. And I did it anyway. He's always said if he can't have me, no one can." She shrugged. "If I go back to him, maybe he won't get so mad anymore."

"There's got to be some other way. I love you." When he heard the words come out of his mouth, Clark knew they were true. "Korena, I love you and want to be with you forever."

"But it can't be, Clark. Don't you see? It can't be. I want to be with you, too, but it's impossible." A tear ran down her cheek. "You just need to forget about me. Forget about me and go back to your life."

Clark couldn't believe what was happening. His dream was turning into a nightmare. "And then what? What happens to you? What happens the next time he hurts you? Maybe he won't stop at just your eye."

She raised her chin. "At least you'll be safe. That's all that matters to me."

"Well, it's not all that matters to me. Not by a long shot. I should be keeping you safe, not the other way around." He swallowed. "Korena, I, I want to marry you."

Her mouth pulled down at the corners, and

she gave him the saddest smile in the world. “You don’t know what you’re saying.”

“I do. I know I’m young, Korena, but I promise you, I’ll take care of you. And I would never, ever hurt you. You’re all I’ve ever needed.”

“Oh, Clark.” She took a shaky breath. “When I met you, I knew I had found my soul mate. I feel the exact same way.” Fresh tears welled in her eyes. “But it doesn’t matter. It’s too late for me. Joey will never leave me in peace. Sometimes” —she lifted her eyes to his, tears beaded on her long lashes—“sometimes I think I should just kill myself. There’s no point in going on. Not if it’s going to always be like this.”

“No.” Clark couldn’t believe what he was hearing. “You can’t do that! You can’t kill yourself.”

She shrugged. “Why not? I have nothing to live for. I can’t have a normal life. Joey won’t let me. I’ll always belong to him, and he’ll always feel that he can do whatever he wants to me.”

Rage ran like fire through his veins. “A guy who can just torment a wonderful girl like you —he doesn’t deserve to live.”

She lifted her tearstained face to Clark’s, her eyes wide. “Do you really think that?”

CHAPTER 43

Northwest Portland

"Don't say a word or I'll kill you," Joey had told Sara when he pressed the gun into her ribs as she unlocked the front door.

She'd let out a gasp and pulled her son in close, pressing his face against her side. The kid let out a little whimper.

"Hurry up," Joey ordered, looking behind them. The street was deserted. "Unlock the door. I want to get inside."

Sara did as she was told. She kept the boy's face pressed against her waist, and the kid shuffled blindly forward. Once they were inside, Joey kicked the door closed, stepped back, and leveled the gun at her.

"Noah," she whispered, tilting her head and squeezing the kid's shoulder, "you need to be absolutely still. Do you hear me?"

There was an almost imperceptible nod.

"And don't look. I need you not to look."

His words were muffled by her waist. "Like hide and go seek?"

"Kind of, baby. Just keep your face there until I tell you."

Joey should have said something right away,

interrupted her. He could feel that he was losing momentum.

Sara lifted her head to face him and looked straight into his eyes, as if the gun wasn't even there.

"Do you want money? I've got some cash. Or I could give you my ATM card and my PIN."

Joey wished she wasn't looking right at him. It would have been a lot easier to shoot her while her face was turned away, and she was talking to the kid. Maybe he would make them kneel on the floor and then shoot them in the back of the head.

Should he lie to her? Would it make it easier to kill them, make her more likely to cooperate, if he told Sara all he wanted was money? He reminded himself to take her purse when he left. Sissy had said to make it look like a robbery gone wrong.

Joey found he couldn't lie, not with her brown eyes boring into him. "I don't want your money."

Sara took a deep breath. "You can do anything you want to me, just leave my son alone. Don't hurt my son. Look, I'll lock Noah in his room. He hasn't even seen your face." She still had her kid's face pressed into the curve of her waist.

Joey gave a slight shake of his head. "I don't want to—" He wasn't going to say the word *rape* out loud, especially not in front of the kid. "I don't want that. Look, lady, somebody wants you taken care of. For good. So that's what I'm here to do."

"And my son?" Her voice had dropped to a whisper.

Joey kept his own voice soft. "If he was here, they said to do him too."

"So Noah's just, just—an afterthought?" Her eyes flashed. "You would do something like that to a kid, and it would be for no reason? Just because he was here?"

Joey didn't have an answer.

"Why are *you* doing this?"

"If I don't kill you, they'll kill me."

"Who?" Sara's brow furrowed. "Who wants me dead?"

The hand holding the gun was shaking now. Joey steadied it with his other hand, wrapping his fingers around his knuckles, just like he had seen a million guys do it on TV and in movies. He was so afraid of shooting her. And her kid. Even if he shot them in the back of the head.

What if they made sounds? What if it took more than one shot? What if they tried to crawl away? He had a feeling they wouldn't die all neat and quick the way it always was on TV.

But Joey was even more afraid of Sissy.

"I can't tell you who it is. Just someone."

Sara's mouth fell so far open that Joey could see the flash of silver fillings in the back. "What? No, no! It's Ian? *Ian* wants you to do this?"

Sissy's boyfriend. The guy who had driven away. Joey didn't say anything.

"But how could Ian—And his son? His own *son?*" Sara doubled over as if she had been punched in the stomach.

Joey thought about correcting her. But in a way Ian had set this thing into motion. So he stayed silent.

"Mommy," the boy protested, twisting his head back and forth. "You're hurting me. Let me go!"

But even though the news had clearly gutted her, Sara was still careful to keep her son's face pressed against her side.

It was pathetic, really. As if Joey could let him live. The kid had seen him in the park, after all.

For a long moment the room was silent except for the sound of the woman's breathing.

Joey knew he should hurry her along. Get this thing done and get out of here. Before one of the neighbors realized just how out of place a beat-up gold El Camino looked parked down the street. Before the mailman came or a friend stopped by.

Sara took a shaky breath, steadied herself, straightened up. Her eyes looked into his. And she didn't see him as an animal, or a criminal. She looked past the melted patchwork skin of his face. Joey felt like she saw inside his soul.

"You can't do this," Sara whispered. "I know you can't."

He pointed the gun straight at her chest, but even with both hands it was shaking so much from side to side that it seemed possible he might miss her altogether.

And there was a long moment that stretched out until it seemed it would break. He looked into her unblinking eyes. Even the kid was quiet.

What was he? What—who—was Joey Decicco? Was he just Sissy's errand boy? Or was he something more?

"Look, just lie down, Sara," Joey found himself saying. "Just lie down. Both of you. And try to look dead."

"What?" Her head snapped back. "Why?"

"I'm supposed to take a photo of you. For proof. And then you have to get out of town. Right now. Just start driving and don't stop. And don't talk to anyone. Not your family. Not your friends. And get as many miles away from here as you can before anyone figures out that you're not really dead."

Sara shook her head. "If we just lie on the ground, we won't look dead. Not dead enough anyway. Look, put the gun away. Put the gun away and I'll help you make it look real."

Sara looked down at her kid and then lifted her hand away, already believing that Joey would do what she had asked. And in that moment, the moment when the gun was still pointed at her, Joey could have shot her.

The kid saw him think about it. His mouth started to open. But then Joey slipped the gun back into his waistband.

Sara walked into the kitchen and began opening up the cupboards. "In high school we did this play," she said over her shoulder, "and we had to make stage blood." She took out a clear bottle of corn syrup and a tin of cornstarch. "Good thing I didn't clean out the cupboards when I moved out. Now all I need to remember is where I kept the—" Her hand closed on a small box. "Here it is. Food coloring. You need red and just a tiny bit of blue."

Joey and the kid watched as Sara used a fork to mix the concoction in a glass with a little water, finally adding one drop of blue, then another until it was just the right color and consistency. And at the end, the three of them were looking at what appeared to be a glass full of blood.

"Cool!" the kid said with a grin.

Joey stuck his finger in and then wiped a trail of "blood" along his forearm. It looked like blood. It also looked like it had been applied, not like it was from a wound. He lapped it off, sweet and sticky, while he thought.

"Can I try some?" The kid bounced on his toes.

"Maybe you could both let some dribble out of your mouths?" Joey suggested. "If we try to put it on your chests or something, I think it will just look too fake."

"Okay, Noah," Sara said, "I need you to try some, but don't swallow most of it. Let it stay in your mouth. We're going to play a little game. That's all. Just a game. For fun."

"To fool Daddy?"

"Yes, honey . . ." Sara's voice caught. "To fool Daddy."

And finally she lay with the child on the wooden floor, her arm half sheltering him, the "blood" running from their slack mouths, their eyes unfocused.

It was a bad photo. But photos from cheap cell phones always were.

It still might be good enough to fool Sissy. Long enough for Joey to get his money and hightail it out of here. Go down to Mexico or someplace warm where $10,000 went a long way. Long enough for Sara to put some distance between herself and Sissy's anger.

Long enough that this photo would never become a reality.

CHAPTER 44

Southeast Portland

Korena came to Clark's apartment a few minutes after he got off work. She had asked him to leave his door unlocked so the neighbors wouldn't hear her knock. Wouldn't peek outside and see her standing there.

By the time she slipped in the door, Clark was already having second thoughts. Had he really told Korena he was willing to do anything to keep her safe from her husband? Willing even to kill? But at the sight of her swollen eye, looking even worse than it had a few hours earlier, his resolve hardened.

She flew into his arms, kissing his face, murmuring "Thank you! Thank you!" in his ear.

Later, in bed, she explained her thinking to him.

"Did you ever see that movie *Strangers on a Train*?"

"No. It's really old, right?" In the gathering darkness, Clark could just make out the side of her face, her perfect cheekbone, the dark pool where the bruise framed her eye.

"Yeah. In the movie, two people who meet on the train each have someone they want dead. They decide to trade murders. And they figure the police will never catch them because the killer won't have a motive. They'll just be a stranger. That's like our situation. I'd be the first person the cops would look at. I can't kill Joey, even though it's in self-defense." She pushed herself up one elbow. "But when you do it, no one would ever tie it to you." She leaned down and kissed his forehead. "You haven't told anyone about us, have you?"

"No." It was mostly true. The day before, Clark had hinted to his mother that he had a girlfriend. His mom had squealed and wanted to know all about her. But he hadn't said much.

"Then it will be perfect. No one knows we know each other. The police will look at me, of course. But I'll make sure I'm someplace busy so I'll have an alibi. And they'll never connect it up with you, because why would you kill a stranger?"

"Uh-huh," Clark said. He wished he could slow things down. Think about them more. "But won't they notice that we're, um"—*dating* wasn't the right word—"seeing each other?"

"We'll have to be careful, sure," she said. "But I'll bet we can work something out."

And then her next kiss turned into something more.

It felt like Clark had been standing forever. His feet hurt. Korena had woken him up at three so that he would have time to pick a hiding spot. He'd had maybe ninety minutes of sleep.

He was dressed in army-green pants and a brown sweater. Not hunter's camouflage, even though he owned some, because, as Korena had pointed out, camouflage would make people look twice.

Clark's back was braced against an old Douglas fir. In front of him was a manzanita bush, with its reddish bark and stiff, twisting branches. And cradled in his arms was his rifle.

He had considered using a .223 round. For a direct hit to a vital area it would be plenty. But what if something went wrong? He had ultimately decided to go with a .308 caliber round, in case he missed the vitals or Joey was wearing a heavy jacket. Even in those cases, a .30 caliber round would be a killer.

Clark had been a hunter since he was twelve. His family ate what they killed. His parents and his cousins and uncles all had trucks with campers on the beds, and during hunting season they took off for a week or two at a time. Slept out underneath the stars. The rules didn't really apply out in the woods. You could drink even if you were a kid. You didn't have to go to school. You didn't need to wash, and you took care of your business behind a tree. And you could eat all the junk food you wanted. Some of his best memories were of hunting trips.

Clark was tucked away in the trees two hundred yards from the little parking lot at the far end of the park. The darkness and the silence reminded him of all the times he had waited in the dawn for a deer to walk by. Forest Park had been left more or less as natural as its namesake, full of trees and ferns. It wasn't the kind of park that had play structures, basketball courts, or off-leash dog parks. Twenty minutes ago a coyote had loped by a hundred feet away, its yellow eyes regarding Clark without fear.

And now a gold El Camino pulled into the parking lot.

An electric shock—equal parts terror and thrill—jolted from Clark's head to his heels. But he had to make sure it was Joey. Korena's ex-husband, who thought that he owned her.

When the guy got out of his car, one look at his face was all it took.

"He's got scars here," Korena had said, touching the perfection of her cheek. "From the fire he set that killed his family. Be careful. Shoot him from far away. You don't want to get close to him."

This guy's skin was a patchwork, some sections pale or ruddier than others. The skin on one side of his face seemed stretched too tight.

Was that what made him be so mean to Korena, those scars? Clark felt a flash of unexpected sympathy. When no one wanted to look at your face, you could feel less than human. You could get angry. When you could hear people talking about you behind your back, or you saw them point and whisper, then part of you was angry all the time.

As Joey waited for what he thought would be Korena, his expression wasn't happy, the way Clark had thought it would be. Maybe it was just hard to tell, what with the scars. But he looked—anxious. His head was turning from side to side as he paced next to the car. Looking for his ex-wife. Expecting to claim her for good.

"I told him I would meet him at Forest Park tomorrow at dawn," Korena had said to Clark. "I told him I was ready to go back to him."

"But why the park?"

"It's where we first . . ." Her voice trailed off. "It was a special place to us. Before. Before he turned all violent."

Clark hadn't wanted to hear any more. It was bad enough to think of her ex-husband hurting her. It was worse to think of Korena welcoming his touch.

Joey didn't look that big, not nearly as big as Korena had said. Someone who was hurting you probably just seemed bigger. He was maybe a little over five foot ten, trim, wearing jeans and a plaid flannel shirt over a black T-shirt. His hair was brown and so curly it stood up around his head like an Afro.

He didn't look like a monster. He just looked like a guy who had had a run of bad luck.

Clark wavered, until he thought of the bruise on the inside of Korena's arm. Her swollen, purple eye. This man wouldn't stop until he killed Korena. *Killed* her. Clark couldn't let that happen.

To reduce any sway, he pressed his back against the rough bark of the tree. He raised the rifle until it was tucked into his shoulder and pointed at the sky. His trigger hand was on the stock and his supporting arm on the fore-end stock. He was well within range. He flipped off the safety.

In a single smooth move, Clark brought the rifle down, tucking his supporting arm into his hip as he did so. His rested his cheek against the stock. As he exhaled, he squeezed the trigger, just the way his dad had taught him years ago.

But Joey must have caught sight of the movement, because he suddenly darted to the left. The bullet zinged past him. And quicker than Clark would have thought possible, the guy was running like a jackrabbit, zigzagging from side to side.

With Clark right behind him.

Then Joey reached into the back waistband of his jeans and pulled out a gun. A gun! Korena had been right. Joey had wanted to kill her. And the only way to stop him was to kill him first.

Rather than turn and fire at Clark, Joey kept running, kept zigzagging, taking big leaping steps. Then he caught his toe on a rock half buried in the dirt. Suddenly he was airborne. His gun flew fifteen feet away.

He landed hard on his hands and knees. He started to get up, but then he looked over his shoulder and saw Clark running toward him, the rifle pointed right at him. He rose to his knees, clasping his hands in front of him like he was praying. Or begging.

"Hold on," he said. "You don't need to do this."

Clark circled around him. Not saying anything. He could have shot him in the back, but that didn't seem right. It would have been cowardly. He had been taught that you owned what you did. You ate what you shot. You served quail breast for dinner and spit the bird shot into your napkin. You didn't hunt deer just for the venison steaks or, even worse, only for the rack to put on your wall. Even the not-so-good bits you turned into spicy deer sausage or pepperoni.

"You're just a kid!" Joey said when he saw Clark's face. "Did Sissy put you up to this?" He snorted a laugh. "You're just as big an idiot as me. She's got us all dancing to her tune. We're just her puppets. So what are you going to do now? Shoot me in my face? Not so easy when you're ten feet away, is it? You can't do it, can you? Can't look right into my eyes and—"

Clark pulled the trigger, and Joey fell back in a boneless sprawl. Flooded with horror, Clark turned and vomited. Nothing came up but strings of yellow bile.

He had to hurry. Grab his duffle bag from back in the trees, stash his rifle inside, and get out of here. But he remembered what Korena had told him. "After it's done, be sure to take his cell phone and his wallet."

"Why?"

"The cell phone will have my number on it. He calls me all the time. I don't need one more thing linking us."

"And his wallet?"

She had shrugged. "If his wallet is gone, they might think it's a robbery."

Clark couldn't imagine a robber going so far as to shoot some guy who had only an El Camino to show for his sorry life. Still, he found the cell phone and wallet in the back pocket of the guy's jeans. He pulled them free, then wiped the phone, the wallet, and his fingers clean on the guy's pants. Trying not to think about the wetness his fingertips had touched.

Should he get the gun? But then what? He and Korena didn't need to protect themselves, not anymore. Not now that Joey was dead. And the gun would throw the police off. Make it look like a fight.

Instead of what it was. An ambush.

Even though he was no longer directly looking at the thing that had once been Joey Decicco, Clark gagged again.

CHAPTER 45

FBI Portland Field Office

In the middle of the afternoon, Dixie, the FBI's receptionist, stuck her graying head into Nic's cubicle.

"Hey, could you talk to this citizen? She and her kid just walked in off the street. She says they're the targets of a murder for hire."

Nic was getting to her feet when Dixie added, "Oh, and I asked Leif if he could assist you." Nic shot her a look, but she was already walking back to her desk.

Dixie was always talking Leif up to Nic and vice versa. She was unaware that her efforts had already been nipped in the bud.

Nic took a deep breath. She and Leif still worked together, she reminded herself. That meant they passed in the hallway, nodded at each other in meetings, and acted like there had never been anything between them. She was a professional. She could handle this.

A haggard woman with messy dark hair stood

in the lobby. She was shifting from foot to foot and looked ready to bolt. One hand gripped the shoulder of a little boy. He had dark hair like his mother, and wide brown eyes that looked more curious than traumatized.

"I'm FBI Special Agent Nicole Hedges."

Nic shook the woman's hand. Her name was Sara McCloud. Leif came up behind Nic and introduced himself as well. Nic nodded in his direction without actually focusing on his face.

"And this is my son, Noah," Sara said.

Leif gave him a little wave.

Nic bent down a little to look into the kid's eyes. "Hello, Noah."

"Hi," Noah mumbled, suddenly shy.

"They told us what you needed to talk about," Nic said as she straightened back up. "Given the subject matter, before we begin, let me get someone to watch your son."

Dixie wouldn't appreciate being turned into a makeshift babysitter, but no kid should have to hear what they needed to discuss.

Sara gave her head a short, sharp shake. "No. I won't let him out of my sight."

Nic recognized a mama bear when she saw one. She wouldn't be any different with Makayla. She exchanged a look with Leif.

"I understand," Nic said. "Let's see if our large conference room is available. That would give us some space to have him in your sight and still give us some privacy." Maybe she could get the boy a pen and some paper from the printer, find a radio and set it to something that would mask their words.

The conference room was free. Not only that, but in the corner sat the rolling cart that held the TV they sometimes used to watch the news or a press conference. Nic turned it on, getting FOX, and then flipped through the channels until she found a *Little Bear* cartoon.

Leif tugged one of the black padded chairs from under the table. He parked the chair right in front of the TV, then leaned down to address Noah. "Why don't you hop up and watch cartoons?"

Noah's eyes widened. Nic followed his gaze. Leif's jacket was unbuttoned, and the kid could see the holster on his hip.

Leif buttoned his jacket closed. "It's okay. I'm an FBI agent. Like a police officer. I'll keep you safe."

Noah gave a tiny nod and then climbed up into the chair and turned to look at *Little Bear*. As he did, he gave the kind of sigh a man might make after coming home from a long day of work and cracking open a beer.

"So tell us what happened," Nic said as the three of them sat down at the far end of the table. She took her notebook from her pocket. Leif did the same.

In a low voice Sara told them about going to the park, seeing a man, and then not paying much attention to him until suddenly he was pushing a gun into her ribs as she unlocked her front door. “He said he *had* to kill me or someone would kill him. He looked—desperate. But also like he didn’t really want to do it. He didn’t even seem to know how to hold the gun.”

And, Sara related, the man had eventually decided not to kill them. Instead he had used his cell phone to snap a photo of them playing dead and sent it to someone.

“I thought hired killers were supposed to be nondescript. You know, someone who could blend into a crowd.” Sara shivered. “No one who saw this guy would ever forget him.”

“What do you mean?” Leif asked.

Sara ran the fingers of her right hand over her face and then held out her left hand, stiff and twisted. “He has burn scars on his face, and his left hand had been burned too. It looked more like a claw.”

Nic made a note. “Were these burns recent, do you think?”

“No. They looked old.”

“You’re right about those scars,” Nic said. “They should make him easier to track down. Do you have any idea who did this?” She had heard that doctors made better diagnoses if they simply asked patients what they thought was wrong with them. It was the same with victims. They often had a better idea about what had happened and why than the professionals. "Who do you think is behind it?"

"Someone burned my house down a couple weeks ago. And I think it was this guy. That would make sense, right? Those *were* burn scars on him. You know, like he was someone who was used to fire. But this thing with the gun, it clearly wasn't his idea. He just kept saying if he didn't kill me, they would kill him."

"Who's *they?*" Leif asked.

"He wouldn't say." Sara's eyes were suddenly wet. She glanced sideways at Noah. He was watching Little Bear walk on a log across a stream. Sara lowered her voice even further, so that it was a near whisper. "But it has to be my ex-husband. The thing I can't believe is that he wanted Noah to die."

"Why do you think it was your—" Leif interrupted himself. "What's your ex-husband's name?"

"Ian McCloud." Sara pressed her fingers against her lips, and her eyes got wider and wetter. A few seconds ticked past before she could continue.

"And the reason I think it has to be Ian is because this guy insisted I couldn't tell anyone where I was going. Not my friends, not my family. Why would he say that if it wasn't Ian?

You're going to tell me my mom or my stepdad or my brother or my best friend wants me dead? No way. So who did this guy think they would talk to? Ian.

"Lately he has been telling me he wants to adjust the terms of the divorce settlement. He makes almost a million a year, but he says he can't afford to pay me what he agreed to. After our home burned down, I told him we needed more money until the insurance paid out. We needed to find a rental, but instead Ian suggested we should move back in with him. Temporarily." Sara's voice began to break. "I thought he was just trying to save money. Now I think he really just said that so he would know where we were when he sent this guy after us."

"Wait." Leif looked up from the notes he was taking. "You're saying you're divorced but living under the same roof?"

Sara shrugged one shoulder. "It's a little weird, I know. We were building our dream house when we got divorced. I moved into the new house, but Ian kept the old one. It has a guest bedroom with its own bath. And Ian said it would be good for him to spend more time with Noah. It was just going to be for a couple of months, until our house was rebuilt. I got the new house in the divorce. Maybe he was mad about that too." She scraped her fingers through her untidy hair.

"How long have you been divorced?" Leif asked.

"Two years."

"Whose idea was it?" Leif asked.

Nic followed up. "Was there another woman?"

Sara's laugh was bitter. "There was always another woman, and there always will be. Ian's good looking, he's well known, he works long hours, and he likes to blow off steam at bars."

"If you don't trust him," Leif asked gently, "then why did you move back in with him?"

"Well, obviously, I never thought he would kill me. Never!" Sara glanced at Noah and lowered her voice. "Sure, Ian can be a jerk. But he loves Noah. At least I thought he did. Now I guess I've learned he just thinks of both of us as nothing more than a drain on his finances."

If Sara was right, Noah's dad had tried to have his own son gunned down in cold blood. Nic glanced at Noah again, but the child was totally absorbed by the TV. Could you even understand that when you were five? How would you make sense of it?

Leif said, "We are going to need to keep you out of sight until we can get this guy with the burn scars locked up and find out who's really behind what happened."

"I told you," Sara said. "It's got to be Ian."

"You could be right. It could be your ex-husband. And if it is, he'll have figured out by now that you're not dead, photo or no photo." Leif paused. "But what if it isn't him? We need to make sure the scenario of you being dead remains believable."

"We could put something out in the media," Nic suggested. "Say the bodies of a woman and child were found, and that the police aren't releasing the names until the next of kin are notified."

Leif nodded. "If Ian is behind it, he'll know it's a lie, because he never found any bodies. But anyone else could well take it as proof."

Sara shivered, and Leif patted her hand with his big square one. Some of the tension left her shoulders.

Nic wasn't aware that she had been watching Leif until his eyes caught hers. Her chest hurt, like her heart was being squeezed. Biting her lip, Nic looked away. This was work, and this was professional, and that was all it could be.

She forced herself to the matter at hand. How could they keep Sara and her little boy safe while they figured out who was behind the would-be hit man? The FBI had a couple of safe houses available, but they were usually used for undercover agents and prosecutors to get together. Not the kind of place where you could indefinitely put up a woman and her kid.

"Do you know anyone in Seattle?" Nic asked.

"Seattle?" Sara shook her head. "No. Not really."

"Good," Nic said. "You should drive up there and stay in a motel until we can figure this out. Find a place off the Interstate with a microwave and a little refrigerator. Stay inside the room as much as possible. And don't contact anyone. Not your friends, not your family, not anybody."

Sara's eyes looked lost. "But how will I pay for it? I used most of my cash last night getting a room, and it wasn't easy finding a place that wouldn't run a credit card. But I didn't want Ian to be able to find us."

"We have a protection fund for witnesses and victims," Leif said gently. "Even a special credit card that can't be traced back to you. Do you have a cell phone and a charger?"

"Yes." Sara closed her eyes and pinched the bridge of her nose. "I keep one in my car."

"Good," Leif said. "Keep it charged and on you at all times. We'll give you our cell numbers. But if it doesn't say Leif Larson or Nicole Hedges or FBI on the caller ID, then don't answer."

CHAPTER 46

Portland Fitness Center

Cassidy was actually early to boot camp class. There she channeled all her energy into squats, jumping jacks, and triceps kickbacks. Being on the trail of a hot story was nearly as good as being in love. She didn't need sleep. She didn't need food. All she needed was lots of coffee, her cell phone, and a few leads.

Elizabeth was wearing the Nike jacket that Cassidy had bought for her. After class, Cassidy waited for her to say something about paying her back for all the clothes she had bought at Nordstrom.

But instead she patted Cassidy's shoulder. "I saw you on the news last night. The story about that Jenna was scary. Are you friends with her?"

"Friends? With Jenna? I guess I'm more like her mentor. But it's starting to look like she was trying to get more airtime by covering stories on her own. Stories she didn't tell anyone else about."

Elizabeth's eyes went wide. "What do you mean?"

"I found a recording on Jenna's voice mail of a guy telling her to meet him at the motel where her purse and keys were found."

"Are you kidding?" Elizabeth's blue eyes got even bigger. "Oh my gosh, it must have been a message from the guy who killed her!"

Cassidy was a little put out that Elizabeth had figured it out so fast. "It sure looks that way."

"Did he say his name or anything?"

"No," Cassidy said. "But the cops are tracing the call to figure out what number it came from."

"And *you're* the one who realized it was on Jenna's voice mail?" Elizabeth said as she leaned over to retrieve her jacket.

Cassidy nodded. "I figured out how to hack into the system."

"Wow! You're like a regular Nancy Drew." Elizabeth slipped her toned arms into the jacket's sleeves. "They don't even need the police with you on the case."

Cassidy grinned. It wasn't until she was in the shower that she remembered that Elizabeth hadn't said one word about paying her back.

Two hours later, Cassidy was sitting at a long table along with the rest of the Channel Four staff, waiting for the nine a.m. story meeting to begin. Normally Eric Reyna, the assignment editor, would already be standing at the whiteboard, juggling a handful of colored dry-erase markers as he led them in planning out the noon broadcast.

But Eric was late. Cassidy couldn't remember

the last time that had happened. Or if had *ever* happened. But she guessed everyone was human. Even Eric.

She took advantage of the time to jot down some interview questions for her next story on Jenna. Jenna's parents and boyfriend had flown in the night before, and they had tentatively agreed to meet with her this morning. They had told Cassidy they were turning down all media requests, but she had managed to frame it as an exchange of information. Now she was impatient for the meeting to get started, because the sooner it started, the sooner it would finish. And then she would grab a cameraman and go.

But when Eric finally came in, he wasn't carrying copies of compiled story ideas to pass down the table. Instead, his hands were empty and his thinning gray hair stood up in tufts as if he had been tugging at it. All eyes went to him.

"I was just listening to the police scanner," he said.

Like all the other Portland radio and TV stations, Channel Four monitored police, ambulance, fire, and public utilities transmissions. Everything from traffic warnings to big breaking stories could start with a staticky transmission heard on the scanner.

"A canoeist just found a body on the Washington side of the Columbia River. According to the scanner, it's a woman in her twenties with long blonde hair. Fully clothed. And with a gunshot wound to the chest."

Anne Forster, the business reporter, sucked in her breath. Otherwise, the room was silent as mouths dropped open and eyes went wide with shock. News was something that happened to other people—not to the folks who covered it.

Jeff Caldwell, the political reporter, finally gave voice to what everyone was thinking. "So it's Jenna, then?"

Eric sagged into a chair. "It will be awhile before it's official, but I would say you're right."

People's eyes automatically went to the corner of the table where Jenna normally sat, bouncing a bit on the blue exercise ball she would roll over from her cubicle and then roll back.

Cassidy began rapidly recalculating what this would do to her story. The chance that she would actually get to talk to Jenna's parents or boyfriend had probably dwindled to near zero, unless she got really lucky. And what would the discovery of the body do to the story? Make it bigger—or smaller?

She finally broke the silence. "Eric, did you send out a cameraman in case we can get footage of Jenna's body being recovered?"

It felt a bit cold to ask, but the B-roll—film without narration—of a body bag being loaded into an ambulance would add depth to the story.

"Andy's on his way out there now." Eric's mouth twisted. "I still can't believe this is happening."

"I think we should cut in," Brad declared.

Normally, the station only interrupted regular programming for national emergencies or crazy weather. Then again, at this time of day, Channel Four broadcasts a string of game shows.

"Let the viewers know. Jenna deserves that. As far as we know, she died in the line of duty."

"We don't know yet that she has died at all," pointed out Alissa Fontaine, Brad's new coanchor. She smiled at him with teeth that seemed too big and too white to be real. Veneers, in Cassidy's opinion.

Cassidy felt the mood shift, from shock and sadness to anger. Directed at Alissa. The outsider.

"There aren't a lot of murders around here, Alissa," Eric said. "Maybe two a month, and 90 percent of those are related to drugs. Something like this—a beautiful girl slaughtered—it's practically unheard of." He took a deep breath and seemed to gather himself. "That reminds me, Cassidy. The scanner also said a guy was found shot to death in Forest Park. No ID yet on the body, but it sounds like it won't take long. They said it looked like he had pretty bad burn scars, old ones, like from a fire."

Forest Park was Portland's crown jewel, a 5,000-acre forest in the middle of the city. It attracted trail runners, hikers, bird-watchers—and the occasional serial killer.

This meant Cassidy's beat would be the big one today and for several days to come. Viewers would want to know everything, not only about Jenna, but also about this dead guy.

If it bleeds, it leads had never been more true as local TV news struggled to stay alive and relevant in a world where anyone could immediately download the latest headlines to their phone and no one had to wait around for the five o'clock news.

People had shorter attention spans and didn't care for reams of dry facts. An exciting or heart-tugging story would always get more airtime than a story about an international trade agreement that would affect millions of people. Leaping dogs at a dog show or leaping flames at a house fire trumped coverage of a city council meeting any day.

And when two bodies—one belonging to a beautiful young woman—were found in one day? Jackpot for the local news.

"I'll see what I can find out from my sources," Cassidy said. "About both of them."

CHAPTER 47

Southeast Portland

"There was so much blood," Clark said. For the millionth time. He was lying facedown on the couch in his apartment, his voice muffled by his arm.

"I know, baby. I know." Absently, Elizabeth rubbed the small of his back. She was watching the local evening news with the closed-captioning turned on. A minute ago Cassidy had been on, and Elizabeth had paid rapt attention.

She'd had to bite her lips to keep from smiling when she read on the screen that a woman and her child had been found murdered in Northwest Portland, but that police were withholding more information until they notified the next of kin. She gloried again in the idea that her rival was dead, as was the child who would always have competed with Elizabeth for Ian's time, attention, and money.

There had been no mention of Joey, or of an unidentified body found in a park. But Clark had said it had been in the back part of the park, the part where few people ventured.

"His head," Clark moaned. "Most of it was just—gone."

Would he never shut up? What was past was

past. You couldn't change it. So there was no use thinking about it. She had learned that long ago.

"You had to do it, Clark. It was like putting down a rabid dog. If you hadn't done what you did, he would have killed me."

Clark continued droning on as if Elizabeth hadn't said anything. "I'll never be able to forget what he looked like."

It was like listening to Eeyore. Who wanted to hear someone who wouldn't stop moaning about how miserable he was?

"Look. You saw what he did to me. The marks that he left on me. On my body." Elizabeth leaned down to whisper in his ear, her breath stirring the hairs on his neck. Maybe she could distract him. "You *saved* me."

"The cops will find me," he moaned.

"No, they won't." Elizabeth rolled her eyes. Couldn't he stop fussing?

"They'll find the shell casings. I didn't even pick them up."

"So? Those only help if they have a suspect. Which they never will. You didn't even know Joey. And let me tell you, there're a lot of people who would want Joey dead. A *lot* of people." The more Elizabeth talked to Clark, the more real her version of Joey became.

"Maybe I didn't even kill the right guy."

She stiffened and lifted her hands away. "What are you talking about?"

"He called you . . ." Clark's voice caught. "He called you Sissy."

"It was just a nickname he used," Elizabeth said, and forced her hands to resume rubbing in slow circles. Her lips found a lie. "Whenever I cried after Joey hurt me, he used to call me a baby and a sissy." It seemed so real to her that tears of sympathy sprang to her eyes.

But Clark continued to complain. "I don't feel right about this. What we did was wrong. Every time I look at you, I think about what we did."

It wasn't like Clark was going to change his mind, Elizabeth realized. It wasn't like he was going to just forget. No way. And it would only get worse once they started talking about it on the news. He would continue to get wound up in his own thoughts. Obsess about it more and more. It would eat at him at night. And in the daytime he would go to work, and people would ask him what was wrong.

And someday he might tell them.

She was going to have to put a stop to this. It was intolerable. For both of them. Really, Elizabeth would be doing him a favor.

"Look, Clark. I know a way to make you feel better."

Clark levered himself up on one elbow. His eyes were red and lost, like a child's. Couldn't he ever be a man? Couldn't he ever stop looking for direction, for love, for reassurance? Couldn't he, just once, make a decision on his own?

"You do?" His face brightened.

Elizabeth opened her mouth and the words slid out. Clearly, with Clark, it was time for the final stage of The Game.

"Last year I was in therapy to help me learn how to deal with what Joey did to me. My counselor taught me this one special technique. It helps you forget about the bad things that have happened in the past and focus on the present. It makes the past be a memory instead of letting it torment you. And it's easy."

Clark swung his feet to the floor. "Can you show it to me? Because I need to forget. I can't live with the guilt." He scrubbed his face with open palms, then slid his fingers up to tug the hair at his temples. "I just keep seeing his face when he begged me not to shoot him." His voice dropped. "And what his head looked like—like—afterward."

"Well, first you need to write down all the negative things in your life. Everything that's wrong with it. Especially things that you have done wrong. But just make a list of anything that's making you depressed."

"Okay." Clark started to move toward his laptop.

"No. On paper. If it's in your own handwriting,

it helps you make a stronger connection with it." Elizabeth almost laughed. She was practically fooling herself.

He took out his sketch pad and turned to a blank sheet. "Should I write down everything? Like how I . . . I killed him? How I killed him because you asked me to?"

Elizabeth hid her annoyance. She hadn't asked Clark to kill Joey. It had been as much his idea as hers.

"Yes. But the thing is, you need to take responsibility for just your role in it. That's part of the therapy. You can only write down what you did. You can't rely on saying that I talked to you about killing him. Because ultimately you made the decision to do it." She made an effort to leach the anger from her voice.

"When you're done making your list, then I'll show you the other half of the exercise. And it will make you forget all about the bad things. It will make you feel good again." She got up and stretched. "While you're doing that, I'm going to take a walk around the block."

"Be careful."

"I will." Once she was out the door, she took Joey's wallet and cell phone from her purse. She ripped up and smashed what she could, then deposited the resulting pieces in a half dozen different Dumpsters.

When she came back twenty minutes later,

Clark was waiting for her. Already looking like he felt a little better.

"Okay, I'm done."

She looked over his shoulder so he wouldn't hand it to her. She wanted just his fingerprints on the paper.

Clark had neatly numbered the list.

Things that make me depressed:

1. My skin is terrible. People don't want to look at it, and when they do, I can see in their eyes that they are grossed out.
2. I only have one real friend. All the people I hung out with in high school seem to have moved on.
3. Even though I tell my parents I'm saving money for college, it's not really working out that way.
4. I don't draw nearly enough, and when I do, I worry that it's not very good.
5. I keep planning on getting in shape, but instead I just watch TV. And I've been drinking a lot of beer.
6. But the thing that is worst of all, far worse, is that I am responsible for the death of another human being. I shot and killed a man in Forest Park. I keep seeing his face. He told me I shouldn't do it, couldn't do it. And I still shot him. Right in the face. And it wasn't anything like killing a deer.

Number 2 gave Elizabeth pause. Was there someone Clark was confiding in? Had he already run to them, spilling his secrets? "Who's your friend?"

He looked shocked. "You are. I meant you."

"Oh. Of course." Forcing a smile, Elizabeth found an explanation. "I guess I expected you to call me your girlfriend."

Clark bit his lip. "I'm sorry. I can change it if you want."

"No, no. That's fine. The list is only for you. And we both know what I am." She kissed him on the cheek.

Pulling back, he looked at her. He offered her a trembling smile. "So now is it time to show me how to change my focus?" His voice arced higher, as if he were holding back tears. "To show me all the good things?"

"First we have to do a trust exercise. Do you know what a trust fall is?"

Clark nodded. "You close your eyes and you cross your arms over your chest and you fall backward into a group of people and they catch you. We did it in middle school."

Hard to imagine why they hadn't just let him fall.

"Well, it's like that, but different, since there's only one of me." She shook his pillow out of the case. "Put this over your head."

"And then what?" His eyes were wide and wet.

"You'll see. That's where the trust part comes in."

As soon as the pillowcase covered his eyes, Elizabeth took the cord from his laptop.

"Like this?" Clark shimmied his shoulders and pulled at the edges of the pillowcase until it was just below his elbows.

"That's perfect." She wrapped the cord around both hands.

Now that Clark couldn't see her, Elizabeth could let her mask slip. Her lip curled back when she looked at him. He sat on the bed, slumped forward, looking ridiculous. Looking pathetic. Like a stupid sack of potatoes. She was doing him a favor, really.

She sat behind him on the bed. He turned his head toward her. "Now what happens?" He sounded excited. As if. Well, now was the time to nip that in the bud.

She looped the cord over his head and yanked it back viciously.

Clark managed to get out a strangled cry. "What?" Or maybe "Why?" His feet kicked out, connected with nothing.

He swung his right elbow back, but Elizabeth was out of reach. His hands reached up, clawed at his own throat under the pillowcase, but the cord was biting too deeply. And already he was growing weaker.

Finally, it was done. She poked him a few times

to be sure, but he didn't move at all, didn't even twitch. When she put her ear against the part of the pillowcase that covered his mouth, she heard nothing.

Elizabeth took the cord and tied it to the bed rail with a double knot. Then she let the body roll off the bed. And that's how she thought of Clark now. As *the body*. As *it*. Its head and shoulders were suspended in midair by the cord, while the butt and legs rested on the floor.

Everything in the apartment told a clear story. Clark, depressed, had flirted with suicide. Maybe he hadn't even completely meant it.

But then suicide had given him a big juicy kiss in return.

Elizabeth looked around the room, making sure she had left nothing of herself behind. The few times she had been in the apartment, she had always been careful what she touched. She wiped down only a few spots. Although she doubted that the authorities would look closely, too many places where surfaces were wiped clean might raise some questions.

Mentally, she dusted her hands. There. Done and done. And done and done and done.

Joey was dead. Sara and Noah were dead. Jenna was dead. And now Clark was dead. And there was no way to tie them back to her. Clark was the last link.

And now he had been snapped.

The cops might wonder why Clark had killed a stranger. And why that stranger had killed Sara and her kid. Or about what had happened to Jenna. But the connection from one person to the next was so tenuous that no one would be able to recreate it and trace everything back to Elizabeth. No one would ever suspect her.

And now she could go back to the life she deserved with Ian. The one where he didn't have any distractions other than wondering what Elizabeth's lingerie looked like. The one where he spoiled her. In a few months, when Ian got over whatever sad feelings he would have about his ex-wife and kid, then they could get engaged.

Elizabeth clapped her hands just thinking about it. Now where would she want to go on her honeymoon?

CHAPTER 48

FBI Portland Field Office

Nic and Leif had spent the afternoon interviewing Ian McCloud. He had professed bewilderment.

"I came home last night and Sara and Noah were gone, no note, no nothing, and she never picked up her cell when I called her. What you're accusing me of is ridiculous! Why would I open my home to her if I wanted to kill her?"

"You would know where she was," Nic pointed out, but the argument sounded weak, even to her.

"And you think that's a good enough reason to spill the blood of my ex-wife and my son in my very own home?" His lip curled in disgust. "You should look at the same people who they were looking at for the arson—her neighbor, her last boyfriend. Look, I have a girlfriend, so I've clearly gotten over Sara. And Sara is the one who wanted the divorce in the first place, not me. She was cheating on me."

"Really." Nic nodded, and she and Leif exchanged a glance.

She knew he was remembering how Sara had said exactly the opposite. Ian was so good-looking, so smooth, that Nic found herself believing Sara. But maybe he was telling the truth. Or perhaps both of them were.

The interview had ended with none of them feeling very happy.

Toward the end of the day, Cassidy had called to request an emergency meeting of the Triple Threat Club. After Nic hung up, she called her mom.

"Can you watch Makayla for a little longer this

evening? I'm going to meet with Cassidy and Allison for a quick dinner."

"Of course," Berenice said. "But I made peach cobbler, so be sure to save room."

Nic was sure the peach cobbler—a decadent family tradition made with peaches canned in heavy syrup, and lots of butter and sugar, then topped with whipped cream—was meant to tempt her into lingering once she stopped by her parents' house. Ever since she had found the lump, Nic had barely said two words to them.

Berenice had a sixth sense for when things were wrong with her kids. Even Nic's game face—which she had been perfecting for years—could fail before her mother's intense gaze. But as much as she wanted to collapse wailing into her mother's arms, Nic planned to keep her cancer to herself for a little while longer. Peach cobbler or no peach cobbler.

As she drove to HUB—Hopworks Urban Brewery—Nic wondered what Cassidy wanted. She had almost turned her down. Cassidy's idea of an emergency usually involved her pumping Allison and Nic for info on a story. But then Nic had realized how much she needed a distraction, any distraction. Tomorrow she was meeting with the surgeon to discuss the next steps in treating her cancer.

Cancer. The word filled Nic with dread. Far better to be at a noisy brewpub with friends than at home with her computer and its overwhelming amount of information, much of it depressing. The night before, Nic had spent thirty minutes reading the blog of a young black woman in Canada who had been diagnosed with the same kind of cancer as hers. A Google search for *invasive ductal carcinoma* had brought Nic to the beginning of the blog, where the woman had posted her diagnosis. Nic had read forward, scrolling through the months, and with each entry she read of the woman's story, her feeling of kinship grew.

At some point Nic decided to skip to the main page for the blog, thinking to read the most recent entry, see how the young woman was doing, and maybe even send her a private e-mail.

But the last entry on the blog had been six months before. It reported the news that the woman's cancer was back, and that she would be undergoing a new round of treatments. And then it just—stopped.

Nic shivered, thinking about it now. It didn't take a genius to guess what had happened. Ghosts on the Internet.

At HUB she had to park in the back lot. Even on a Thursday night, the brewpub was hopping. Open and airy, it catered to Portland's version of bikers—the non-motorized kind—with pizza, organic beer, a kids' menu, and bikes and bike parts used as part of the decor.

She found Allison and Cassidy already seated in one of the wooden booths.

"I was so sorry to hear about Jenna," Nic said as she slid in next to Allison.

Cassidy bit her lip. "Yeah, everyone at the station is pretty much in shock. We're used to making the news, not being it. That's one reason I wanted to get together with you guys. Jenna's murder is now a federal crime, right?"

"Right. The body crossed state lines," Nic said. "We don't know if it floated over to the Washington side of the Columbia or got transported over there. They found abrasions on the shoulders and lower legs—looked like they had been made with some kind of rope. The working theory is that the body was wrapped in something and dumped in the water, but the current pulled it loose. It doesn't matter what the killer's intent was or where they put the body in the water. All that matters is that Jenna was killed in one state, and her body ended up in another."

The waitress came up and asked if they were ready to order. Nic let Cassidy and Allison choose the pizza—she wasn't even hungry—and while they ordered beer, she just asked for water. Some studies had linked alcohol to breast cancer. In a couple of months she would probably be guzzling wheatgrass juice and eating only raw foods.

After the waitress left, Cassidy said, "So could you guys just keep your ears open for any new angles about Jenna's death? Right now, I've just got the same story as every other station. The family is in seclusion and not talking to me, even though they had agreed to before they found the body. I tried to pitch it to them as 'You can help our viewers remember Jenna as she was, not just as a victim,' but they were too torn up. And even though Jenna worked at our station, which you would think would give us an automatic angle, we're coming up dry. We've already run the footage we have of her so many times that it doesn't have much impact. Eric and Jerry are planning a half-hour tribute to her. But I'm the crime reporter, not the lifestyle reporter, and right now not a lot of info is coming out. Of course, I'll keep you guys in the loop if I hear anything at work—but can you do the same for me?"

Nic and Allison nodded. There were times that they could share tips with Cassidy, or vice versa. And there were times when they couldn't. It was a fine line, and one they tried not to cross.

"I heard there wasn't any trace evidence on the body," Nic offered, "other than the ligature marks. The river washed it all away. And they traced that phone call—but it just led to a disposable cell phone bought at Target with cash.

They're seeing if they might still have video from the checkout, but it's a long shot. So I'm afraid I'm not going to be much help."

Cassidy's hands went to the back of her short blonde bob. Nic didn't even know if Cassidy was aware of her habit, but whenever she was stymied, she twisted strands of hair at the back of her head—a spot the camera never saw.

"Yeah. Everything just feels—stuck." Cassidy picked up a new hank of hair and began to twist it around her finger. "So while I've been trying to figure out a new angle on Jenna, I've been concentrating on the other story of the day—that guy they found shot to death in Forest Park. What a crazy day! I mean, how often does this city have two murders in a single day?"

Since it was a city crime, Nic hadn't heard anything about it. She refrained from pointing out that Jenna's murder had probably taken place five days earlier.

Allison asked, "What is it with bodies and Forest Park?"

Ten years earlier, a serial killer had dumped the bodies of prostitutes in the park. And only a few months before, the three women had all been involved in a missing person's case that came to a sad ending at the park.

"It's accessible *and* isolated," Nic pointed out. "What more could you ask for? Five thousand acres, right in the middle of the city, with well-used trails and places only the deer go. It's a great place to dump a body."

"This guy wasn't dumped," Cassidy said. "I'm hearing he was shot at close range with a rifle. Once in the head."

Nic winced. Sometimes she wished her mind wouldn't insist on supplying her with pictures. "Can't be too much left to look at."

"Not of his face, no. And they couldn't get prints off his left hand because it had been badly burned a long time ago. But I heard they got prints off his right hand and were running them through IAFIS."

Sara's words echoed in Nic's memory. *He has burn scars on his face, and his left hand . . . looked more like a claw.* She straightened up. "Wait—this guy had been burned? Are you sure?"

Cassidy's brows pulled together. "I didn't see him myself. I just heard he had old scars on one hand and what was left of his face."

"Just a second." Nic grabbed her cell phone and went outside, as Allison and Cassidy watched her curiously. She called Leif. "I think I just found our would-be hit man. Only somebody hit the hit man." She explained what Cassidy had learned.

"I'm actually still at the office," Leif said. "How about if I call Portland police and get an ID for this guy? I'll call you back."

When Nicole came back to the booth, Cassidy said, “So what was that all about?” Allison was also looking at her expectantly.

Nic gave them a truncated version of the story of Sara and Noah and the guy with the gun, with no names or distinguishing information. “But you have to keep this on the QT. Whoever ordered the hit thinks this lady and her son are dead. And if it gets shared prematurely, then they might still end up that way.” She gave Cassidy a warning look.

“Just stop it, Nicole.” Cassidy crossed her arms. “I don’t understand what is wrong with you lately. It’s like you don’t—you don’t trust me anymore.”

Well, she didn’t. She didn’t trust anyone.

But then Allison surprised her by adding, “And you’ve been awfully distant lately. Nic, what’s wrong? And don’t tell us it’s nothing.”

The long silence was finally broken by the waitress bustling over with their pizza and three heavy white plates. But once she left, no one made a move to take a slice. Instead, Allison and Cassidy simply regarded her. Waiting patiently.

And Nic’s resolve began to crumble. “Okay. You want to know the truth? The truth is that I’ve . . . I’ve got breast cancer. They think it’s in the early stages, and there are a lot of treatments available, and they say they think they can get it all. But the truth is that I’m so . . .”—

the words caught in her throat—". . . so scared."

"Oh, honey," Cassidy murmured. And then Cassidy did something that Nic had never thought she would witness. She pressed a button on her cell phone until it chirped off. Then she fastened her big teal eyes on Nic.

Allison followed suit.

Her friends gave Nic what she needed. They listened more than they talked. Even Cassidy. And when Nic couldn't find the right words or found herself overwhelmed with emotion, they didn't rush to fill the silence. Instead they waited, patting her hand, their own eyes filling with tears. They listened to her vent and handed her their napkins when she started to cry.

"Let me tell you something." Nic decided to lay it all out for them. What she wanted—and what she didn't. "I don't want to hear about juice fasts or acupuncture. Let me figure those things out on my own. And I don't want to hear that I'm strong. I don't want to hear that I'm a survivor. I don't want to hear that God never gives you a burden you can't carry."

Allison surprised her by nodding in agreement. "I've learned that sometimes the only way out is through. And just because you get through, it doesn't automatically mean you're strong. You might look like you just went a dozen rounds in the ring and lost every one of them. Just because you're still standing doesn't mean you feel like a winner. It just means that you weren't given any alternative."

"Except dying," Nic said, "and I'll never choose that. Not while Makayla is still so young." She looked at her friends. "Can you guys promise me something? Will you still treat me like I'm me? Will you guys still be you? Not change?"

Cassidy and Allison nodded. Somewhere along the way, the three of them had started tearing into the pizza, eating as if they were famished.

No one was perfect, Nic realized. Her friends cared. They were doing their best. And that was all anyone could ask for.

"You guys know me. I'm a private person," she said. "If there's one thing I don't want, it's the look of pity you get when you tell someone you have cancer. And then that will be all anyone wants to talk about. Since cancer is the *last* thing I want to talk about, I'm going to keep this to myself as much as I can. Of course, I'm already losing a lot of my privacy whether I want to or not. In the last two weeks, I swear all I've done is show my boobs to strangers."

"Too bad it's not Mardi Gras." Cassidy's expression was deadpan. "You'd have a great collection of beads."

First Nic started to laugh. Then Cassidy and Allison joined in. The three friends laughed harder than the joke warranted. Hard enough that Nic found herself blinking back more tears. Only these tears were healing.

"What about Leif?" Cassidy finally asked.

Nic wiped her eyes with her already sodden napkin. "I have too much on my plate right now. There's no room for a man."

"But we're not talking about *a* man," Cassidy protested. "We're talking about Leif."

Nic didn't answer. Some things were too close, even for her friends. She was the only one who hadn't turned off her phone. Now it buzzed on her hip. The display read *Leif Larson*, giving her a bit of a start. Speak of the devil. She took it out onto the front patio.

"They've identified the guy with the burn scars," Leif told her. "It's some guy named Joseph—Joey—Decicco. He has a history of setting fires that stretches back to when he was a teenager. He's also got a string of psychiatric diagnoses behind him, plus stays in mental hospitals and the occasional prison. But no history other than arson."

"Any links between him and McCloud?" Nic asked.

"None that show up in the computers. McCloud never defended him, which I thought might have been a possibility. I called Sara and ran his name past her, but she didn't know it. I'm getting his photo to send to her cell phone, but I'm thinking it's the right guy. They even found a handgun a few feet from his body, and I would bet it's the gun he threatened her with. But all the pieces still don't quite fit together."

"One of the biggest pieces," Nic told Leif, "is why."

CHAPTER 49

Hopworks Urban Brewery

As soon as Nic went out on the patio with her cell, Cassidy grabbed Allison's hand, her eyes wide.

"I can't believe it! Cancer. *Cancer*. I didn't know what to say."

"Who would?" Allison rubbed the bridge of her nose with her free hand. "But I think we did okay." She gave Cassidy's hand another squeeze and then released it. "Right now, I think that all Nicole really needs from us is to listen to her. And how often does Nic *really* tell us what she's feeling? How often does she even complain?"

"How often," Cassidy added, "does she cry?"

The two women looked at each other, and Allison said what they both were thinking.

"Never. Nic never cries. Even when she told us about what those guys did to her ten years ago, she was dry-eyed." She sighed, and her breath shook a little. "Right now, let's just try to give her space to talk, like she said. If she wants to complain, let's just listen. I mean, if anyone deserves some self-pity, it's Nicole. And later we can help her put herself back together again."

Allison knew that some people needed you to be strong for their own reasons. And many wouldn't—or couldn't—give you room to be weak.

And that's where she and Cassidy could come in. As true friends who offered compassion and understanding, and who were willing to acknowledge the moments when it seemed impossible to go on. Just as Cassidy and Nic had done for Allison when she lost the baby, or Nic and Allison had done for Cassidy when she got caught up with the wrong man—and then the wrong prescription.

Allison wanted to caution Cassidy against suggesting some funky healer or aura masseuse, but she couldn't think of a tactful way to do it. Besides, Nicole had already told both of them that she wasn't looking for that kind of advice. For herself, it would be all too easy to answer Nicole's fears with platitudes, to say, "They have so many treatments now" or "Everything will be fine" or even "I'll be praying for you." But as the Bible said, faith without works was dead. She could and would pray for Nicole, but she would also prove the truth of her belief that

God was in even this by the help she gave Nic, the ear she offered.

Nicole came back to the booth. "We've got an ID on the body," she announced. "The fingers on his left hand were pretty useless as far as prints were concerned. But they managed to get a match off his right. So we know who he is. Joseph—Joey—Decicco. And Leif went over his records with me. They're pretty interesting. How this guy got to be a hired killer is a puzzle. He's got an arrest record dating to his teens—all for the same thing. And it's not murder."

Allison thought of the burn scars. "Arson."

"Right. It's true that he's caused three deaths in the past. When he was fourteen, he was playing with a lighter in the basement of his house, and the resulting fire got out of control. That's where he got those scars. The fire killed his family—his mother, stepfather, and a younger half brother. Decicco himself suffered severe burns. And guess where he ended up after he was discharged from the burn unit."

Allison shrugged. "No idea."

"The Spurling Institute. Didn't you tell me once Lindsay was there?"

"Yeah, for nine months, when she was sixteen."

Lindsay had been a chronic runaway. Before she was sentenced to Spurling, she had been shacked up with some fifty-year-old, boosting stuff to feed her drug habit. Really, Allison thought, maybe Lindsay *had* come a long way.

"Your sister's three years younger than we are, right?" Nicole looked up, thinking. "That would put her there at the same time as Decicco. I'll try to get my hands on his records, but as I'm sure you know, Spurling was closed a decade ago."

Guilt washed over Allison, as it had so many times before. After two months at Spurling, Lindsay had managed to slip a letter out with a sympathetic staff member, begging Allison to help get her released, or at least transferred. She claimed that physical and mental abuse was rampant. But when Allison and her mother had talked to the director of Spurling, he had smoothly explained Lindsay's claims away. They were lies, he said, lies meant to manipulate them into letting her out into the world where she could continue down her destructive path. They followed his advice and did nothing. Believed the director's own manipulative lies.

Four years later the school was shut down by the state of Oregon. The allegations were hair-raising. And when Allison tried to stutter out an apology to her sister for not having listened, all Lindsay had said was, "Whatever."

"So could you talk to your sister?" Nicole asked now. "See if she remembers him? See if there's more about him than the records we can get?"

"Sure. You said it's Joseph . . . what?"

“Joseph—Joey—Decicco.” Nicole spelled it, then shot Cassidy a narrow-eyed glance.

Cassidy gave her a lopsided smile. “Don’t worry. I know not to say anything until it’s public information. But Allison—ask Lindsay if she wouldn’t want to be on TV.”

Allison’s first impulse was to do no such thing. Lindsay loved reality TV. She didn’t see how it reduced everyone until they were small enough to fit inside a plastic and metal box. Allison couldn’t see how being on TV would benefit Lindsay at all. Then again, Allison had promised herself that she would start letting her sister make her own decisions. Let her figure out how to stand on her own two feet. Or how to fall.

“What we need to figure out is how a guy like that became a hired killer,” Nic said. “I mean, how many unsolved murders are there on the books? Maybe there’s more to this Decicco than we know about.”

“Yeah, but he *didn’t* kill this woman and her kid,” Cassidy said. “So you don’t know that he’s a killer.”

Nicole blew air out between pursed lips. “Maybe he just took a look at the child and decided he couldn’t do it. That doesn’t mean he hasn’t been successfully killing adults for years. I’ve met killers who would make a point of stepping over an ant on the sidewalk and then gut someone’s grandma without even blinking.”

"Yeah, but a firebug?" Cassidy picked up a crust from Allison's plate and began to nibble on it.

Allison didn't even blink. Cassidy had few scruples when it came to food.

"People like that, it's fire that turns them on. Not killing people."

"But people who like to start fires also like to control things," Nicole said, her face animated.

Allison wondered if she welcomed the chance to think about something other than her cancer.

"That's one reason they like fire so much, because they can control it. And there's nothing bigger than controlling life and death."

"Maybe this Decicco guy tried to burn down her house." Cassidy spoke around another mouthful of crust. "You know, Jenna covered that arson fire. Maybe she figured out this guy was behind it and contacted him. She was hoping it would be a story. Only he killed her. And then maybe Decicco snapped and decided to kill anyone who might know that he was behind the arson. It makes a lot of sense."

It did and it didn't, Allison thought. Pyromaniacs loved fire in and of itself. They weren't criminals so much as mentally ill. Why would a guy with a history of arson suddenly switch to killing people—even if he was worried about going back to prison? That was a big step. But it was hard to argue with Jenna's death or with

Sara saying Joey had stuck a gun in her face.

"But didn't you say Jenna called in sick?" Nicole asked. "Or at least a woman claiming to be Jenna?"

Cassidy nodded.

"Do you think it was really Jenna?"

"The weekend receptionist probably doesn't know Jenna well enough to be able to tell her voice. But she didn't seem to have any doubts that it was a woman."

"This Decicco sounds like he didn't have any friends," Nicole said. "So one question is—who called in?"

Cassidy shrugged one shoulder. "Maybe he just pitched his voice higher. Or heck, my phone at home came with a button that lets you make your voice higher or lower."

Allison added, "The other question is—if Joey killed Jenna, then who killed Joey?"

"Could he have killed himself?" Cassidy asked.

"No." Nic grimaced. "Close-range shot to the head—but the bullet didn't come from the gun they found at the scene. And no gunshot residue on his hands."

The waitress came up. "Are you ladies going to want dessert?"

"Of course we are, right?" Cassidy looked around the table. Nothing ever dampened her appetite. "How about that brownie sundae I saw on the menu. Didn't it say it was organic?"

The waitress smiled. “The brownie, the vanilla ice cream, the whipped cream, the chocolate and caramel sauces, and the walnuts.”

“Organic means no calories, right?” Cassidy winked at the waitress. “And since we’ll be splitting it three ways, I think it will actually end up being negative calories. We’ll probably lose weight eating it.”

“Your math sounds pretty good to me.” The waitress grinned back as she tucked her order book back into her apron pocket and picked up their now empty plates.

On the drive home Allison had a lot on her mind, but not so much that she couldn’t spend the drive praying out loud for Nicole. She prayed for Nicole’s health and her healing, for her doctors, for her daughter and her family, and for her friendships. Prayed that she would know what to do to help her friend.

When she walked in the door, she smelled cookies baking. She went back into the kitchen.

“Lindsay, can I ask you something in confidence?”

“Of course.” With a smile, Lindsay slipped off the oven mitts.

Allison realized she rarely asked her sister anything—just told her. “When you were at Spurling, do you remember a guy there named Joseph Decicco?”

"Joey?" Lindsay look up and then to the left, her eyes unfocused. "Yeah. We called him Joey Cheeks. Because of his name, and because of what had happened to, well"—she touched her own relatively smooth skin—"his face. He had scars on his face from burns and skin grafts, and his left hand didn't really work."

It was definitely the same guy.

Lindsay tilted her head. "Why do you want to know?"

"This is the part you have to keep in confidence. Joey was found murdered yesterday in Forest Park."

"Oh no." Lindsay put her hand over her mouth.

"The thing is, it looks like he might also be connected to at least one murder."

"Murder?" Lindsay's eyes widened. "Joey Cheeks?"

"So that surprises you?"

Lindsay's face softened. "Actually, it does. I mean, sure, he was in Spurling for killing his family. But he didn't mean for it to happen. Did you know about that?"

"Nicole told me a little bit about it. He was playing with fire, and it got out of control."

"Yeah, it was an accident. There were only a couple of real killers at Spurling."

"There were killers there? Real killers?" Despite the sweet smell in the air, Allison felt a little sick to her stomach. "What do you mean

—like they killed someone in a fight over drugs? A robbery gone bad?"

Lindsay pursed her lips. "There were some like that, sure. But there was one girl who took Joey in as her pet, and she was a real killer. An on-purpose killer. Her name was Sissy. She killed two little kids when she was thirteen."

"Thirteen?" Allison tried to picture it. Were you even capable of understanding murder when you were that young? "What happened?"

"She said her four-year-old cousin had come to live with her and her grandma. Sissy didn't like him getting all the attention, so she killed him and made it look like an accident. Except that same day, the day she killed her cousin, she was babysitting another little kid, a three-year-old. And Sissy started worrying that the girl was going to tell on her when she got older. So a couple weeks later she killed her too."

"How did she kill them?" Allison asked. Thinking smothering. Or some kind of poison.

"She drowned them. She drowned them both."

Allison was horrified. "And this Sissy just told you all this?"

Sending Lindsay to Spurling had been like sending her to a hard-core prison. The only life lessons she had probably learned there were to be a better criminal.

Lindsay shrugged. "She told everybody. It was

part of the therapy. You had to talk about what you had done and show how sorry you were. But Sissy? It was always a lie when she said she was sorry. She never meant it. Really, she *liked* to talk about how she had killed those kids. She wanted to keep us all in line. Everyone there knew that Sissy would do whatever she wanted. She messed a couple of people up pretty bad while she was at Spurling. Some she hurt physically, and some she hurt"—Lindsay tapped her temple—"up here. Played with their heads. She lied all the time. Sissy always had these big stories about how she was related to royalty, how she had been in a movie, how she had almost died. She had Joey thinking that she loved him, but then she'd tell on him when he broke a rule, or make fun of him behind his back. Everything was like one big game to Sissy."

"Really?" Despite herself, Allison was fascinated by this digression. A thought nagged at her, but she was too worn out from the long day to follow it. She forced herself to refocus on the question. "So when you think about the Joey you knew, does it surprise you to think that he grew up to be a killer?"

"Well, it was a long time ago," Lindsay said. "But the Joey I knew only loved two things in this world. Fire. And Sissy."

CHAPTER 50
Channel Four

The police had already taken away Jenna's computer, but that didn't mean that her files were gone. Staff at Channel Four shared a server where they were supposed to back up their work every night. But as with the phone system, Cassidy had discovered that there were varying levels of compliance. Jenna, however, seemed to have backed up her files religiously.

Cassidy had already taken a quick look through Jenna's computer the morning before it was seized. But now she had a better idea what she was looking for: any connection between Jenna and this dead guy, Joseph—Joey—Decicco.

Searching the server for the name Decicco turned up nothing. But the word *arson* turned up dozens of files—including the draft of a script Jenna had been working on only the day before she was killed.

Studio—OC—Jacobs. Fire officials now say the fire that destroyed this home in Southwest Portland was intentionally set.

VO—server video: swfire.01—More than forty firefighters battled the flames that erupted two weeks ago, but the house was a total loss. But this fire turns out to be more than just a case of arson. Instead, it's a twisted tale of revenge—and murder. And we caught the would-be killer on camera.

===============

Server—video+
audio (file: swfire.07)

(In cue: "Burning down the house was supposed to teach her a lesson . . .")

(Out cue: ". . . and tonight, she is in fear for her life . . .")

Caught on camera? If Jenna had gone to the motel alone, then how had she planned to get footage?

Andy said Jenna had been asking about hidden cameras. When Cassidy finally tracked him down, she found him outside, loading camera equipment into one of the station's vans.

"Andy, didn't you say Jenna asked about lipstick cams?"

With a grunt, he heaved in a black duffle bag. "Yeah, she wanted to know where we rented them. I told her we usually go to this store called the I Spy Shoppe. With two Ps and an E on the end. Why?" His eyes narrowed. "Do you have a line on what happened?"

"I'm not sure yet." Cassidy was already taking her keys from her purse. "I'm following up on some connections."

The I Spy Shoppe turned out to be housed in a strip mall in Southeast Portland, sandwiched between a Thai restaurant and a tanning salon.

A bell tinkled when Cassidy went inside. The store was a single square room with blank white walls and industrial gray carpeting. There was a cash register, a counter, and a dozen glass display cases. Behind the register, a brush-cut clerk was reading a magazine. He didn't even bother to look up when Cassidy walked in.

The nearest case held a dozen items made to hide keys or valuables. A fake rock. A hollowed-out candle. A giant *can* of Fritos. It all looked unconvincing. A key holder that was supposed to resemble a pile of dog droppings seemed more likely to appeal to a nine-year-old boy than to deter thieves.

The items in the glass case the clerk was standing behind were sleeker and more expensive looking, designed to appeal to men with James Bond fantasies. At least Cassidy hoped they were fantasies, she thought as she waited for the clerk to look up from his reading. Car bomb detectors, night-vision goggles, vehicle trackers. A briefcase that would shock anyone who attempted to force it open with 10,000 volts. Was this stuff even legal?

"Excuse me," Cassidy finally said when the man continued to ignore her. "I'm thinking you might have sold something to my coworker." She took out the photo of Jenna she had scanned into her computer earlier. "If so, I need to know what it was."

She expected him to say he couldn't provide any info. After all, this was a spy shop. Or shoppe.

Instead his lips curved into a half smile as he regarded the photo. "I remember her. Tall, long blonde hair, with these legs that went on—"

"Yes, yes." Cassidy waved her hand to cut him off. She didn't like to think of how he had clearly slavered over Jenna but hadn't even bothered to look at *her* twice. "I take it you don't know that she's dead."

His eyes bulged. "What?"

"Her body was found in the Columbia River yesterday. She was murdered. Now I'm helping the authorities try to figure out what happened. And to do that, I need to know what she bought here."

His face had gone pale. "It was one of our cameras. It's popular with parents who want to know what the babysitter really does."

"Well, Jenna's not a parent. She works—worked—with me at Channel Four. So was it like one of those stuffed teddy bears?"

"Nah. It's made to look like a smoke detector." He turned to the case behind him, took out a box and opened it up. Inside was a tan plastic smoke detector. Or at least what looked like one. "You attach it to the ceiling, and it records video on a memory card. It's motion activated. And she sprang for the deluxe version. That records audio too."

"Did she say what she wanted it for?"

He shrugged. "As far as I can remember, she just wanted to know if it would be good for recording a conversation between two people."

Jenna must have gotten the camera as insurance. A silent witness to whatever had gone on in that motel room. But instead Joey gunned her down.

But what had happened to the disguised camera? Had Joey spotted it, killed Jenna, and then ripped it down and destroyed it? Or—Cassidy felt a surge of excitement—could it still be there, mounted to the ceiling? Innocent looking. Invisible.

"Thank you very much," she said. "You've been very helpful."

"So you're following the same story that Jenna was?"

"That's right." Cassidy's hand was already reaching for the handle of the door.

"No offense, lady, but have you thought that doing that might get you killed too?"

At the Barbur Bargain Motel, the yellow crime-scene tape was gone from the doors to the two rooms Jenna had rented. Cassidy knocked impatiently on both doors but got no answer.

She hurried into the motel's office. Behind the counter was the same Grecian-formulaed guy she had interviewed just two days earlier. “Hello. I don’t know if you remember me, but I’m Cassidy Shaw. From Channel Four.”

His lips pinched together. “I remember you. I talked to you on the phone. And then you came out and did a story on that girl of yours.”

“That’s right. Now I need to get back in those rooms she rented. I think she might have left something there.”

He crossed his arms. “We already told the cops. The only things she left behind were her purse, car keys, and car.”

Cassidy wasn’t about to tell him what she was looking for. Not until she had her hands on it. “It’s something that wouldn’t be obvious. But it could be important in solving her murder. So can you help me out?” She gave him the smile that worked on 99.9 percent of the people she met.

The motel manager was clearly in the 0.1 percent. His eyes narrowed. “Help you out? After what you did to me? You described my motel as”—he made air quotes—“a location where police have made a lot of prostitution busts. Let me tell you, missy, that was not good for business. A lot of people like to stay here because it’s close to the hospital or they need a place to stay for a couple of days, but all of a sudden they’re canceling and going someplace else. My bookings have dropped by half.”

"That's not because of my report." Cassidy tried to appeal to his common sense. "That's because someone was murdered here. *That* wasn't my fault. It wasn't your fault either. It just happened."

"You're the one who made a big deal about it." He shook his head. "I don't care what kind of line you try to feed me, lady, I'm not letting you in there."

CHAPTER 51

Bridgetown Medical Specialists

As Nic was parking her car in the parking lot attached to the medical office, her BlackBerry buzzed. With a sigh, she slipped it from her belt and said hello.

"Nicole? It's Cassidy." Cassidy's words were so fast, they ran into one another. "You need to come to the motel where Jenna was murdered. I just found out she bought a spy camera that looked like a smoke detector. I think she installed it at the motel. And Nic, I think it's still there! The owner won't let me in, but if it's still there, then it might have recorded Jenna being shot—and whoever killed her."

It was a relief to think about something other than herself. Nic would much rather put the key back in the ignition and drive over to the Barbur Bargain Motel than to go see Dr. Adler. But she made herself get out of the car and press the button to lock the doors. "I'm actually at the surgeon's."

Embarrassment colored Cassidy's voice. "Oh, I'm sorry, Nic. I completely forgot."

"That's all right." She knew how single-minded Cassidy could be in pursuit of a story. "I'll call Leif and ask him to look for it."

When Nic explained the situation to Leif, she kept her voice matter-of-fact. "Cassidy's right. It could be important. If you do find anything there, could you call Allison?"

"Sure thing."

Leif hesitated, and Nic knew he wanted to ask her where she was and why she couldn't do it. But in the end, he settled for simply saying good-bye.

"These are very individual choices, Nicole," Dr. Adler said. They were seated in his office, and for once Nic had all her clothes on. "There is no wrong decision. In your case, you could opt for either a lumpectomy or a mastectomy. If we do a lumpectomy, we'll remove the cancerous tissue and conserve as much of your breast as possible. Then you'd have radiation once a day for six weeks. A lumpectomy plus radiation is about as effective as a mastectomy."

Even though she had already read the same thing on the Internet, Nic dutifully wrote *lump + rad = mast* in her notebook.

"So if you choose to go with the mastectomy, you probably won't need radiation. And a plastic surgeon could rebuild your breast as part of the same surgery."

Nic ordered her head to nod again. It was still hard to believe that she, Nicole Anne Hedges, was sitting in a padded chair in a breast surgeon's office, looking at the crow's-feet that radiated from Dr. Adler's kind eyes or the unruly black curl that stuck up on the crown of his head like a rooster's comb. And when it was too hard to look at Dr. Adler's face, focusing on the back of his computer or the wall behind him with its framed diplomas and arty photograph of a hovering blue dragonfly.

And it was nearly impossible to believe that she had an alien presence growing inside her that had a mind of its own and wanted to kill her. It was like something from a science fiction movie. And as much as she liked and trusted Dr. Adler—which she did—Nic would rather have Sigourney Weaver from the old *Aliens* movies by her side. Kicking down doors and blasting anything that moved.

But instead, Nic asked in a reasonable voice, "Radiation—is that what makes your hair fall out?"

"No. That's chemo. Radiation side effects are usually minimal."

She made another note. "Would I have to miss work with radiation?"

"Probably not. While you have to go every day, it only takes a few minutes. Patients tell me it takes longer to change out of their clothes than to get their radiation therapy." Dr. Adler tapped his pencil on his desk. "But even if your lymph nodes are clear, you may still need chemo. It depends on what kind of cancer you have. And you're young, which means you're at higher risk of recurrence. There are tests that can help you decide."

Chemotherapy. On the Internet, Nic had read that chemotherapy could cause early menopause. The Internet told her all kinds of things she would rather not know. For example, that breast cancer was the second leading cause of cancer death among African American women. And that black women died at a 20 percent higher rate than white women.

If Nic had chemotherapy, then Makayla would probably never have a brother or sister. Only a few weeks ago she had found herself staring at Leif during a meeting and wondering what a child of theirs would look like. Now all that was gone, dust.

Nic took a deep breath and told herself that the important thing was to make sure that Makayla still had a mommy.

But the worries crept back in. Chemo meant that Nic would lose her hair. It wasn't so much the hair, it was that everyone would know. People at work. Maybe even strangers. Nic kept herself to herself. Would there come a time when she might as well be wearing a billboard that said CANCER VICTIM?

Her eyes burned, but she blinked rapidly until the feeling went away. This morning she had woken up to a wet pillow. She had told herself she had just drooled in her sleep. She certainly hadn't been crying.

"I thought breast cancer was just breast cancer," she told Dr. Adler now.

"That's what we used to think, but we're learning that there are a lot of different kinds out there. Some are more aggressive than others. We try to fingerprint and identify each breast cancer as an individual cancer, rather than having just one blanket treatment for all types."

"How will you know what I have?" All her reading had just left Nic confused.

"Part of it will come through the pathology reports on the tumor. And we'll send some of the tissue out to a specialized lab to look at the genetics to help us decide about chemo. We'll also look at the lymph node the tumor drains to, to see if it's spread." Dr. Adler continued to talk about Nic's choices, but it was all a blur. If she wanted a mastectomy, then they could use an implant or take fat from her belly or even her butt. But even if she opted for a lumpectomy, he still might need to do a mastectomy if he opened her up and found the cancer had spread further than they thought.

"Take a few days to think about your options," he said finally. "Consider what's right for you."

How much of this was just rearranging the deck chairs on the *Titanic*, Nic wondered as she walked out of Dr. Adler's office holding a pile of pamphlets and brochures. She didn't care what happened to her breasts. She just didn't want to die.

She was dragging by the time she got to her parents' house to pick up Makayla for her swimming lesson. Her daughter was in the den, doing her homework. Finding her parents alone seemed like a sign. Nic knew she couldn't put off telling them forever, especially since she would soon need to spend the night in the hospital while Dr. Alder removed the cancer and a lymph node or two. And it had gone better than she thought, telling Allison and Cassidy. She had ended up feeling loved and supported.

Her parents were sitting in their matching recliners, watching the news. Nic took a deep breath. "Mama, Daddy—I have something to tell you."

Her dad aimed the remote control at the TV and switched it off.

Berenice gave Nic a look that only a mother could give—part knowing, part annoyance. "Is it about that young man you're dating? Because we already know."

"What?" Nic blinked, knocked off course.

"Your cousin Ducky saw you two inside a restaurant."

Nic gave her head a little shake as if it would help her rearrange her thoughts. "Leif and I work together. Just because I share a meal with someone doesn't mean I'm dating him."

"Oh, really, Nicole." Berenice's eyes narrowed, and Nic suddenly remembered how it was a failing proposition to try to slip anything past her mama. "You're trying to tell me that you'd have breakfast with any of the other agents on a Saturday? Ducky said this guy was feeding you with *his* fork."

A million thoughts flew through Nic's mind. Did her parents mind that Leif was white? Did they erroneously think the two of them had spent the night before that breakfast together?

Then her mother smiled. "Why didn't you tell us? You haven't dated since—since the incident."

Surprised, Nic blurted out, "You don't mind that he's white?"

She had asked both her parents, but as usual, it was Berenice who did the talking. "We've heard you talk about Leif before. He seems like a good man. What does it matter if he's black, white, or polka-dotted? If we told you to wait for chocolate love, well, this is Portland. You might just end up an old lady living by herself with four chocolate cats." Berenice bit her lip, suppressing a smile.

Reality crashed in on Nic. It didn't matter what her parents thought of Leif. It was already over.

"You're right. Leif is a good man. But I've told him I can't see him outside of work anymore. Because there's something else going on in my life. And that's what I really have to tell you. Mama, Daddy—I found a lump the other day."

Their expressions began to slowly falter.

"I have breast cancer."

"Oh no," her father groaned. Her mother pressed her fingers to her lips.

Nic hurried to reassure them. She glossed over the details, painted the brightest scenario, rattled on about breakthrough, cutting-edge treatments. Still, her mother began to weep quietly, and her father's eyes looked like wounds.

Nic finished by saying, "Don't tell anyone. At least not for a while. I need time to think about this on my own. The more people who know, the more questions I'm going to have to answer, and the more advice I'm going to get. And right now, I just don't have the energy to deal with any of that."

They nodded numbly.

Nic went into the kitchen, where she grabbed two paper towels and brought them back. "Here, wipe your eyes. I need both of you to act like nothing has happened. It's time for me to take Makayla to her swimming lesson, and I don't want her to know that anything is wrong. At least not today. I don't want to tell her about this until after they've taken it out and the doctors can tell me more about what I have ahead of me."

Her parents nodded and wiped their faces. But their expressions were so strained and false that Nicole hurried Makayla out in record time. Eager to get her out of the house before she could ask questions. Eager to get to her lesson, where everything was black and white. Sink or swim.

CHAPTER 52

FBI Computer Forensics Lab

At first glance, the FBI's computer forensics lab looked like a cluttered high-tech office. The curved metal desks all held two or more computers. The difference was what was on the computers. As Leif led her to a workstation, Allison caught a few glimpses of the images on the screens. What she saw was enough to sicken her soul.

"Sorry," Leif muttered. "Eighty percent of what they do here is child porn."

No wonder so many of the desks had framed pictures of children or families on them, Allison thought. All facing away from the computer screens and toward the people working. You would want to be able to look at something to counteract what you saw on the screen.

Leif stopped at a desk where a man with a shaved head was watching something unspeakable. When he saw them coming he hit a few keys, and the image mercifully blinked off. He slipped off his headphones and turned to them.

"Allison Pierce, this is Paul Trumbo."

They shook hands as Leif slipped the smoke detector out of a pink antistatic bag. He handed it to Paul.

"This is supposed to be a hidden camera."

"Clever," Paul remarked, turning it over in his hands. "Haven't seen one of these before." From his desk drawer he took a zippered kit, opened it, and selected a miniature screwdriver.

After he had removed the back, Paul plucked out a tiny black memory card the size of a thumbnail. He inserted it into a reader that looked like a flash drive. A few seconds later the memory card reader was connected to a computer with a thirty-inch screen. With a couple of clicks they were in business.

The three of them leaned closer. The image was in color and surprisingly clear. In the foreground was the bed, neatly made with a garishly patterned spread. In the background, the door. In front of it, a man with tight brown curls, his back to the camera, tapping his foot. He raised his right arm to look at his watch. Allison saw that the fingers of his left hand were twisted, frozen in a permanent red claw.

"Do we know who that is?" Paul asked.

"I believe we're looking at Joseph—Joey—Decicco," Allison said. "His body was found in Forest Park yesterday. He was shot in the face at close range with a rifle."

Paul winced.

"And he must be waiting for Jenna Banks— that woman who worked for Channel Four, whose body was just recovered from the Columbia River," Allison said. "Her blood was found in this room. She's the one who bought the camera."

From the computer came the faint sound of a knock. Decicco sprang forward and opened the door.

The three of them had a brief glimpse of a woman wearing a baseball cap pulled low. But then she stepped out of the frame so that all they could see was Decicco and a slice of her shoulder.

"Shoot!" Leif muttered. "The angle's wrong."

Allison held up her hand. The video might be bad, but the audio was still fairly clear.

"Hey, sweetheart." Her voice was low. She stepped into the frame for a second, long enough for Allison to confirm her impression that the woman was young and slender. In her arms she held a red flowered nylon shopping bag. There was the smack of a kiss, and then she stepped back. Decicco slowly raised his hand to his cheek.

"I really, really appreciate what you did for me, Joey. I mean, you totaled her house. They know it's arson, of course, but there's no one to pin it on. I'm sure that's making it hard for her to sleep at night, not knowing who did it."

Allison stiffened.

Paul looked at her and then hit the Pause button.

"I don't know who that is," she said, "but I'm 99 percent sure it isn't Jenna."

"Curiouser and curiouser," Leif commented.

Then Paul hit the button again, and the tape resumed playing.

"It burned easy," Decicco said, and even in the weird echoey way the microphone had recorded it, Allison heard the longing in his voice. "Wooden structure, no rain the week before." He raised his hands, wiggling his fingers. "It was just *whfff.*"

"Well, she lost everything." The woman's tone began to turn from pleasure to anger. "But then she was all 'Boohoo, poor me' about it to my boyfriend. And Ian's such a nice guy that of course he started offering to buy her more stuff. No, it's not enough for her that she has insurance and can get all new stuff anyway. She's trying to double-dip. Now the stupid chick is staying in a hotel that's probably way nicer than her house ever was."

In the corner of the frame, the woman's right hand clenched into a fist.

"She's got a housekeeper to bring her fresh towels and put clean sheets on the beds every day, and a pool her bratty kid can swim in any-time he wants. When I heard that, I realized it's not enough. Not nearly enough."

It was clear that this tape had been made before Sara and Noah moved back in with Ian. If this woman hadn't liked Ian paying for a hotel, how would she have felt about their moving in with him?

Allison found herself mentally urging the woman to take just a half step forward so that she could see her face. There was something about her that nagged at Allison. But all they could really see was her shoulder and the brightly flowered shopping bag she was holding.

"Not enough?" Decicco echoed. "What'd you mean, Sissy?"

Sissy! Allison blinked. It was the same girl—woman, now—that Lindsay had talked about. Decicco's only friend at Spurling.

"You know, you're the only one who still calls me that." Her tone was a mixture of amusement and annoyance. "Everyone else calls me by my real name."

Which is . . . Allison thought.

"I like Sissy," Decicco said, maddeningly. "So what is it you want me to do?"

The woman called Sissy pulled a handgun from the shopping bag. "You need to kill her," she said, putting the gun in Decicco's hand. "Kill Sara and make it look like a robbery gone wrong. Take her wallet, her watch, her jewelry. Anything you want. Just as long as it's fast." She reached inside the bag again and pulled out a bulging manila envelope. "Here's a thousand and the address for the hotel." She handed it to him. "I'll give you the rest when it's done."

Allison wondered if she had ever planned on giving him the money.

"Didn't you say she has a kid?"

"What about him?" Her voice was offhand.

"Will he be there?" There was hesitation in Decicco's voice. "At the hotel?"

"I don't think so. Ian said something about him going to kindergarten half time. But if he is, you have to do him too. Just get in, do what you need to do, and get out."

The hair rose on the back of Allison's neck.

"How old is he?" Decicco asked.

"The kid?" The woman sounded like she had already lost interest. "Four or five." Her voice hardened. "Don't go getting all soft on me now, Joey. That woman needs to die, and I need you to do it. End of story. Oh," she said, clearly remembering something. "I brought you a little something extra."

Allison and the two men strained to see what Sissy took out. It was a light-colored round plastic container, about six or eight inches high, with a flat top.

"What's this?"

She pulled off the lid. There was a smile in her voice. "My homemade pasta salad. Enjoy!"

A chill crawled over Allison's skin.

Decicco took the container. He sounded a little dazed as he said good-bye, holding the gun, the manila envelope, and the pasta salad. The door opened and closed, without ever allowing them a clear glimpse of the woman who had just asked Decicco to gun a woman and her child in cold blood.

"We didn't get Ian's girlfriend's name, did we?" Leif asked grimly.

"No," Allison said.

"Did you notice how he always has his back to the camera?" Allison asked the two men.

"Jenna must have told him about it," Leif

said. "Maybe it was even his idea. Maybe he thought it would be insurance."

"Only it didn't work," Allison said. Decicco had been caught between a rock and a hard place. "And if Jenna told him about it, then where's Jenna?"

Decicco put the gun and the pasta salad into a duffle bag and then left.

The tape went black. "I feel like I know that Sissy person from someplace," Allison said. "But—"

The camera kicked in again as Jenna opened the door and entered the frame. With her eyes fixed on the camera lens, she made for a chair in the far corner. At the sound of a knock, she started and looked at the door. She called out, "It's okay. I don't need anything." And repeated it several times, with variations, before she finally opened the door.

A woman holding a tall white stack of towels pushed her way into the room. Jenna stumbled backward. The towels fell to the floor.

And now Allison could see who it was. And why she had sounded so familiar.

And on the tape, Elizabeth trained a gun on a babbling Jenna. Allison's thoughts raced as she made the connections. Elizabeth who taught at Cassidy's health club. Elizabeth who had also been Sissy. Sissy who had killed those two children. Drowned them.

Drowned them.

Pools.

She looked at her watch. 6:48.

"Leif—what time does Nic's daughter have her swimming lesson? Isn't it now?"

The two men turned their faces to her, startled. From the computer there was the sound of a gunshot, and suddenly Jenna's body flopped on the bed in the foreground, dark blood running from her mouth and nose.

But Allison wasn't looking at Jenna. She was punching a number into her phone.

By the time she realized that she had set something terrible into motion, it was too late.

CHAPTER 53

Portland Fitness Center

Nic sat on a wooden bench in the hall outside the swimming pool area. With Makayla at her lesson, Nic was free to look through the various pamphlets and brochures Dr. Adler had given her. Each described one of the many ways they could attack the cancer. Cut her open. Pump poisons through her veins. Beam radiation at her. To cure her, it seemed like they would have to nearly kill her first.

On Nic's hip, her BlackBerry began to vibrate.

She looked at the screen and then accepted the call. “Hello?”

“Nicole—where . . . *buzz* . . . you?” If she hadn’t seen Allison’s name on the display, Nic wouldn’t have recognized her voice. It was higher pitched than normal, faster.

And completely broken up. The reception was terrible on this floor of the gym. Presumably to help it hold the weight of the two swimming pools, the floor was half set into the ground, and the walls were made of thick concrete. Nic got to her feet and began moving toward the window at the far end of the hall, hoping for a better signal. “At the gym. Why?”

“And . . . *buzz* . . . Makayla?”

Guessing at the question, Nic answered, “She’s having her lesson.”

“Nic—listen. Jenna did tape Decicco meeting with . . . *buzz* . . . ordered Sara’s murder . . . *buzz* . . . wasn’t Ian. It was Elizabeth.”

Nic pressed the side of her head against the window so that the back of the phone was directly against the glass. “What are you talking about?”

It didn’t make any sense. She must have missed half a sentence or more. Why had Allison started talking about Jenna and Decicco but then switched to Elizabeth? As in the boot camp instructor? As in Makayla’s swimming teacher?

"Elizabeth's dating Ian." Allison's words were still edged with static, but her tone was unmistakable. "But there's something else you . . . *buzz* . . . Elizabeth murdered two children when she was . . . *buzz* . . . drowned them."

Nic started to run.

Later, she would replay the scene over and over. Would everything have gone so wrong if she hadn't panicked?

Nic had trained herself to approach her job with dispassion, but now terror pushed all reason aside. Her low-heeled shoes slipped on the wet blue tiles as she sprinted the length of the Olympic-sized pool. As if she were in a nightmare, it seemed to take her forever to reach the therapy pool tucked in the separate room behind the main pool. The lifeguard turned in his tall chair to watch her run past. His mouth opened into an O as her jacket flapped back and he saw her gun.

As she ran, Nic reached back and tapped the grip of her Glock. Not surreptitiously, but to tell her the exact position of her weapon. She might need to draw it fast.

When Nic ran through the open doorway into the room, Makayla was at the far end of the short pool, her upper body resting on a yellow foam kickboard. Behind her, the sun had slipped below the level of the horizon, the floor-to-ceiling windows already growing dark.

Elizabeth was fifteen feet nearer, her back to Nic, encouraging Makayla to kick to her.

At the sound of Nic's clattering footsteps, they both turned to stare.

"Makayla, get out of the pool right now," Nic ordered. "Use the ladder behind you."

Makayla tilted her head to one side, her expression puzzled. But she didn't move.

Elizabeth did not suffer the same kind of paralysis or confusion. Not wasting any time in talking, she just knifed through the water. Straight toward Makayla.

"Get out of the water now, Makayla!" Nic screamed. "Get away from her. The ladder's behind—"

Elizabeth erupted from the water. Seeing her wide smile, Nic's blood chilled.

"Oh no. Come on, sweetie, you're coming with me." Wrapping one arm across Makayla's chest, Elizabeth jerked her off the board.

Without the safety of the flotation device, or the pool bottom beneath her feet, Makayla was suddenly drowning in fear.

"Mama!" she screamed, her wild eyes rolling so far the whites showed, her mouth opened in a scream. "Help! Mama!"

Without a second's hesitation, Elizabeth pressed her lips together and dropped to the floor of the pool. Dragging Makayla along with her. The water closed over both their heads.

In one motion, Nic set her gun on the tile and dove into the water. Not even bothering to kick off her shoes.

The chlorine burned her eyes, but Nic fought to keep them open. She saw water churning, long dark legs kicking, her daughter's open mouth and wide eyes.

Makayla, who was so afraid of drowning. And Nic had just handed her over to her murderer. Her daughter's last thoughts would be filled with terror.

Nic had to put her head up to breathe, sucking in as much air as she did water. Coughing, she launched herself forward again.

On land, Elizabeth would have been no match for Nic. But Nic had always been clumsy and anxious in the water. Now she tried to grab her daughter, but Elizabeth shoved Makayla behind her. Then Nic felt Elizabeth's fingers knot viciously in her hair. Her strong hands pressed her down. Nic kicked out her legs but connected with nothing. She tried—and failed—to bring her feet underneath her.

No air. *No air*. Somehow Nic managed to heave her head above water, snatch a single gulp of precious air. The room was suddenly filled with white, red, and blue light from a car's revolving light bar, washing over the pool, dancing on the waves, reflecting and multiplying.

Someone was coming. But would they come soon enough? And then Nic's head was pushed under again. She was weaker this time. It was harder to fight. She let herself stop moving. She would fool Elizabeth. Pretend to be dead. And then surprise her.

Except that Nic wasn't certain how much she was pretending.

Suddenly, the hands were gone. Gone. With a gasp, Nic lifted her head above the water. Just in time to see Elizabeth drag Makayla up the stairs and out of the water—and grab Nic's Glock.

Then Elizabeth turned, pointed it at Nic, and pulled the trigger.

CHAPTER 54

Channel Four

During the six o'clock local news, Cassidy had given viewers the latest updates on Portland's two murders. All the while wishing she knew what the latest really was.

After all, she was the one who had figured out that Jenna had purchased a hidden camera and that it was still at the motel. But she hadn't even been allowed to look at whatever images it had captured.

Driving home, Cassidy called Allison, who wasn't making any sense.

"Leif and I are on our way to get Nic and Makayla at the gym."

Cassidy strained to hear Allison over a siren in the background.

"What? What does that have to do with the tape?"

"It's *Elizabeth,* Cassidy. Elizabeth is behind it all. She killed Jenna and Deciccio. She ordered that woman and her kid to be killed."

"What?" The thought was impossible to grasp. Cassidy tried to hold on to it, but it slipped away from her. Still, she automatically merged into the right lane. The freeway exit for the street that led to the gym was only a mile away.

Allison launched into an explanation of how everything was connected—Elizabeth and Lindsay, Joey and Elizabeth, Jenna and Joey, Elizabeth and Ian.

"I was watching the tape, Cass, and I see Elizabeth! Shooting Jenna! And then I think—Makayla. Makayla is taking lessons from Elizabeth right now. I called Nicole and warned her, and she ran off to get Makayla. We've got Portland police and FBI agents scrambling over to the gym. Leif and I are almost there. I just pray we're not too late. I've got to go."

Cassidy took the exit at far more than the

posted speed limit of thirty-five. She hadn't followed everything Allison had said, but she had gotten the gist.

Elizabeth. Funny. Fascinating. Beautiful.

Elizabeth.

A killer.

A sociopath.

A human scorpion.

And Cassidy had let her ride on her back.

She pulled into the gym's parking lot, her thoughts swirling. Elizabeth had played Cassidy like a virtuoso. Everything Elizabeth had said had been calibrated to make Cassidy do and think exactly what she had wanted.

She had gotten Cassidy to buy her a whole new wardrobe. She had pumped Cassidy for information, lied to her, tried to turn her against her friends.

But what Elizabeth didn't understand was that you didn't mess with Cassidy. And you especially didn't mess with her friends.

This was all her fault, Cassidy thought as a car raced past her, a police light strobing blue on the dash. She had to make it right. She had to think of some way to fix it. If anything happened to Nicole or Makayla, she couldn't live with herself. She skidded to a stop.

The car with the police light drove up over the curb and onto the lawn until it was facing the big glass wall of the swimming pool. Automatically grabbing her purse, Cassidy got out of her car and started to run. The driver's side door of the other car flew open and Leif leapt out, sheltering behind the door, holding a gun in both hands. Inside the car Allison leaned forward, her hands on the dash. The pool was churning with a struggle. As Cassidy watched, Elizabeth dragged Makayla out of the pool and then snatched up a gun from the tiles.

Then Elizabeth turned and fired at the pool, the bullet as loud as a thunderclap.

"No!" Leif shouted, a shout that was very nearly a scream.

Cassidy's heart stopped when she saw what Elizabeth had done.

Nicole's body now lay motionless on the bottom of the pool.

But Cassidy didn't have time to grieve, because Elizabeth, still holding the gun, was dragging Makayla toward the emergency exit. Sirens rose and fell behind Cassidy as more police cars began to converge. She realized it was already too late for Nicole.

She couldn't let it be too late for Makayla.

Cassidy ran to the edge of the building and pushed her way into the bushes planted in a line next to it. As she scrambled through the narrow gap, she rummaged frantically through her huge black bag. Past pens, lipsticks, candy bars, mascara wand. Where was it? Where was it?

Everything she touched was either too slender or too long to be what she needed.

Then her hand closed on the cylinder.

Pepper spray. The guy at the I Spy Shoppe had called her back to the counter and told her she needed it to keep herself safe. At the most, she had imagined using it to fend off a mugger in a parking lot. Not attacking the woman she had counted as a friend. Trying to stop her from killing a child.

Because Cassidy knew that Elizabeth would. She would use Makayla as a bargaining chip to get out of here. And then discard her when she stopped being useful. Not even looking back at her broken body as she walked away.

Cassidy flicked off the cap with her thumb. Dozens of cop cars were squealing into the parking lot, but it was too late. Elizabeth pushed the door open with her back, and the alarm began to blare. Cassidy pushed her way out of the bushes, staring at the woman who she had thought was her friend.

Elizabeth looked her in the eyes. "Cassidy," she started to say, still following some vestigial impulse to try to manipulate her. As if she could explain away the gun in one hand and the terrified girl she held with the other.

"Sorry, I'm not listening to you anymore." Cassidy lifted her hand and sprayed Elizabeth directly in the face.

But the pepper spray was far from pinpoint. Cassidy sprayed herself and Makayla too. The three of them fell to the ground. Gasping, coughing, choking, eyes and nose burning. More than burning. On fire.

Cassidy heard more than saw the cops swarm them. One pulled Makayla away, another snatched up the gun, a third grabbed Elizabeth, and a fourth yelled at Cassidy that she was under arrest.

CHAPTER 55

FBI Portland Field Office

Allison walked into the meeting room. Nicole was waiting for her. After everything that had happened on Friday, Nicole had taken a three-day weekend, but her eyes still had dark circles under them. She stood up.

Allison gave her a tight hug, then pulled up a chair. "Are you still coughing up pool water?"

"I think I've finally got it all out of my system," Nicole said.

"I'm sorry I sent you into a panic." Allison looked down at her hands. "It's just that when I realized it was the same girl Lindsay had known at Spurling . . ."

Nicole pressed her lips together. "I usually

have a pretty good poker face, but once I knew the truth, all I could think was to get Makayla away from that . . . that monster."

"I've been thanking God every day that you both survived." Allison raised her head and met Nicole's steady gaze. "I still can't believe you're alive after she shot at you. I was sure you were dead."

"Well, if I hadn't watched that one *Mythbusters* on TV with Makayla, I would be." Nicole shook her head, looking bemused. "They were seeing if diving under water could really protect someone who was being shot at, the way it does in old movies. It turned out to be one of the few myths they've tested that is actually true. They had someone stand at the edge of a pool and shoot down into it. Most bullets lost their punch by three feet and came apart by five. When I saw Elizabeth point the gun at me, I just had to hope that I could get far enough down. That pool's only five feet deep. I guess it helped that she was shooting at an angle. The bullet never even touched me."

"You're very lucky," Allison said, and again thanked God for it.

Nicole's mouth twisted into something like a smile. "I can't decide if I'm blessed or cursed. You know, it's like—I got cancer, but it probably got caught early. Or—my daughter nearly got murdered, but then she was saved. So am I lucky or unlucky? That kind of thinking can make for some looong nights." She took a deep breath. "Speaking of which, right before I took Makayla to her swim lesson, I told my parents about the cancer."

"You did? Oh, Nicole, that must have been hard."

"They took it pretty well. I mean, if I put myself in their place, if I imagine how I would feel if Makayla told me the same thing, I think I would have gotten a lot more upset than they did. Maybe it took a little while to sink in. Yesterday they told me they started a prayer chain for me at their church." Nicole shrugged. "I guess it can't hurt."

Allison patted Nicole's hand. "I have to admit they're not the only ones with that idea." She had submitted Nicole's name on Sunday.

"Well, we all do what we can to protect those we care about, don't we?" Nicole put her hands over her eyes for a moment, then took them away. "I used to lie awake at night and think about Makayla getting leukemia or being hit by a car. Part of me thought that if I worried about those things, I could make it so they didn't happen. I know, I know. Rational Nicole, doing something that was definitely irrational. And clearly, it didn't protect her." She managed a weak smile. "Or maybe I should have worried about different things. Like being nearly killed by her sociopathic swimming teacher."

"How's Makayla doing?"

"She's been sleeping in my bed. And we've been talking about it a lot. The gym is horrified, of course. They've located a therapist who actually works with people in the water. Only this time I'm going to be there too. We'll be starting lessons again about ten days after I have my lumpectomy. Give it time to heal before I get into the water."

Allison was surprised. "Do you think that will be too fast for Makayla?"

Nicole bit her thumbnail. "I actually don't think it's fast enough. Last time I let her go four years, with her fears getting bigger and bigger every day. If I let that happen again, then she'll never feel safe in a pool, or a kayak or a canoe or even on a boat. Not even by the time she's an adult. I'm actually going to take the lessons right along with her. It's a miracle neither of us drowned in that pool."

Allison nodded. It was indeed a miracle.

Nicole took a deep breath. "So enough about me. Do you want to know about Elizabeth?" From the table, she picked up a thick manila folder with a large red stamp on the outside that read EXPUNGED. "I had to get special clearance from the Justice Department for you even to look at these. You can't take notes, you can't photocopy them, and they can't leave this room."

"I know." Allison couldn't keep her eyes off the file. "And we can't use them at trial. But I appreciate you tracking them down. I just keep going around and around in my head, trying to understand what makes someone like Elizabeth tick."

"I've just spent the last two hours looking through the files, so let me give you the highlights." Nicole opened to the first page. "Elizabeth's name used to be Elizabeth Hewsom, but when her cousin started calling her Sissy, it stuck."

"Sissy," Allison echoed. "Lindsay told me that's what they were still calling her at Spurling. When I heard that on the tape, I was shocked."

Allison looked at Nicole's beautiful face, her slanted eyes and high cheekbones, and wondered how she could have gone forward if Elizabeth had succeeded in ending her friend's life.

"Elizabeth didn't have much of a home life. Her parents never married and seem to have spent most of their relationship taking out restraining orders on each other. When she was seven, her father shot her mother and then himself. Elizabeth said she was a witness."

"Oh, how terrible." Allison felt an unexpected pang for the girl Elizabeth had been. Had she been born a monster or had circumstances made her one? Or had she chosen her path?

Nicole shrugged. "Well, we'll never know for sure if she really did witness it. Elizabeth clearly knew that brought sympathy for her. And she has a long record of falsely accusing others of a variety of activities, either in bids for sympathy or simply to get them in trouble."

She turned a few pages. "When Elizabeth was thirteen, her four-year-old cousin Mikey came to live with her and her grandmother when his parents ran into some personal troubles. By all accounts Mikey was an extremely attractive child. And Elizabeth was expected to take care of him. Instead, a few months later she drowned him in the duck pond when they were on an outing at the zoo. Elizabeth had everyone believing it was a tragic accident."

"That's the part Lindsay told me about," Allison said. "She knew about his death and how a little girl might have witnessed it. And Lindsay said that's why Elizabeth killed that second child—because she was a witness."

"That's right," Nic agreed. "The same day Elizabeth murdered her cousin, she was also babysitting a neighbor's three-year-old, Hannah. A few weeks later Elizabeth told Hannah she was going to teach her how to swim. Instead she drowned her in a neighbor's backyard pool while the folks were at work."

Allison pursed her lips. "I don't even know how you were able to read that part. I mean, when you think about what nearly happened with Makayla . . ."

"*Ironic* isn't even the right word, is it?" Nicole scrubbed her face with her palms, then let them drop with a sigh. "When no one found the girl's body right away, Elizabeth tripped herself up being a little too helpful to the FBI. She actually led them to Hannah's body. The girl was wearing a yellow swimsuit that her mother said did not belong to her. Her clothes were next to the pool, neatly folded. The autopsy revealed no signs of sexual abuse. They might have chalked her death up to another accidental drowning—except they did find bruises on her body. And when they looked at Elizabeth, they found scratches and bruises on her arms and legs."

"It's still so hard to believe. A thirteen-year-old multiple murderer." Allison had heard of a few kids who had killed that young, but she couldn't remember any with more than one victim.

"That's why the judge sent her to Spurling. They had a reputation for performing miracles. Of course, after the school was shut down, it was clear the only miracles they performed were on their own numbers."

Allison grimaced. "Lindsay has told me a few stories."

"Elizabeth was released from Spurling when she turned nineteen, because back then Oregon law forbade incarcerating female juvenile offenders over the age of eighteen. After she graduated she successfully petitioned to have her juvenile record expunged. At that time, even murder and sex crimes could be expunged. And she changed her name to Elizabeth Avery."

"And does Elizabeth Avery have a criminal record?"

"No." Nicole flattened her hands against the manila envelope.

"Do you think she went straight?" Allison asked.

Nicole's smile was devoid of humor. "Are you kidding? I think she switched to crimes that people might not be so willing to go to the cops over. Like Cassidy told me that Elizabeth tricked her into buying her a whole new wardrobe by claiming she had forgotten to bring her credit cards to Nordstrom. And she even had me writing checks straight to her for the swimming lessons, instead of to the gym. I think the more we dig, the more we'll find."

"Then why do you think she turned to murder?"

"I forget that you haven't met Ian McCloud, her boyfriend. He's a tall, dark, handsome, rich, well-connected lawyer. When Elizabeth met him, I think she saw him as the one thing that would complete her. A sociopath like Elizabeth is empty inside. She thought if she married Ian it would show to the world that she was the perfect person she always longed to be—beautiful, rich, assured, admired, catered to. And she was willing to do anything to make that dream come true."

There was a knock on the conference room door, and then Leif stuck his head inside. The last time Allison had seen Leif, he had had his arm around Nicole while she clutched Makayla and wept. But now their relationship seemed strictly back to business. Although Allison secretly hoped that wasn't the case.

"I've got something for you guys," Leif said. "Portland PD got in touch with me a couple of hours ago. They were called to the scene of a suicide this weekend. Some kid named Clark Smith who worked at a grocery store. He left a note—in what his parents say is his own handwriting—about what was wrong with his life. He was found hanging from his bed, a pillowcase over his head, and the cord from his laptop around his neck and tied to the bed."

So far, Allison wasn't hearing anything to explain why Leif had interrupted them.

"Don't suicides sometimes do that?" she asked. "Cover their eyes? It's like they don't want to see what they are doing."

"Yeah. But want to know what was on the list of things wrong in his life? He says he killed a man in Forest Park."

Nic's head jerked back. "This guy's the one who killed Decicco?"

"It looks like."

"Why would he do that?" Nic frowned. "Does the note say?"

"No." Leif shook his head.

"Elizabeth is behind this. She has to be," Allison said, thinking of how she had manipulated them all.

"His parents say there is no way this kid committed suicide. No way. His mom says he was saving money to go to art school. And get this—" Leif pressed his lips together and then said, "She says he told her that he had a new girlfriend. The first girlfriend he'd ever had."

Elizabeth. It had to be. But how would they ever prove it? Allison was determined to pursue justice for every victim she could.

"I'm going to go back over the scene with the evidence recovery team," Leif told them. "If there's anything there, we'll find it."

"Thanks, Leif," Nic said.

After he left, Allison thought that Nicole seemed open to talking, so she decided to take advantage. "I've been thinking about your surgery Friday. Are you nervous?"

"I trust my doctor," Nicole said, leafing through Elizabeth's file and not meeting Allison's eyes.

It didn't really answer the question, but Allison

could tell it was the only answer she was going to get. "Are you sure you don't want one of us at the hospital with you?"

"I'm sure."

"Cassidy and I both love you. You know that, don't you?"

"Yeah." Lifting her head, Nicole gave her a smile that was equal parts joy and sadness. "I know."

CHAPTER 56

Portland General Hospital

As she lay on the gurney being pushed down the hospital corridor, Nic realized she did not expect to wake up from the surgery.

This was not a logical conclusion based on research. It was a gut reaction, so deep and primal that reasoning with it did no good. No matter how many times Nic told herself that all signs pointed to the cancer being in an early stage, or that she trusted Dr. Adler's expertise, she was still convinced that she was going to die during surgery. It didn't matter how much reading she had done on the Internet, how many pamphlets she had perused, or that no one else seemed to think that her heart would stop right on the table.

She still believed she was going to die.

As she watched the ceiling tiles slide by, Nic realized she had lied to everyone, including herself, about how terrified she was. Even fighting with Elizabeth in the pool hadn't been as bad as this. Then, Nic had been all action. Now she was forced to wait. Forced to wait for what a secret part of her was convinced would be her end.

But still she had persisted in lying, telling Cassidy and Allison and her parents that she was fine, and that she did not need or want anyone at the hospital for what was just the first step on a long journey. Now she doubted she had fooled anyone.

Least of all herself.

She had lied in an attempt to turn her bravado into the real thing. She was like one of those alchemists in the Middle Ages that Makayla had studied, the ones who believed they could turn lead into gold.

During the admissions process, Nic had still managed to act calm and composed, an act she maintained as she was prepped for surgery. But as the anesthesiologist's assistant pressed the button to open the double doors leading to the surgery suite, she began to cry.

It wasn't fear that she would wake up without her breast, or that she would wake up to hear that the cancer had spread far more than Dr. Adler had thought. It was the idea that she wouldn't wake up at all. That it would all end here, today.

A team of gowned and masked people lifted her from the gurney to the operating room table. The last thing Nic saw were the blindingly white lights of the two large operating room lamps. What a cliché, she thought, as the anesthesiologist put the mask over her face and asked her to count backward from 100. Her last sight on Earth—or anywhere else for that matter—was going to be the same lamps she had seen in every movie or TV show about someone going under the knife.

Then Nic slid down into a dreamless hole.

Nic swam to the surface. Opened her eyes. The light was too bright and her eyelids too heavy. She let them fall closed.

A minute or an hour later, Nic woke up again. She didn't know what time it was or even, for a moment, where she was. She had no sense that time had passed, no memory of anything. Her stomach was roiling, and her breast and underarm throbbed. Her breast! She brought her fingers up to her left breast, ignoring the pain of the IV needle stuck in the back of her right hand.

Still there. With a three-inch-long incision in it, and another in her underarm, but her breast was still attached to her.

She let her eyelids flutter open.

An old Korean lady with two long braids was

sitting next to Nic's hospital bed. She smiled at Nic, and the skin at the corners of her eyes pleated like fans.

"Hello," Nic said. She wasn't surprised. She wasn't anything. She was in a kind of limbo, one filled with dull marvels like not losing her breast and finding a stranger sitting in her room.

The older woman held a finger to her lips, then took Nic's hand. Her own hand was dry and warm.

At her touch, Nic came a little more awake. She was really and truly alive. Alive! She hadn't died.

She didn't realize that she was talking out loud until she heard herself. "I didn't die," she said hoarsely.

The older woman just smiled and gave her hand a gentle squeeze.

Nic wanted to say something more, but her throat wouldn't let her.

It hurt to swallow. She felt like she had been punched in the throat. Like she hadn't kept her guard up in boxing and had caught an elbow or a fist.

"Thirsty," Nic managed, and the older woman let go of her hand, stood up, and got the white plastic water bottle, emblazoned with the hospital's logo. She bent the flexible straw and put it between Nic's lips.

"Thank you," Nic said after several long

swallows, and the woman set the bottle back down. Nic felt like she knew her, but she didn't know from where.

"A friend of yours sent me," the older woman said, as if Nic had asked a question. Her soft voice was oddly reassuring.

Nic could have asked what friend, but she was too tired to do more than nod. The fear was gone. She realized how much space it had taken up inside her head.

"I am here to pray for you."

Nic should have protested, but no words came to her lips.

The older woman raised one eyebrow. "Is that all right?"

"Sure," Nic said in a rough whisper. It still hurt to talk.

The old woman took Nic's hand in her own, bowed her head, and began to murmur. The words were so soft that Nic couldn't make them out. So soft they almost sounded like music.

Peace spread through Nic, as if she had been lowered into a warm bath. Her throat eased, and the two incisions stopped throbbing.

After an amount of time that might have been ten minutes or a hundred, the older woman got to her feet. She gently placed Nic's hand on top of her belly. Then she smoothed out the covers and tucked the blanket under her chin. Nobody had tucked Nic into bed in decades, but it felt good. With a smile, the older woman leaned over and said softly, "Nicole, you are going to be okay."

Then she turned and walked out of the room.

At first Nic couldn't move or speak. It was like she was paralyzed. In the places where she had hurt—her throat, the back of her hand, the two surgical incisions—there was warmth where the pain had been.

Finally she pressed the button for the nurse.

"Who was that lady?" she said when the nurse came in. She wore blue scrubs and was carrying a short clear plastic cup with two pills in it.

"Who was who?"

"That older woman who was sitting with me when I woke up." Nic cleared her throat. "Was she a chaplain or something?"

The nurse's brow furrowed. "What are you talking about?"

"The woman who was here. Sitting with me. She was maybe Korean? She had two long braids, and she was wearing a red sweater. She just left."

"Now?" The nurse's voice was amused. "Honey, it's the middle of the night. No visitors are allowed after eight."

"Then it must have been someone who works here. Maybe a housekeeper? Somebody. Or a volunteer?"

"No volunteers come in at night either. It's just

us nurses, and there aren't enough of us to do what needs to be done, let alone sit with someone." She laid a cool hand on Nic's forehead, as if checking for a fever. "Some people have really vivid dreams as they come up out of the anesthesia."

"It wasn't a dream. She was here. She was real. She held my hand." Nic remembered the warmth of her grasp, the rasp of the woman's dry skin.

"I'll call security." The nurse reached for the phone.

"No." Nic put her hand over the receiver. "It's fine."

And she realized it was.

CHAPTER 57

Firehouse

A week after her surgery, Nic sat with Cassidy and Allison at a wooden table in the Firehouse. The weather was warm enough that the garage door—left over from when the restaurant had really been a firehouse—was rolled up over their heads.

"I feel like a fool for having liked Elizabeth," Cassidy said, not meeting their eyes. She picked up a cherry pepper stuffed with fresh mozzarella and anchovies from the plate of appetizers.

Nic knew how upset Cassidy was when, instead of eating it, she began to toy with it.

"Can you guys forgive me for dragging her into our lives?"

"How were you supposed to know she was a sociopath?" Allison patted the back of Cassidy's free hand. "Elizabeth had years and years to perfect her lying."

"She was like the plastic fruit my grandmother used to keep in a basket on her dining room table," Nic said. She popped a fried olive into her mouth. "More perfect than the real thing."

Sure, Cassidy had introduced them to Elizabeth, but Nic was the one who had chosen to hand her daughter over to a child-killer. Obviously, her antennae hadn't been up either.

"Even Lindsay feels guilty that she didn't recognize Elizabeth from her photo at the gym," Allison said.

"Hey, the only people I can recognize anymore that *I* went to school with are you guys," Nic said. Allison's comment about Lindsay made her curious. "How is your sister doing, anyway?"

"Lindsay? I guess she's holding her own. She's staying sober. She's not seeing Chris. At least I'm pretty sure she's not." Allison puffed air out of her lips. "She's not actually doing much more than baking cookies and trying to help around the house. But I'm slowly realizing I can't make her live the life I think she should. And just staying away from her old life is a pretty big achievement."

Allison sounded like she was trying to convince herself, Nic thought. She had high standards, which was what happened when your dad died when you were young, your mom started drinking, and it turned out to be up to you to hold the family together.

The waitress set down their drinks.

"To the Triple Threat Club!" Cassidy said, raising her glass of red wine. Nic tapped her water glass against it and then against Allison's glass of white.

"I didn't used to belong to any clubs," Nic said. "Now I guess I'm in two. But people pay their dues to get *out* of the Cancer Club, not in."

"How are you doing?" Cassidy asked.

Nic picked up another olive. "I've gotten almost all my tests back. Stage 1 cancer, the tumor was under two centimeters with clear margins, and the lymph node they took out was negative, so that means it hadn't spread."

"That's all good, isn't it?" Cassidy asked, a little anxiously.

"It's about as good as it can be." Nic hoped that what she said was true. The only way to know for sure that you'd survived breast cancer was to die from something else. "Good news, that is, if you set aside the fact that I had something growing inside me that didn't want to stop and didn't care if it killed me in the process."

The thought still shook Nic. She had been close to death before, but her opponent had always been a person she could see, touch, hurt back. It was hard to grasp that this killer had arisen from deep within herself. That she had *grown* it. Birthed her own monster. As if she were her own worst enemy.

Nic still didn't know what to think about the Korean woman who had been in the room after she woke up from surgery. Had there even been a woman? Had she dreamed her up? All she knew was that the woman's prayer had brought her an unexpected peace. She had only told the night nurse about the woman and her visit. And no one but Nic knew about the older woman's pronouncement that she would be okay.

"I still need to do radiation," she continued, "but I guess the side effects from that are usually pretty mild. But before I start that, there's one more test we need the results from. It tells you whether or not it would help to have chemo to make sure the cancer never, ever comes back." She attempted a smile. "If I do have to do chemo, will you guys go wig shopping with me before I lose all my hair?"

"You could be a redhead," Cassidy joked.

Then her expression faltered, and Nic knew

she was remembering Elizabeth's red hair.

"Or a blonde." She ruffled her fingers through her own hair. "We blondes have more fun, after all."

"I would love to see the guys at work if I showed up in a blonde wig." Nic grinned as she imagined it. "Half of them would fall all over themselves pretending not to notice. The other half would either love it or mock it. And a tiny percentage might want to wear it themselves."

"Have you told anyone at work yet?" Allison said as the waitress set down their entrees.

She looked innocent, but Nic knew she really meant *Have you told Leif?*

Nic answered by not answering. "Right now, I don't want everyone up in my business. I'm keeping it on a strictly need-to-know basis." She took a bite of her hanger steak. "My incisions are healing, and I finally have clearance to shave my left underarm. But my breast is never going to look the same." She pretended to pout. "I guess my secret dream of becoming a topless dancer is over."

The other two women laughed, and Nic joined them. It felt good to laugh. Good to feel that there was more in the world than fear.

"We got you this," Allison said. She handed over an ivory-colored envelope.

Inside was a card with a photograph of wild-flowers on the front. Nic was touched. She had told Allison once that wildflowers were more beautiful than your standard roses and daisies. She admired them for their beauty and strength, for the way they grew even though they hadn't been planted.

Nic opened the card. Inside was a quote from Maya Angelou: "I can be changed by what happens to me, but I refuse to be reduced by it."

Blinking back tears, Nic unfolded the coupon that had been tucked inside the card. It was a gift certificate for spa services.

"You can get a massage, a pedicure, a facial—anything you want," Cassidy said. She took a bite of her gnocchi. "We figured you could use a little bit of relaxation."

Nic looked from Cassidy to Allison. "Thanks, you guys."

"After all you've been through, you deserve it." Cassidy's voice roughened with emotion.

Nic's eyes suddenly felt wet. She had cried more in the past two weeks than she had in the previous ten years. She raised a cautioning hand. "Stop that! We're here to celebrate. We're all alive. And Cass, you saved my daughter. You have no idea what that means to me. Makayla is more important to me than my own life. But thanks to you—to all of us, really—we solved the crimes and caught the bad gal. And I hope she rots in prison."

Even without being able to bring up Elizabeth's

two earlier murders in court, they still had more than enough to make sure she got sent to prison for the rest of her life. They had the video of her shooting Jenna Banks, as well as of her ordering the murder of Sara McCloud and her son. A half dozen people had witnessed her attack on Makayla.

Joey Decicco was the one death it would be difficult, if not impossible, to pin on her. Even though everyone was sure she was responsible, at the time of the shooting Elizabeth had been leading two-dozen women—Cassidy among them—in a boot camp class.

But Allison had told Nic that she intended to try to prosecute Elizabeth for Clark Smith's death. The FBI's Evidence Recovery Team had managed to find a single print of Elizabeth's on the bed rail. And in the same sketchbook in which Clark had written out what was meant to look like a suicide note, they had found a pencil drawing of a nude woman. A woman, everyone who saw it agreed, who looked a lot like Elizabeth.

Taking a bite of her salmon, Allison said, "For someone like Elizabeth, I think prison might be worse than the death penalty. She's not a very patient person. And she likes to control everything."

"I hope she hates it," Nic said, so forcefully that a woman at the next table looked over her shoulder. She lowered her voice a tad. "I hope she loathes it. I want her to think every day about how if she hadn't made the choices she did, she could be enjoying the sunshine and" —Nic lifted her fork—"hanger steak, and instead she's got fluorescent lights and mystery meat."

"Her and Foley," Allison said. "They'll both hate prison."

"Do you think he'll be convicted?" Cassidy asked.

"Nic and I will make sure of it," Allison said. "Because if we don't, he'll just do it again. Someone like that, they'll never stop."

When they finished their meal, they made a show of looking at the dessert menu. But there was really only one choice that met the informal rule of the Triple Threat Club: the Bittersweet Deep Chocolate Torte with Cocoa Nib Chantilly.

"What's chantilly?" Cassidy stage-whispered.

"I think it's like whipped cream," Allison whispered back. "And even if it's not, I'll bet whatever it is, is good."

And when the waitress set it down, along with three forks, and Nic took a bite, she decided it was very good.

And so was life.

ACKNOWLEDGMENTS

Mom and Dad, your lives continue to inspire. Bill O'Reilly, my mentor and friend (though don't expect me to admit that on air), Roger Ailes (to whom I owe so much), and Dianne Brandi (whose judgment is infallible). And David Winstrom, Kevin Magee, Neil Cavuto (all inspirational as well as successful and, more important, good folk).

Our book agents, Todd Shuster and Lane Zachary of the Zachary, Shuster, and Harmsworth Literary Agency, and Wendy Schmalz of the Wendy Schmalz Agency—you made the Triple Threat happen. And the wonderful folks at Thomas Nelson: Allen Arnold, Senior Vice President and Publisher of Fiction (a true visionary); Ami McConnell, Senior Acquisitions Editor (who defines the word *superwoman*); and Editor L.B. Norton. Thank you Natalie Hanemann, Belinda Bass, Kristen Vasgaard, Daisy Hutton, Corinne Kalasky, and Becky Monds . . . your enthusiasm is infectious. And the Thomas Nelson sales team continues to inspire: Doug Miller, Rick Spruill, Heather McCulloch, Kathy Carabajal, and Kathleen Dietz, just to name a few. And the fantastic marketing team of Jennifer Deshler, Eric Mullet,

Katie Bond, Ashley Schneider, and Heather Cadenhead.

Thank you Don and Deirdre Imus; Mickey; Scribbles; Joe Collins, paramedic/firefighter; D.P. Lyle, MD, who is a mystery author in his own right; Alida Rol, MD, gynecologist; Bob Stewart, retired FBI agent; and other FBI agents and security professionals who wished to remain anonymous. And THANK YOU to all the women who shared their personal experiences with breast cancer. We will win the fight!

All of the mistakes are ours. All the credit is theirs. Thank you!

READING GROUP GUIDE

1. The prosecutor in Elizabeth's first trial (when she is a teenager) says that harsh sentences deter teens from committing similar crimes. Considering the teens you know or have met, do you think that is true for most teens?

2. What should the primary purpose of the justice system be: punishment, deterrence, rehabilitation, or the protection of future victims? How important are the other aspects? Is our current justice system accomplishing that?

3. In Matthew 25, Jesus says, "For I was hungry and you gave me something to eat, I was thirsty and you gave me something to drink, I was a stranger and you invited me in, I needed clothes and you clothed me, I was sick and you looked after me, I was in prison and you came to visit me," and then adds "I tell you the truth, whatever you did for one of the least of these brothers of mine, you did for me." Have you ever visited anyone in prison? Would you ever consider it?

4. Do you think difficult experiences—like Allison's miscarriage —happen for a reason? Do you believe that such events can teach us?

5. Have you ever crossed paths with someone you believe is a sociopath—someone manipulative, impulsive, who frequently lies and lacks empathy for others?

6. Some scans have shown sociopaths' brains operate differently than normal brains. Do you believe that some people are born without a moral center? If so, should they be subject to the same kinds of sentences as people with normal brains?

7. What should the system do with sociopaths? In current studies, mental health treatment has proven ineffective and sociopaths who are forced into it frequently prey on others receiving treatment. Sociopaths are often imprisoned, but is it fair to expose the other prisoners to them?

8. Cassidy and Nicole argue over Cassidy's pursuit of ratings. Is it difficult to be moral and be ambitious in your business?

9. Nicole discovers she has breast cancer. Has breast cancer touched your life? Have you ever considered joining a group who helps those dealing with a life challenge?

10. Cassidy struggles with feeling lonely and empty. Do you know people like Cassidy? What would be the best thing Cassidy could do to help herself?

11. Lindsay is another person who may or may not be to blame for her actions. Have you ever dealt with someone with an addiction? How many times should you forgive an addict? Does tough love work? Was Donna wrong for turning her daughter away? Should Allison have taken Lindsay in? Would your answers be different if Allison and Marshall had a child?

Center Point Publishing
600 Brooks Road • PO Box 1
Thorndike ME 04986-0001 USA

(207) 568-3717

US & Canada:
1 800 929-9108
www.centerpointlargeprint.com